)W

Dedicated with love to
David, Matthew, Helen and
Gwilym, and to the people of Llŷn.

*If we had a keen vision and feeling of all
ordinary human life, it would be like
hearing the grass grow and the squirrel's
heartbeat, and we should die of that roar
which lies on the other side of silence.
As it is, the quickest of us walk about
well wadded with stupidity.*

(*Middlemarch*. George Eliot)

Hearing the Grass Grow

First edition published in 2008 by Broad Leys Publishing Ltd.

A catalogue record for this book is available from the British Library.

ISBN: 978 0 9061 3741 3

Cover design: Jane Smith
www.janeillustration.co.uk

Printed by Antony Rowe Ltd.

Special thanks to my husband David for his unfailing help and support throughout the writing of this book.

Broad Leys Publishing Ltd.
1 Tenterfields,
Newport, Saffron Walden,
Essex CB11 3UW, UK.
Tel/Fax: 01799 541065
Website: www.blpbooks.co.uk

Hearing the
Grass Grow

Katie Thear

Broad Leys Publishing Ltd

Introduction

I was born in a small village on the Llŷn peninsula of North Wales, an area separated from the rest of the country by the Rivals mountains. During those war-time years there was comparatively little through traffic or industrial development, and even the nearest train station was ten miles away.

It was an idyllic existence on a traditional smallholding, protected from many of the stresses of life, despite the war. It was only after moving to Liverpool that I realised what a haven it was. It has remained as my ideal ever since, a magical place where much of the original culture and gentle tolerance are still to be found.

It seemed natural for me to draw on these memories for my first novel, and to remember the heartfelt words of a Llŷn poet:

Felly Llŷn ar derfyn dydd,-
Lle i enaid gael llonydd.

And so Llŷn at the end of the day,-
A place for the spirit to find peace.

(J. Glyn Davies)

Katie Thear, January 2008

Please note: There is a guide to the houses and
people in this book on page 305.
For a Welsh Pronunciation Guide, see Appendix II.

1.

The gnats weren't biting today. It was a truce declared under the eye of a soporific sun. But the chorus of the grass played on! Endless voices tuned and hummed, now in harmony, now in cacophony, but always in unison with the beating of her heart.

The skylark was a speck, so small that Catrin had to squeeze her eyelids to keep it in focus. Insects fly high in fine weather. That's what John Prys said. You always know when it's going to rain because then they fly low and swallows skim across the lane and cows sit down in the fields. But you never see skylarks hopping on the ground. She wondered why that was. John Prys would know. John Prys knew everything! Cutting down the hedgerow growth ... slow, steady strokes ... pause, wipe his forehead with a large, work-roughened hand ...

'Well now, as I see it, it's like this ...'

John Prys knew everything! He knew that toads had a precious jewel in their heads. But you must never catch and kill one to get it! Toads might seem ugly on the outside but if you looked into their eyes you could see their inner beauty. She had seen it! Lying flat on her stomach in the dappled, tangy cloister of the rhubarb, she had seen it! Face to face with an early evening toad, she had seen it! Slow, squat, bulbous and beautiful, it crept from some damp, secret crevice and paused.

Catrin held her breath, willing herself not to move or touch it - for touching toads gave you warts - and looked into its eyes. She gasped. It was true! Amber flecks glinted and flashed fire in the brown depths, like precious agates in dark, unfathomed caves. The toad swallowed suddenly, its throat convulsing in a silent gulp, while the great eyes disappeared, only to reappear a second later, molten, magnificent and still.

John Prys knew everything! He knew that the first butterflies had been splashes of paint from the Creator's paintbrush. He'd laughed to see them flicking and flitting across the sombre skies of His new creation and He'd let them be. He'd let them be because they'd made Him laugh. He'd let them be to make people laugh, said John Prys, in case we take ourselves too seriously.

John Prys knew everything! He knew about skylarks. He'd told her, her cousin Winnie, Ifan next door and Rose the evacuee from down the lane, about the skylark and the monk from the monastery whose green ruins lay just beyond the village. One day the monk had left the monastery to walk up the hill that watched over the quiet fields of Llanwrtan. At the top he heard a skylark singing. Looking up into the great blue dome of heaven, he saw it rise and fall, and fall and rise, its timeless song transforming the morning landscape into a strange world of unforeseen shapes and colours and magnitude.

For a long moment the monk stood, filled with the song and resonance of the bird, struck by a wonder that knew no name. Then, with a light step and heart, he went back to the monastery.

There was a strange monk at the gate! All the monks were strangers. No one knew him! After much discussion one ancient brother recalled a story he had heard when he was a novice, of how a monk had walked up the hill one morning, many years before, and had never been seen again. A hundred years had passed while the monk gazed enraptured at the skylark!

Catrin blinked. What if a hundred years had passed while she had been lying here? She turned her head so that one ear pressed against the meadow grasses, making a nearby grasshopper fall silent. The humming field momentarily held its breath. She held hers. There he was again! Rasping his legs together, he chirruped for the world to listen while the sun shone and the distant surf beneath the headland murmured in response. What if a hundred years had passed?

Ty Fron's stone and turf wall around the kitchen garden still looked the same. Beyond a tall stalk of quaking grass that shimmered endlessly in her breath, a column of smoke aspired upwards, almost in a straight line. Megan Prys always had a fire, even in mid-summer.

'You never know when you might need it', she claimed. 'A kettle should always be on the hob, just off the boil'.

Yes, that was her fire, sure enough. Even if a hundred years had gone by, Megan Prys would still be there, brewing cups of tea, bathing bruised knees and hanging out endless baskets of washing with chapped hands reddened by the laundering winds of time.

All the village children went to play at Ty Fron. No one knew why. It had always been so. John and Megan Prys had no children of their own, but they had all the village children around Ty Fron. No one else had such a good barn to play in, or hay that smelled so sweet.

'It's the bedstraw that does it', said Megan Prys. 'While the little lady's bedstraw grows in the field it's not anything particular to look at, except little white stars almost lost in the green, that don't smell much. But, cut and dried, it smells like the sweetest hay there ever was. Good for people and animals is the little bedstraw. Even the finest ladies don't object to it in their linen cupboards, adding fragrance to their sheets and embroidered handkerchiefs.'

What if a hundred years had passed? What was a hundred years like? Was it forever? And they lived happily ever afterwards. The beautiful princess had slept for a hundred years in her white laundered, bedstraw-fragrant sheets. She'd pricked her finger but the prince had awoken her with a kiss - on the lips not on the cheek, according to Winnie, because kissing on the cheek doesn't count - and they'd lived happily ever afterwards.

Catrin could not remember a time when she had not been. Nor could she imagine a time when she would no longer be.

'I shall live for ever', she said out loud, momentarily drowning the sounds of lark, surf and humming field. There was a shocked silence as the landscape considered the statement. But soon the voices reconvened, chirruping, buzzing and humming again in blissful disdain.

How long was a hundred years? Old Guto Rowlands was nearly a hundred they said, but no one was really sure. His skin was like that of Bryn Llywelyn's pet tortoise that his Uncle Wil had brought home from sea. And his head on its stringy tortoise neck poked backwards and forwards from bent old shoulders shrouded in a brown shell of blanket, smelling of lavender, tobacco and old people. He looked as old as time as he sat in his sunny front porch. Maybe he was Old Father Time himself, disguised as a tortoise or Rip van Winkle. Yet, Guto had been a boy once. He'd told them so!

'When I was a boy', he said in his croaky tortoise voice that shrilled and cracked like a winter phlegm throat. 'When I was a boy, there were dragons in the mountains. They used to fly down and roast a couple of sheep for supper. The smell of roast mutton would fill the night air and the sound of their great roaring and the beating of their wings were like thunder. Folk would bar their shutters and wouldn't dare peep through the cracks in case they saw the dragon breath that would turn them into pillars of stone'.

Catrin shuddered with delicious horror as she, Winnie, Ifan and Rose sat in Guto's porch, their eyes like saucers fixed on the wrinkled parchment face with its swimming, rheumy eyes that seemed to look back and back to a time that was, but was no more.

'Where are the dragons now?', asked Winnie breathlessly, twisting the red ribbon from one plait round and round her finger until both were almost the same colour. 'Do they still come down?'

'No, mach i', he said sadly. 'They've gone long ago, but only to sleep in their caves, mind! They sleep with Arthur the king and his knights in high Eryri. They sleep there until Wales needs them. When she does, Myrddin will come back from Enlli and wake them with one blow of his great staff on the echoing stone down there on the beach. Then, look out Germans! Arthur, his knights and the dragons will drive you back into the sea - and the English too, I shouldn't wonder.'

'So the dragons are on our side then?', volunteered Catrin.

'Well of course they are, twp!', said Guto, exasperation cracking his voice until it piped away into a whistling cough. He wheezed as he regained his breath. 'Dragons are Welsh aren't they, not English or German?'

'Why did they eat Welsh sheep then?', she persisted stubbornly. 'Why not English or German sheep?'

Guto paused, his watery eyes moving from side to side in unison with the silent muttering of his lips as he reflected on this seeming imponderable. Then, with a flash of inspiration that stilled the restless furtiveness of his eyes, transforming them into cunning brown pellets, he added: 'They didn't eat *all* the sheep, see! It was just one or two, now and again and only those that belonged to people who didn't say their prayers', he finished triumphantly.

Catrin nodded gravely. The logic of the argument was indisputable. Everyone knew that terrible things could happen to those who didn't say their prayers. She resolved to pray harder that night in case any of their seven sheep were turned into mutton before their allotted time. She had once prayed for a weakly triplet discarded by its mother at lambing time and it had survived as a bottle-reared orphan. That it had subsequently grown into a bad-tempered creature always wanting to butt, and had been despatched to Pwllheli market and the butcher's knife as

14

a result, was an aspect that was hastily glossed over in her reminiscence.

It was unlikely that her family would be a target for marauding dragons because we all say our prayers, she reasoned. But there are some who might! This knowledge had been reinforced the following Sunday when her attention was suddenly jerked back from an agreeable face-pulling competition across the aisle with Ifan by a stomach-lurching pronouncement from the pulpit.

'Remember Lot's wife!', thundered Mr Elis Jones, the Minister, as he warmed to his theme of damnation of erring souls who did not say their prayers. Lot's wife had been turned into a pillar of salt by two great dragons, Sodom and Gomorrah, after they had reduced her sheep to fiery mutton.

'Remember Lot's wife!', thundered the Minister again, and Catrin did!

She rose from the headland and made her way back home, past Ty Fron and down the small lane that led to her home at Pant Uchaf. The smell of cowpats mixed with summer tar filled her nostrils, while a wren twittered a flighty warning of her approach.

Time stretched to infinity for eight-year old Catrin Hebon of Pant Uchaf, Llanwrtan, in that year of Our Lord, 1943, in the ancient dragon land of Llŷn.

2.

Standing by the washing line strung between an apple tree and the end wall of the washhouse, Bethan Hebon caught sight of her daughter between the billowing freshness of the second-best sheets.

'I'm down here by the washing, cariad', she called, stooping to retrieve a towel from the woven basket with the handles that were always threatening to come off. 'Things are drying so quickly today. This is the third lot already!'

She paused to wipe her hands on her wrap-around pinafore then caught a stray strand of hair that was obscuring her vision on one side and tucked it behind her ear. She smiled at Catrin as she approached.

'Are there any messages from Ty Fron?'

'No, Mam. I didn't call by the house. I've been looking at the sky and things. Is there anything to eat?'

'You'll be having your dinner soon. Go and wash your hands and lay the table now. Take an apple from the store if there's a hole in your tummy. This tablecloth has come up nice. I put it in to soak for a while last night and that tea stain has gone.'

'Mam, how long do people live?'

Caught by the unexpectedness of the question, Bethan paused then held out her arms to Catrin.

'It depends, cariad', she said, hugging her daughter to her damp, soap-smelling pinafore. 'Some people live to be very old, while others die younger, and then there are accidents and illnesses. But you don't want to worry about things like that. You'll grow up to be a beautiful lady and live to be very old, with lots of children and grandchildren, too'.

'Will I live to be a hundred, Mam?'

'At your age, cariad bach, you'll live forever! Now give me a hand with this basket and we'll go and help with the dinner. Nain's done the potatoes and Auntie Mari's home already.'

It was but a short distance, past the well and round the corner, to the house. Catrin dropped her end of the basket at the door and ran off to the barn on the other side, where the apples were stored. She'd better get one for Winnie as well, otherwise she'd say it wasn't fair.

'Don't forget to close the lid!', called her mother.

The barn was dark and cool. A swallow darted from its nest high in the rafters, arcing through the top of the broken window in a flash of dark blue, white and orange. The smell of hay was strong and sweet, but the lure of apples led the way to a large wooden chest in the corner. As she lifted the lid, Catrin's nose was assailed by their tangy sweetness. They were some of the best apples in the area, according to Nain. She said that her father had planted the Keswick Pippin tree on the first day of a new year when all the Celtic spirits of the land were there to help it grow. There were many apple trees in the orchard - early eaters, cookers and late storing ones, but nothing with fruit as good as these. Carefully Catrin selected two of the biggest and smoothest. One mustn't be bigger than the other!

Nain was tending the big saucepan on the black-leaded range, while trying to negotiate the recumbent figure of Pero the dog on the rag mat. Profoundly deaf, she heard little of the conversations that went on around her, yet never seemed to miss much.

'Wash your hands and lay the table', she called as Catrin entered. 'Are there any messages from Ty Fron?'

'No, Nain', enunciated Catrin carefully, shaking her head vigorously to emphasise her response, then went to the corner where a large water pitcher stood near the hand washing basin.

The smell of new potatoes with mint hovered like a benediction over the warm, busy kitchen. Mari, in a Land Army uniform with a hastily donned pinafore had just finished shelling the broad beans. She bore a strong resemblance to her older sister Bethan, but was plumper in the face and darker haired. There was the same way of lifting the head and gesturing with the hands as she spoke, but the nervous hesitation and gravity of manner in Bethan, was absent in Mari. In her was an innate bubble of irreverence that was never far from the surface. Her dark eyes sparkled with merriment and her facial expressions always mirrored exactly what she felt. Where Bethan could, and often did conceal herself behind a mask, Mari was an open book.

'What a morning!', she proclaimed, as Catrin came in clutching the apples. 'You'd think they'd never seen cows in Germany, the way those prisoners handled the poor beasts. They hadn't any idea. Though there was one who said he'd stayed on a farm on holiday once, but he was really a clock repairer. Said he didn't know much about animals. Funnily enough, though, he was the best at handling them. He was quite gentle really, even though he has such strong hands. His name is Werner.'

She broke off thoughtfully and Bethan looked at her sister suspiciously.

'You're not getting ideas about a German prisoner of war are you Mari?'

'Of course not! What do you take me for? I've got better things to do than moon about an enemy prisoner.'

But Bethan still looked uneasy. She knew her romantic sister only too well. Winnie's father, an English sailor Mari had met in Bangor before the war, had disappeared as soon as he discovered that Mari was pregnant. Loyal to him at first, with pronouncements that he would soon return, Mari had gradually realised that words spoken during nocturnal passion were frequently rescinded in the cold light of day. In recent years, she had taken to claiming that he probably would have come back but the war had now undoubtedly claimed him, as it had so many lives and loves. He had receded into the mists of time and become a fondly reminisced figure.

'Your father was a fine, strong man', Mari would tell Winnie as the cousins listened spellbound in the kitchen. 'So strong he could lift me with one hand, right up high! And then he'd laugh and say he was never going to let me come down again, at least, not until I'd promised to give him a kiss. He was English, but a fine man for all that. And passionate! I wish I could tell you how passionate ... '

'Hisht Mari!', Bethan would say disapprovingly. 'Not in front of the girls!'

'Where's Winnie?', asked Catrin.

'She's in the parlour sorting out buttons. Tell her to close the box and come and give you a hand with laying the table', said Auntie Mari.

'Oh!', exclaimed Catrin and ran out of the house to the barn. Hurriedly she closed the lid of the apple store and ran back. Winnie was just putting her head around the house door, a half-eaten apple clutched in one hand.

'Where have you been?'

'Just to Ty Fron and back. I got you an apple.'

'Thanks, but my throat still hurts. I can't swallow without it hurting.'

Taking a tiny bite, she gave a demonstration of the agonies involved in consuming the apple. The contortion of face as she struggled to swallow made Catrin's throat tighten in sympathy, but the dramatic effect was spoiled a few moments later when the erstwhile invalid took a large bite and ate with every indication of relish.

Winnie had been confined to the house yesterday and this morning with a sore throat. The extra attention and administration of a jealously guarded portion of homemade treacle toffee had been marred however, by being made to gargle frequently with salt water. She was now ready to acknowledge that she was better.

'Come and lay the table, you two! What's going on?'

The cousins ran inside and began a well-practised routine. A small check-patterned cloth was placed on top of the oilcloth that was never removed from the table. There were some houses where they just ate off the oilcloth, but not at Pant Uchaf! The blue check linen cloth alternated with a red check one during the week, but on Sundays the best-but-one damask of pure white was brought out. The *very* best white cloth with the intricate drawn thread work was only used on the parlour table on special occasions. Christmas day, the Minister coming for tea, deaths and the crowning of kings were deemed to be occasions of sufficient gravity. Catrin and Winnie had experienced some but not all of these occasions, although Auntie Mari had seen to it that they were well versed in the ramifications of the abdication and crowning of kings.

'Torn between his love for a woman and his country, there's a choice for any man to have to make, and him only flesh and blood, despite being a king', she would tell them dramatically, while Bethan eavesdropped nervously in case her romantic sister should elaborate too much on the demands of the flesh.

'That Mrs Simpson isn't much to look at, mind! I don't know what he saw in her. She's much too thin and she's no breasts to speak of. There's nothing for a man to get hold of between the sheets!'

The table was soon ready, the broad beans cooked and the new potatoes piled in their skins into a great bowl in the centre. There was freshly churned butter to go with the beans and potatoes, and a jug of buttermilk to drink.

Winnie remembered at the last minute to put an empty dish for the peelings by the side of the potatoes. Nain would not be amused if that were forgotten.

'They may put left-overs on the oilcloth and sweep

them onto the floor for the chickens to peck in some houses', she would pronounce with dignity. 'But not here.'

The girls took their places on the high-backed oak settle against the wall on one side of the table, while Mari and Bethan sat on chairs opposite. Nain settled herself into the wooden armchair at the head of the table. She still thought of it as her husband's chair. The grave, kindly man who had presided over the household had been dead for eleven years, but his presence was still strong.

'A hearth needs a man', she would declare, always insisting that Bethan's husband, Richard, sat at the head of the table when he was home on leave from his ship.

'It's your chair, Nain', he would protest, laughingly, but the old lady was adamant. Now, she placed her hands together and they all bowed their heads to say grace.

'What have the Germans been doing today, Mari?', enquired Nain as she peeled a potato delicately and dipped one end of it onto the small pat of salted butter on her plate before transferring it to her mouth.

'Trying to learn one end of a cow from the other, Mam', shouted Mari, mouthing each word expressively for the old lady's benefit. 'You wouldn't credit the way they don't know anything. Hans used to be a bank clerk in Dresden. Then there's Peter, a schoolteacher from Berlin and Werner the clock repairer from Hamburg. Funny how they all did different things before going to be soldiers. Not a lot of choice I suppose. Poor things, I feel sorry for them really. I don't suppose they wanted this silly war. Now they end up as prisoners of war in Llŷn.'

'They're better off than when they were fighting', said

Bethan. 'They're not locked up or anything like that.'

The arrival of the German prisoners of war to work at Hendy, the big farm where Mari also worked, had created a great deal of interest and engendered much discussion in the village. Here was the dreaded enemy, face to face! Would they be safe in their beds now? Doors were never locked at night. They were always left open during the day unless it was the depths of winter. Anyone was welcome to walk into a house after the customary call, 'Oes yna bobl?' What would they do now with Germans in their midst? Germans were tall, blue-eyed and blond like the Saxons who'd once ravaged Britain and forced the Welsh from their lost lands into the mountains of the west. They were ruthless killers who clicked their heels and saluted like Romans before shooting you. They raped women, tortured men and murdered babies. They were the enemy to be driven back with blood, toil, tears and sweat. What were they doing in Llanwrtan?

When the three prisoners arrived, the village was agog to see them, but mystified to find that they looked just like ordinary people, tired and a bit shabby. It was true that there was one who was tall and blond but his eyes were grey and he smiled a lot. None of them showed any inclination towards violence. They didn't even click their heels and salute. That was disappointing, but gradually the village relaxed as their fears and suspicions subsided.

The prisoners were initially housed and locked up at night in a Nissen hut from where they were released each morning by the Home Guard in the person of Sergeant Thomas. Soon however, they were given quarters at the farm where they worked so no confinement was needed.

'Where would they bloody go, anyway?', asked Sergeant Thomas of his cronies in the Red Lion. 'Stands to reason that they can't swim to Germany, and who in their right mind wants to go there when they can live in Llanwrtan? I've got better things to do than guard prisoners who are not going anywhere?'

His listeners charitably kept quiet about the fact that Sergeant Thomas had been consistently late in arriving to release the Germans from captivity. Samuel Jones, the irate farmer at Hendy, had finally made it clear that he needed his workers first thing in the morning, not halfway through it. It was better for the prisoners to live on the farm and bugger the military rules! What was Sergeant Thomas going to do about that?

Sergeant Thomas had been the first to acknowledge that the concept of the military mind was indeed a contradiction in terms. He was also relieved not to have to get up at dawn in order to open the Nissen hut. A slight bending of the rules was not only sensible but also in keeping with the local tradition of cooperation. It was generally agreed that as there is no such thing as a straight line in nature, the same must also be true of human society. Everything had to be flexible in order to accommodate the complex interweavings upon which all communities depend.

A compromise was agreed upon. The prisoners would stay on the farm and promise not to try and escape. They would also be given a day off on Sundays, as long as they stayed within the confines of the village. It was a compromise that met with everyone's approval, including the Germans. That higher authority in far-off England might object was briefly considered and then rejected. It was not their business. They didn't live here. They would never know anyway.

The only English in the village were two child evacuees from Liverpool and a retired businessman from Bootle who had had a holiday caravan permanently parked on one of the farms since before the war. 'Just tell them to bugger off', had been his advice when that was sought within the confidential precincts of the Red Lion. 'Or just answer in that indecipherable language of yours and they'll soon give up.'

'Did you say that one of those Germans mends clocks?', said Nain suddenly, pausing as she was about to reach for another potato.

'Yes, that's Werner, the one from Hamburg', said Mari. 'He's the tall blond one with ...'

'Well get him to come here and fix the grandfather clock', interrupted Nain. 'He might as well do something useful besides trying to milk cows at Hendy.'

The clock that stood in the parlour had ticked and chimed the hours for several generations. Lovingly tended and polished over the years, it had stopped suddenly at a quarter to three one afternoon. Everyone within its sphere had paused. Something was wrong! A familiar sound that was the backdrop to their lives was no longer there. Bethan declared that the silence at night kept her awake. It was as if an old friend had been taken from them.

No tinkering had made a difference and the clock still stood, mute and sad, a shadow of its former self. The Minister, on one of his visits, had commented that the horizontal hands of the clock were now a reminder of Christ's outstretched hands on the cross. Nain, while dutifully acknowledging this pious sentiment, was heard to mutter after his departure: 'Duw, I'd rather it told me the damn time.'

'It would have to be a Sunday', said Mari. 'I'll ask Werner to tea next Sunday and he can do it then. I'm sure he'll be able to fix it. He's nice to talk to as well and his English is improving. He knows quite a few Welsh words, too. Have we got enough ingredients to make a cake? It'll be really …'

'You can't ask him to tea! He's a prisoner of war', broke in Bethan. 'They're supposed to work not fraternise. Anyway, what would people think?'

'They'd think we were being charitable', said Mari indignantly. 'And sensible for getting the clock fixed. Anyway, they went to tea at the Choirmaster's house the other Sunday. They're going to join the choir. Did you know?'

William Jones the Choirmaster had been delighted to discover that the three Germans could sing. He'd been passing one of the fields where they were harvesting potatoes when he was stopped in his tracks by a sudden full-bodied harmony of one baritone and two tenor voices soaring in unison. That they were singing a German song of dubious taste about a well-endowed fraulein was immaterial. A good voice is a gift to be treasured. World wars could not be allowed to interfere with the serious business of making music. It mattered not that they spoke German and only a smattering of English. He would see to it that they would soon be singing gloriously in Welsh, the language of heaven.

'Tell him to come then!', said Nain, whose ability to distinguish between an invitation and a command had never been strong.

Catrin and Winnie were agog with excitement. They had only seen the Germans from a safe distance. In fact, the two of them with their friends Ifan and Rose had recently hidden behind a haystack at Hendy in order to have a closer look at the prisoners. If they were spotted they had an excuse ready prepared. Catrin would say that they were bringing a message to Mari from her sister Bethan at Pant Uchaf.

There was no sign of Mari but the Germans were in the farmyard having a smoke, enjoying a respite between potato picking and the evening milking. Their conversation was a mixture of laughter and strange jagged utterances that were fascinating to the children's ears.

'They say 'ch' just like us', said Winnie just as one of them gave a particularly loud and hoiking 'ch' before aiming a stream of saliva to one side of the tractor. Ifan was impressed and immediately decided to practise and perfect that particular manifestation as soon as he could.

'It sounds like swearing', said Catrin, recalling that Ifan's grandmother had said she'd heard on the wireless that Hitler swore a lot. He'd been particularly angry on one occasion because the newsreader said that he was damning everyone, she'd reported. The fact that this was based on her imperfect translation of the Dam Busters' raid report in May of that year was a fact that no one had had the heart to reveal.

The children giggled and then saw to their consternation that the prisoners had turned to look in their direction. One of them got up and advanced towards them.

'Quick, run for it!', said Rose, all thoughts of the prepared excuse forgotten. 'They've seen us.'

Like young gazelles they'd flown across the fields to the safety of Ty Fron's barn, leaving the Germans looking after them with considerable amusement.

In the sanctuary of the barn the children had discussed their narrow escape and how they needed to exercise caution next time. There was no question about there being a next time. The strange aliens held a fascination that had to be acknowledged. They could not be in Llanwrtan without being investigated.

As the mid-day meal came to an end at Pant Uchaf and Mari prepared to go back to Hendy, Catrin and Winnie, barely able to suppress their exhilaration, raced next door to Ifan before going on to Rose's house to impart the news. A German was coming to tea on Sunday and they could come too. Nain had said it was alright as long as they behaved themselves. It was a real German and they'd see him up close.

'We'd better learn to do German things then. We can start with saluting, clicking our heels, walking goose steps and doing 'ch' spits', said the ever-pragmatic Ifan.

3.

Mari climbed over the stile and picked her way carefully past the brambles to the path at the side of the pasture field. There was a well-trodden network of footpaths around the village and outlying farms. Generations of feet had forged then followed the direct routes from one homestead to the next, but it was a network reserved for the few.

Visitors would invariably traverse the lanes, never having been introduced to the secret byways. When Dai Rowlands the postman had been informed that an inspector from central regional office was coming to accompany him on his round, the news had initially caused consternation. Dai invariably followed the footpaths, frequently stopping for a cup of tea at this house and that, while passing the time of day in the manner that is a recognised part of social interaction. The inspector would expect a period that left no time for such pleasantries. He would have little understanding of such complexities. What was Dai to do?

It was his wife Blodwen, the post-mistress, who had come up with an inspired solution. 'Take him the long way round', she'd said. 'He won't know the difference.'

So, the long way round along the lanes had been negotiated without any pauses for tea - the various residents having been forewarned not to issue invitations on that day. To Dai's satisfaction, the long route minus tea breaks took the same amount of time as the short route with requisite stops. The footsore inspector duly logged the result and went back to his central office well satisfied with his day's work.

Mari came to the end of the field and negotiated a pig gate to enter Hendy's farmyard. As a member of the Women's Land Army she would normally have been posted away from home, but what would be the sense in that? She was needed by her daughter Winnie and by the rest of the family at Pant Uchaf. She could help out at Hendy, of course she could, but she would still go home to have her dinner each day and sleep at home. Initial protests had soon evaporated. Samuel Jones, the owner of Hendy, knew better than to go against time-honoured village attitudes and, besides, it turned out that Mari's commanding officer had an influential cousin living in the village.

'Alright Mari?'

Samuel Jones's greeting accompanied by a nod as he came out of the farmhouse was as invariable as the seasons. It was a question that required no answer other than a smile and a nod in return. Mari often wondered what would happen if she took the query literally and responded accordingly. What would be his reaction if she said that she was fine, apart from having had to darn her best stockings yet again late last night, that Winnie had a sore throat, that they were short of sugar and she had a period today? It would be his usual, 'That's alright, then', she was sure.

In Samuel Jones's world everything was assumed to be alright unless there was overwhelming evidence to the contrary. Even then, there was always a way round most things. One of the milk churns was missing. Well find it then! One of the cart's axle pins was playing up. Well fix it then! There are just a few rows of potatoes left to harvest. Well go and get them in then! Blossom is about to calve. Well why didn't you tell me sooner?

Yes, when it came to his cows, his lovely girls, Samuel Jones was of a different demeanour. He knew all ten of them by name and visited them in their stalls when they were being milked. He would stroke them and talk to them fondly about the glossiness of their coats and the beauty of their soulful eyes. Nothing was assumed to be alright with the milking herd. Nothing was too good for Samuel's cows.

'Fine, thanks, Mr Jones', said Mari giving him a nod and a smile.

'That's alright, then.'

On her way to the dairy, Mari paused to throw a smile in the direction of the three Germans who were just emerging from the farmhouse kitchen. They responded with smiles and cheery waves. Unlike Jacob Lewis, Hendy's ancient farmhand, Mari was popular with them all.

Jacob regarded the presence of the three Germans as an unwarranted invasion, a situation that was not helped by their lack of a communal language. Jacob's command of English was sparse at the best of times and, in his opinion, anyone who did not speak Welsh, the language of heaven, was hardly worthy of respect. Mari had found herself in the role of impromptu translator from Germanic pidgin English to Welsh and vice versa, a situation that evoked friendly hilarity from the prisoners and dark mutterings from Jacob. Samuel Jones was content to leave such diplomacies to Mari with his usual, 'That's alright, then!'

In the porch entrance to the dairy Mari took off her coat and shoes and donned a pair of short rubber boots and a white overall that was hanging on the peg. Finally she pulled a white cap onto her unruly curls.

Samuel's wife, Beti, was already in the dairy, inspecting the large skimming pans where some of the morning's milk was settling before the cream was skimmed from its surface. She was an unusually tall woman in an area where most of the indigenous population were short. That, together with her fair now greying hair and blue eyes, was generally regarded as evidence that her father had been an English visitor to the village, unable to resist the temptations of a dark-eyed local siren. Her mother had subsequently married a local man and given birth to five short, brown-eyed children, but all the siblings had been regarded and treated equally. Illegitimacy was not regarded as being unusual or particularly serious in Llŷn. It might be a bit unfortunate, yes, and the chapel might not approve officially, no, but if a child had arrived, it was here to stay, wasn't it? Make the best of the situation; that was the sensible thing. Most of the families in the surrounding villages were related to each other, anyway.

Both of Beti's sons were now in the forces, Gethyn at sea and Bleddyn in the army. There were few moments in the day when she did not think of them and worry about them. The presence of the German prisoners in the household was not a problem, however. She did not regard them as being personally to blame for the conflict that had separated so many families. In her usual, rather grave manner, she had made them welcome while making it clear what was expected of them in terms of behaviour.

Dormitory accommodation had been made available for them in an annexe attached to the farmhouse. They were to make their own beds with clean sheets provided once a fortnight. There was an earth closet behind the stables. This was to be emptied regularly onto the midden. A storeroom was turned into a washhouse, with the pump in the yard providing water that was carried in for their ablutions. Water could be heated up on the small range at one end of the annexe. Everything was to be kept clean and tidy. All their meals were taken with Samuel, Beti and Jacob in the large kitchen of the farmhouse. Muddy boots were to be left in the porch by the side door before they all sat down to eat. Grace was to be said before anyone started and there was to be no swearing or smoking in the house.

With their army training the prisoners were quick to settle into a routine that took in all the requirements. They were happy to concur with Beti's rules, especially as she was an excellent cook and always treated them fairly. When Hans had gone down with a feverish cold that kept him confined and shivering in his bed, Beti provided him with an extra blanket and ensured that he had the appropriate medicine. He was grateful for the cool hand on his forehead and the readiness with which she tended him.

Samuel Jones was a fair man, too, in his own gruff way, although he made it clear from the start that he would brook no disobedience, slacking or bad behaviour.

'Any of that and you go straight back to England where you came from and no mistake', was his explicit warning. 'I'll not have trouble here.'

There was no trouble. The three worked hard and were relatively content with their lot. Even the occasional skirmish with Jacob became an almost pleasurable pastime.

'How's Winnie's throat now, Mari?', asked Beti, turning to reach for the cream skimmers on the shelf .

'A lot better, thank you, Mrs Jones', said Mari as she rolled up her sleeves and scrubbed her hands in a bowl of water taken from the small boiler that provided the dairy with its hot water. 'She'll be back to school on Monday, and not before time, too, according to Nain.'

She laughed as she took one of the skimmers from her employer, then swirled it backwards and forwards in the hot water of the boiler before proceeding to skim the cream from the milk in one of the setting pans.

Mari enjoyed the dairying activities, even turning the handle of the butter churn as it rotated and swished, buffeting the particles of cream until they magically coalesced into butter. After rinsing and salting, it was then worked and finally put into a wooden mould from where it emerged as a rounded pat. Mari knew that in the towns, people had to eat margarine, a strange-tasting product that was as far removed from butter as chalk was from cheese. But then, they had no choice, poor things.

'Those little evacuees seem to be doing alright at school', said Mari. 'They know a lot of Welsh now. Just as well really because no one understands their English.'

This was less to do with an innate lack of understanding of English on the part of the villagers, but rather with an inability to comprehend the children's Scouse accents.

'They talk through their noses all the time, that's the trouble. It must be all the grime in the air in Liverpool that does it. You've been there haven't you Mrs Jones?'

Beti nodded, thinking of the ruin and desolation she'd seen two years before when visiting the great city.

'You wouldn't believe how much bombing they've had, especially around the docks. Whole areas are nothing but brickfields. They had to get the children out of there.'

There had once been more evacuees in the village, but most had now returned to their homes, once the tide of war had begun to turn against the aggressors. Only two now remained, one because his family had perished in the Blitz, the other whose mother had either disappeared or showed no inclination to have her back.

'Would it be alright if I asked Werner to tea next Sunday, Mrs Jones?', asked Mari. 'Mam wants him to mend the grandfather clock because he's a clock repairer really, not a soldier, isn't he?'

'I suppose so. It's his day off after all. Yes, I'm sure that'll be fine, Mari. Your Mam will be glad to have the clock working again, even if she can't hear it.'

They finished the cream skimming and then went on to make preparations for the evening milking. Most of the milk would be put into large metal churns that were placed at the farm gate for collection by the milk lorry. It was then taken to the central dairy in Pwllheli to be pasteurised and bottled. Some was kept for their own use, as well as for making butter and cheese. There were also a few villagers to be supplied. They usually brought their own lidded cans to be filled, although one old lady insisted on bringing a jug every day.

With the preparations complete, Mari went out into the porch, took off her overall, cap and boots and put on her outside wear. Werner and the others would be in the potato field now. She could ask him there. She paused suddenly as she laced her shoes. She'd need to speak to him alone. What could she say? An unexpected feeling of shyness made her pause again. What's the problem? It's a perfectly natural thing to ask. Mam's clock needs repairing. That's all there is to it. Pulling the laces tight, she told herself not to be so silly. Get on with it!

'I don't know if we'll have enough sacks for the potatoes', said Jacob gloomily as she emerged into the farmyard. 'Half of them have disappeared. Somebody's been helping himself, I shouldn't wonder.'

'Why would anyone want to steal our sacks, Jacob?', she laughed. 'Come on, I'll help you find them. Have you had a look in the stable-loft?'

Grumbling that at his age, no God-fearing person should be expected to climb into stable-lofts, he followed in her wake.

'Could be sabotage ... anything to help the war effort ... their war effort ... the Huns, that is', he muttered

'Oh come on, Jacob!', said Mari. 'Look, you stay at the bottom of the steps and I'll throw the sacks down to you.'

She climbed up nimbly and soon located the sacks piled neatly in a corner of the loft. Jacob was an awkward old sod. But that's not all there is to him, she reminded herself. Different, uncomplaining words could also flow from him when the inspiration of verse took hold. Some of his strict metre, 'cynghanedd' poetry had even won him a chair at a local eisteddfod. If anyone in the village needed a poem to celebrate a life occasion, it was to Jacob that they turned. There were few households without one of his compositions to mark a birth, coming of age, marriage or death. Some even had them framed on the wall, which Jacob thought infinitely preferable to the usual, floridly decorated 'God is Love' that hung on many parlour walls.

As Mari threw the sacks down to the shabby old figure at the bottom of the steps, she pondered as she had done many times before, on the mystery of how a bard could be concealed in such an unlikely frame. For he was a true bard! His ability to take a mundane subject and ascribe to it qualities of fineness and sensitivity, expressed in words that gave the spirit wings, were remarkable.

The Welsh language is a cloak of invisibility, she thought, remembering what her late father often used to say. The outside world knows little about the treasures that lie hidden in its ancient depths. Its words, names, forms and structures hold the basic history of these islands, long before the Anglo-Saxons came, before even the Romans came. But it's that very cloak, said to have been a gift of Merlin the magician, that has protected the language and culture, and kept it safe through all the centuries. Many English people do not even know of its existence. Wales to them is just another part of England! But, fair play, the Welsh have not made much effort to inform them, thought Mari. We always want to keep things secret and hidden away. It's our own fault, really.

She remembered a pleasant English academic who had once stayed in the village for a few weeks before the war. He had made strenuous efforts to get the villagers to talk about the legend of Merlin's association with the area, and whether there were any other long-standing traditions such as the practice of bardic poetry, but had met only with polite and firm rebuffs.

'No, I don't know anything about that', was the usual response. Jacob had studiously avoided him. 'Duw, tell him I'm a half-wit', he had said to Blodwen at the post office, when she informed him that the academic had seen some of his poetry on her wall and wanted to meet him. On the one occasion when Jacob had spotted the Englishman coming towards him, he had adopted a posture and facial expression that he thought appropriate for a rural imbecile and hastily shuffled past. It was a sadder and no wiser man who had returned to Oxford on the morrow morn.

As she reached the bottom of the steps Mari looked at the old man fondly. 'I expect that even an old sack holds a poem for you, Jacob?'

He brightened immediately. 'Give me a few minutes, girl, and I'll tell you what those woven threads have to tell, sure enough. Are you expecting me to take the sacks to the field?', he added.

'Oh give them here! I'll take them', she laughed. 'You'll be seeing to the pigs, I expect.'

He plodded off happily, already with the words, forms and music taking shape in his mind. The pigs would be the first to hear his poem; Mari would be the second.

She set off towards the potato field, rehearsing what she was going to say to Werner. Clutching the pile of sacks closely to her and looking down at the ground as she considered, she cannoned straight into him as they both rounded the corner of the barn at the same time.

'Oh it's you', she gasped breathlessly as she struggled to get up. 'I was just bringing you these potato sacks.'

'Me also, I vas coming to get', he explained. He put out his hand and helped her up. 'You OK now? You sure you not hurt?'

'Yes, thank you. I'm fine. I … I just wanted to say … I mean … well, would you like to come for tea on Sunday, on your day off?', she gulped in a rush. There, she'd said it! '

'It's not me', she added. 'I mean, it's Mam. She wants you to fix her grandfather clock for her. Can you do that? Would you like to come?'

'Nothing vould give me more happy', said Werner carefully, anxious that he should get it right. 'To make clock go and to tea with you vould be the most pleasure.'

He smiled with a sense of achievement at his growing command of the English language and bent to retrieve the last of the potato sacks.

'These I carry for you now, please?'

'Yes, thank you. That's alright then', said Mari feeling rather pink. 'Come on!'

4.

Megan Prys folded the last of the washing into a pile to await the ironing. There! It had dried well but now it was time for a welcome cup of tea.

Her husband, John, was down on the beach collecting seaweed for the kitchen garden. Jess, the old mule was sure-footed and patient while her panniers were being filled with the slippery harvest of the strand. Carefully she would negotiate the path as she brought back her load of kelp and bladderwrack to be stacked in the corner of the field where the rain could wash out some of the brine. Then, mixed with straw and manure from the stable and the cow byre, as well as the contents of the earth closet and household chamber pots, it would rot down slowly until it was ready for the kitchen garden.

The vegetables at Ty Fron were legendary! Carrots were a green and orange fanfare that burst triumphantly from the ground, while peas and beans almost podded themselves, so luxuriant was their growth pressing against the succulent pods. Huge and tasty potatoes gleamed white, like floury treasures waiting to be unearthed from the hidden pockets of the earth.

'There's still a bit of salt left from the seaweed, d'you see', John Prys would explain. 'Pests don't like it. Ach y fi, they say and then they go off to look for other vegetables instead of Ty Fron's.'

Some of the village children had gone down to the beach with him. Gathering the slippery seaweed was not their favourite pastime, but he had promised to show them how to collect limpets.

'Pigs like nothing better than limpets fresh from the rocks', he told them. 'But it's best to boil them first. Those old pigs sometimes even crunch the shells as well, but first, you have to get at them.'

He smiled at their eager faces and added, 'I'll show you how.'

It was not an easy task. George, one of the Liverpool evacuees, rushed up to the nearest rock revealed by the outgoing tide and grasped a limpet, but try as he might, he could not move it.

'Gerroff, you bugger!', he shouted at the recalcitrant mollusc, but to no avail.

'No swearing now', chided John Prys, putting a finger to his lips and looking at each child in turn, a signal that attention was required from all them.

'Now then, why can't you get it off the rock?'

'Cos it's a limpet and dey get stuck on rocks. Dat's what limpets do', said George.

'Yes', nodded John Prys. 'But why can't you get it off?'

'Cos it's bl ... Cos it's stuck', said George again.

'Yes, but why can't you get it off the rock?', asked John Prys yet again, smiling at the increasingly irate George.

'I don't bl ... I don't know. Why don't you tell us?'

John Prys put his finger to his lips again and then pointed theatrically at the limpet. 'Because you've told him that you're here', he said mysteriously.

He held up an admonishing finger again as George was about to interrupt. 'You have to creep up on a limpet and then strike it on one side before it realises you're there.

Once it senses your presence, it clings on even tighter and nothing will make it let go.'

He took a small, narrow hammer from his pocket and aimed it at another limpet. A quick, sharp tap on its side, and it fell to the ground.

'There', he said, looking round at the ring of wide-eyed faces. 'That's how you collect limpets.'

Megan Prys finished her tea and went to get things ready for the ironing. She ought to be able to get that done before John came back for dinner. The meal would not take long to prepare. *Brwas* was one of his favourites; fine oatmeal mixed with bacon fat, then soaked in hot water with salt and pepper. With bacon pieces placed on top and finished off in the oven, it provided a tasty and substantial dish for an appetite sharpened by the tang of the sea.

She placed a piece of charred old blanket on one side of the kitchen table and then covered it with a folded sheet. Two flat-irons were put, in turn, on the range hob where the kettle had been, and swung over the fire to heat up. As she waited for the first, she mused on what Bethan Hebon had said to her the previous day.

An evacuees allocation officer had come from Bangor, and had been seen in the village. No one seemed to know what he wanted. Surely, they were not thinking of evacuating city children again? The worst of the bombing had stopped now. Perhaps the authorities had managed to trace some relatives for George and Rose, the two remaining evacuees in the village. It was ...

A sudden knock at the door followed by a hesitant,

'Oes yna bobl?', interrupted her musings. It was Rose, the little evacuee girl from Liverpool. She lived in Bwthyn, one of the cottages by the chapel, but when not at school, spent most of her time playing in Ty Fron's barn, along with many others of the village children, or she was to be found at Pant Uchaf with her friends Catrin, Winnie and Ifan. Megan wondered why she hadn't gone down to the beach with the others.

At one time, there had been eight evacuees in Llanwrtan, including a brother and sister who had been boarded with Megan and John Prys at Ty Fron, but most had now gone back to their parents. Megan and John, with no children of their own, missed them, although they still corresponded regularly by letter.

Eight year old Rose and nine year old George were the only ones not to have returned to Liverpool. George's mother and grandparents had been killed in the devastating Blitz of 1942, and his father had been posted missing in Tobruk. No other members of his family had yet been traced. Rose had no father and her mother had disappeared. As far as anyone knew, her relationship with her daughter had been tenuous at the best of times. An unmarried mother, she had found it difficult to support Rose. The little girl had spent most of her early years on her own during the day, or left with a series of temporary minders. As a result, she was shy and withdrawn, but had undoubtedly come out of herself since coming to Llanwrtan. The dirty, thin-faced urchin with straggly fair hair and blue eyes had developed into a pretty little girl who was gradually gaining in confidence. Much of this was to do with her acceptance by Catrin, Winnie and Ifan into their exclusive group. There had been reservations at first.

'She's English, she can't be one of us', had been Ifan's initial reaction, but Winnie had pointed out that her Dad had been English, too, and he had been a fine man. Her Mam had said so!

'And my Dad is a sailor on an English ship that sails from Liverpool, England', added Catrin. 'So the English must be alright, really. They can't help being Saeson.'

The final decision to accept Rose was made when she demonstrated that she could waggle her ears, a feat that had impressed them deeply, for none of them could master that particular phenomenon. There was no further question of exclusion and Rose had been accepted as a member of their gang.

'Sit down, mach i', said Megan kindly. 'Do you want some buttermilk or would you prefer tea?'

'Tea, please', said Rose hastily. Although by now she was well-versed in village customs and was reasonably fluent in Welsh, she had not developed a taste for the ubiquitous buttermilk.

Holding her cup with two hands, she settled herself carefully on the small settee by the fire and gazed solemnly at the glowing coals. Megan could see that something was bothering her but refrained from asking what it was. Let her introduce the subject in her own time, she thought, as she began to iron.

The fire crackled cheerfully and a cricket began to sing in the hearth, as if in reply. The hiss of Megan's iron as it smoothed over the damp cloth placed over one of John's shirts was the only other sound, but the atmosphere was friendly and congenial. There was no pressure to say or to do anything.

'I like it here', said Rose suddenly.

'Do you, cariad? I'm glad to hear that. There's always a welcome on this hearth for you, as you know'.

'I don't want to go back', said the little girl miserably. 'I want to stay here'.

She turned towards Megan with tears brimming in her eyes. 'Can I come and live with you, Mrs Prys? My mother doesn't want me and I don't want to go to Liverpool and Australia.'

Megan looked at her in surprise. What on earth did she mean by going to Australia?

Rose suddenly burst into tears and Megan hastily put down the iron and went to sit by her on the settee. She took Rose's cup and placed it on the hearth, then put her arms around her and stroked her hair as the little girl sobbed uncontrollably.

'Here you are', she said, handing Rose a large handkerchief as the sobs gradually subsided. 'Do you want to tell me about it?', she asked gently.

'A man came from Bangor', said Rose in a tremulous voice after blowing her nose on the handkerchief. 'He said I have to go back to Liverpool and then to Australia with lots of other children, but I don't know where Australia is', she finished with a wail.

'You don't have to go anywhere you don't want to, cariad', said Megan firmly. 'Don't you worry. I'll go and speak to Mrs Thomas this evening and find out all about it. We'll sort things out.'

Eluned Thomas was the villager at whose house Rose was boarded. A kindly widow, she had done her best for Rose, but was becoming increasingly disabled with rheumatism. She was also getting on in years and was not best placed for bringing up an impressionable young girl.

'Oh, thank you, Mrs Prys. I knew you'd help me', said Rose brightly, all traces of tearfulness now vanquished, apart from a slightly red nose. 'Everything is going to be alright now. I know it is. I'll lay the table for you when you've finished ironing', she added. 'And if there's anything else I can do to help, I'll do that as well. Shall I go and collect the eggs first?'

As Rose set off happily to the hen-house, carrying the wicker egg basket, Megan watched her go through the window. She was touched by the little girl's trust in her ability to sort out problems, but wondered whether she could really do anything. Rose's mother would surely be the one to decide on her future. Had she been found? And what was this talk of Australia? She sighed. She would give anything to help the little girl, but how?

Later that evening, after the milking was done, Megan set off for Eluned's house, as she had promised. She passed several of the villagers who all gave their customary greetings. It was a peaceful time for a leisurely stroll after the work of the day was done. Calling on family, friends and neighbours for an evening chat was a common pastime.

'He came from Bangor to say that they've found Rose's

mother', said Eluned, as she and Megan sat drinking tea in her tiny kichen . 'A right jarff he was too', she added, using the local expression for one with a big opinion of himself. 'He says that she's taken up with an American serviceman who wants to marry her, but he doesn't want Rose. She's agreed to give Rose up for adoption, it seems. Isn't that a really unnatural thing for a mother to do? The orphanage in Liverpool will be taking her until the next stage is sorted out.'

'What next stage and what's this talk of Australia?'

'If the mother really does give her up and there's no one else to take her, the orphanage has a scheme that's been set up with the authorities in Australia', said Eluned. 'Apparently, British orphans are to be shipped out there from Liverpool and found new homes. It's supposed to be a chance of a new life for them.'

'But what if they don't want to go?'

'I don't think they have much choice in the matter, poor little things. It's what the parents say first, and then it's the authorities if there are no parents. I told that old jarff, Mr Hetherington from Bangor, that I'd adopt Rose if she wanted to stay with me, but he told me that I wasn't a suitable candidate. I suppose he means that I'm too old and rickety. I can't bear the thought of her going all that way to the other side of the world, and what if her new guardians are cruel to her? She's come on so well since she's been here. Llanwrtan is her home now. Oh, Megan, surely there's something we can do?'

'We'll find a way', said Megan determinedly, patting her hand. 'It's just a matter of knowing the right way of going about it.'

John was sitting by the fire, reading, when she got back. The seaweed harvest had been successfully deposited in the field and they'd found some serviceable wood on the beach as well. The planks left by the tide had been dragged up and placed on rocks above the tideline so that others would know that they had already been claimed. Jess the mule had done enough hauling for one day, but she would be ready in a day or two. Meanwhile, there was no rush to collect the wood. No one would take it from the rocks. It was one of those unwritten laws that the whole community knew and respected.

'How's Eluned's rheumatics?', he asked. 'And did you find out about little Rose?'

'She's not too bad. Her rheumatism is worse in winter, so she wasn't complaining too much in this weather. She's very worried about Rose, though. You remember I told you that an evacuee allocation officer from Bangor had called? Well, it was to say that they've traced Rose's mother and she has to go back to Liverpool.'

Megan proceeded to tell her husband everything she had found out from Eluned. John had been distressed to learn that little Rose had been so upset when he came back from the beach. In John's world, small children should know no fears or worries. Childhood should be a blessed time of magic and wonder. There was plenty of time to learn about rationality and the realities of life.

'Oh, John, do you think we could have her here? Could we adopt her, do you think? I know that she wouldn't be your child. I failed you in that, didn't I?', she added sadly, thinking back to the tiny stillborn son to whom she had given birth some years after their marriage. Shortly afterwards they had been told that she could never have another child.

'Megan, cariad, it's you I married and it's you I love before anyone or anything else in this life. I'll always love you, to my dying day. There never has been and there never will be anyone else for me. When fate decided that we would be childless, it was not anyone's fault. It's just how it is, but we still have each other.'

He reached over and kissed her and held her close. He could feel her trembling slightly as she tried to hold back her tears.

'If you are really sure that you want to adopt little Rose, then we'll do it. She will be our child', he continued gently. 'We'll give her all the love we're capable of, and we are capable of a great deal of love, aren't we?'

'Oh, John, I do love you', said Megan as her tears began to flow freely. 'I don't know what I'd do without you.'

'Well, that's settled then', said John. 'Tomorrow I'll start making enquiries and I'll get some advice on what we need to do. It might not be easy, mind. We'll have to convince a lot of people that we'll make suitable parents.'

5.

Hans stood by the gate that led onto the headland, gazing out at the shimmering line that was the sea's far horizon. A curlew called plaintively to its mate as it winged overhead, seeming to voice the conflict of the watcher. On the rocks below a couple of cormorants stood with wings outstretched as if holding them out to dry. It was without doubt a beautiful place, but a prison all the same. A beautiful prison from which there was no escape.

He tried to visualise in which direction Germany lay, and where Dresden was in relation to where he stood. What was Greta doing now? Was she thinking of him? Did she wonder where he was and whether he was safe?

The Red Cross had assured him that news of his capture had been sent to Germany, but he had received no letters. Could he trust them to be telling the truth? Were Greta and little Wilhelm safe? Would his little son even remember him by now?

A wave of raw emotion surged through him suddenly, tightening his throat so quickly that he could barely breathe. Tears formed a hot and blinding curtain that obscured his view before they trickled down his cheeks. 'Oh Greta, my love, how I miss you both', he whispered with a sound that turned into a strangled sob.

He turned and looked over to where Werner and Peter were about to close the far gate of the pasture field, now that the cows were out to graze after milking.

'Come on Hans! We haven't got all day', called Peter, holding the gate open for him.

Hastily wiping his eyes, Hans walked over to the other side of the field, to join them. It was alright for them. They didn't seem to mind being here. What did they know about families, anyway? Neither of them had anyone close. They didn't know anything about the gut-wrenching loneliness that came, particularly in the early hours of the morning, when the day still held its breath, before even the bloody farm cockerel was awake to greet the dawn.

He strode scowling though the gate, without a word, while the other two looked after him with some concern.

'What's the matter with him?', said Peter, securing the gate as he spoke. 'He's been funny all week.'

'He's probably depressed and missing his family', said Werner. 'You know what he's like. Leave him alone for a bit. He'll probably come through it.'

'Yes, but I'm not sure that going for a walk late at night is a good idea. He could land us in trouble. We could end up being locked in every evening.'

'I didn't know he went out at night', said Werner in surprise. 'When did that start?'

'A couple of nights ago. The first time I thought he'd just gone out for a piss, but he was gone for nearly two hours. He went out again last night, but I don't know when he got back because I fell asleep.'

Werner nodded. After a hard day's work an undisturbed night's sleep was inevitable, as far as he was concerned. In fact, he couldn't remember a time in recent years when he had slept so soundly as he did these days.

'Maybe we ought to have a word with him about it.'

Unfortunately, that was easier said than done. Every attempt to engage Hans in conversation met with rebuff.

'Look, Hans, you can't go on like this. You're going to get yourself and us into trouble', said Werner in exasperation, after trying all sorts of approaches. 'Talk to us, for God's sake, man. We only want to help you.'

'There's nothing you can do. Just leave me alone!'

'Leave him, Werner!', said Peter, as Hans shrugged away Werner's concerned hand from his shoulder and went off for a solitary smoke. 'We'll keep an eye on him tonight and see what happens.'

Even the best-laid plans can come to nought, however, when the grip of Morpheus tightens itself unrelentingly around corporeal frames. Despite their good intentions, neither Werner nor Peter heard Hans slip away into the concealing darkness, nor were they aware of his return some hours later in a state of high excitement.

It was a relief to them to find that Hans was his old self again the following morning. Depression was a funny thing; it could lift just as easily as it had settled, thought Werner. Hans seemed to be in a rare good mood, perhaps more cheerful than he could ever remember. It wouldn't do to rock the boat again. Better leave things be!

Samuel Jones was already in the milking parlour when the prisoners brought the cows from the byre. Carefully he inspected and stroked each one in turn, telling them that they were undoubtedly the best cows in Wales and that he was the most fortunate of farmers in having such a magnificent dairy herd. Mari looked over to where Werner was looking on in amusement and gave him a wink. They had seen the routine many times before.

Werner was delighted to hear that Mari would be helping them pick apples in the orchard after milking. She was an extremely pretty girl and fun to be with. She seemed to bring sunshine with her wherever she went. He found himself increasingly attracted to her, but was she equally attracted to him? Did it bother her that he was a prisoner of war? An invitation to tea at her house was more than he had dreamed of. It was ...

'Come on, get moving there! Those apples won't pick themselves', said Samuel Jones once the milking was over, and with a truculence that had not been apparent with the cows. 'And don't forget, treat them like eggs! Bruised ones won't keep.'

The shady canopy of the orchard was a welcome respite from the farmyard where the flagstones were already giving up the heat of the morning sun. As Mari and Werner walked towards the first of the apple trees, with Hans and Peter following in their wake, the Embden gander and his harem of geese hissed towards them, necks craned forward and wings outstretched. The gander gave his clarion call of warning but Mari, who was well accustomed to his threats, merely shaped her right hand into a goose-head and moved her arm up and down in front of him. At this aggressive sign, the gander backed away, taking his harem with him, while expressing his displeasure from a safe distance.

'His bluff you call', laughed Werner. 'But maybe we

give him some apples, so face he does not lose.'

'Oh, you and your face-saving. Males are all the same; they must never lose face', laughed Mari in turn. 'Come on, then, let's give them some face-saving apples. Would you like one, too?'

'Me? I have not the face to save, but always I take an apple from the beautiful Eve in this garden of paradise.'

'Flatterer! Here you are, catch! Now, let's make a start. We should be able to clear at least six trees of keeping apples before dinnertime. Don't forget to treat them like eggs. They mustn't be dropped and bruised. Those trees over there can have the apples shaken down and dropped as much as you like, though, because they're the cider ones. We'll finish off with them.'

It was hot and tiring work, climbing up and down the ladders, picking the egg-apples and placing them carefully in the waiting baskets. It was a relief to them all when it was the turn of the cider apple trees. They rushed towards them and proceeded to shake them vigorously, laughing and dodging in protest as some of the small apples fell on their heads. Werner was glad to see that Hans, too, was joining in the fun.

Lowry Morgan, on her way to discuss a chapel sale of work with Beti, heard the laughter as she passed the orchard. She glanced over the hedge just as Werner took hold of Mari's hand and then raised it to his lips. So, that was how things were developing at Hendy. She wondered what Mari's family would have to say about it. No good would come of it, she was sure of that!

6.

Catrin looked at her friends and then addressed them fervently: 'We have to go on a pilgrimage. You're supposed to go three times and we haven't been once yet. Besides, we have to have something interesting to tell the German when he comes on Sunday. I don't suppose he knows about pilgrimages.'

They had spent some time perfecting their salutes, heel clicks, goose steps and 'ch' spits, but felt that in addition to these welcoming gestures, they needed to offer the exotic visitor something from their own culture.

It was Friday afternoon after school and the four of them, Catrin, Winnie, Ifan and Rose, sat in the hidden fastness of an apple tree in Pant Uchaf's kitchen garden. Three great branches, hairy with grey-green lichen, flexed their strength from a trunk that stood like a great dryad protecting its young. Reinforced with planks, salt-bleached driftwood and hay, the bower was to the children a fortress fastness secure from prying eyes and stern injunctions. The world outside the lichened lair ceased to exist. Like a chastened seasonal worker it waited outside, cap in hand.

Construction of the den had been carried out with military precision. The planning stage consisted of a drawing on the large section of slate used to block the gap where the corrugated iron had fallen away in reddish parings on one side of the hay barn. A piece of chalk, secreted in a nimble sleeve when the attention of Mrs Myfanwy Humphries, School, was diverted, ensured that the planners were suitably equipped for their architectural inspirations. It was easily done!

'Can I clean the board duster for you Miss?'

Delivered with all the innocence of a cherub with Shakespearean pretensions, Winnie's ploy ensured a strategic position by the blackboard.

A sudden, 'Why can't I do it Miss?', from Catrin on the other side of the schoolroom was an inspired sally that diverted the teacher's attention for that vital microsecond. Quick as an eyebrow twitch the chalk was purloined and safe in the sleeve.

Mrs Humphries wasn't daft! Her eyes salvoed back from Catrin to Winnie and then volleyed and thundered between them. Something was wrong! She knew it. Those Pant Uchaf cousins were as quick as toadstools. But the dark eyes were guileless, the postures those of eager novices anxious only to please respected elders. The schoolroom, seasoned in the arts of military tactics, watched with deep interest.

'Neither of you will do it! Give the board duster to Jane Edwards. She will clean it'.

The pronouncement was delivered with the satisfaction of a Solomon several jumps ahead of potentially errant petitioners. The disappointed, 'Oh Miss!', like a Greek chorus from Winnie and Catrin, was deeply satisfying. It also ensured that the sleight of hand that transferred both board duster and chalk to Jane's conspiratorial hand went undetected.

It was only when the conspirator returned, with duster divested of its chalky residue on the playground wall and the chalk safely ensconced in a hole in the rowan tree by the school gate, that Mrs Humphries realised the extent of the treachery. Her precise fingers, reaching for the chalk on the blackboard easel's ledge in order to portray the intricacies of long multiplication, encountered emptiness. Her fury knew no bounds. But the evidence had flown! The serried ranks of innocents could not be breached. The gall of defeat was bitter!

The plan, drawn by Ifan with considerable artistic flair, indicated a need for building materials and furnishings. An ignorant world, viewing the same creation, saw what appeared to be a starfish standing on one tentacle, containing a cup within its digestive system.

Everything had to be acquired in conditions of the utmost secrecy. No one must know! Talking costs lives! It must not be like the place where the King and Queen's jewels from the Tower of London were stored to keep them safe from Blitz who was trying to steal them. Everyone knew that they were in one of the disused passages of a slate quarry in Blaenau Ffestiniog where Twm Eurig's Auntie Marian lived. The den must be secure from Blitz, Germans and anyone else outside their camaraderie.

Catrin's mother discarded a battered tin tray with a peeling picture of King George V and Queen Mary. Ifan's mother threw away four old cups, while John and Megan Prys left a couple of old plates and some short planks where they were sure to be found. Eluned Thomas gave Rose an old brown glazed teapot without a lid, with instructions for her to throw it away. Throw it away, indeed! It was the piece-de-resistance! It was the centrepiece of a ceremony that took place whenever the four met in the sacred bower. First the password 'Rommel', then the pouring of the buttermilk, followed by a special invocation.

The cool, tangy, tongue-grasping buttermilk from the great glazed earthenware pot with the slate lid in Pant Uchaf's outhouse emerged from the teapot in a steady stream of solemnity. Rose contrived to arrange that her portion was the smallest acceptable amount that she could swallow quickly without causing offence. Cups were held aloft and clinked together to a chorus of, *'Iechyd da a twll dîn bôb Sais.'* It was an expression that they'd heard Bob Evans use when, somewhat bleary-eyed, he'd emerged from the Red Lion one lunchtime before leaving to rejoin his ship in far-off Liverpool, England. The cheery injunction for good health and an irreverent reference to English arse-holes seemed to them a perfect invocation.

'We have to go on a pilgrimage', Catrin repeated. 'John Prys says there are twenty thousand saints buried on Enlli. If you go there three times you don't have to go to Rome'.

'Where's Rome?', asked Winnie.

'The other side of England and the Holy Land', said Ifan, a statement that engendered general admiration at the extent of his knowledge.

'It's so far away that you only need to go there once and it takes years to get there. That's why they let people from Llanwrtan go to Enlli instead because it's nearer, but you have to go three times to make up for it. That's what John Prys says'.

'Enlli', John Prys had said one warm morning when the children had tired of catching lizards in the turf and stone bank. 'The island of Enlli is one of the most holy places of ancient Wales. It is there that Myrddin whom the English call Merlin lies. It is there that the bones of twenty thousand saints are buried. Men and women with a spiritual search have for generations made the pilgrimage to Enlli. The very air is rarefied. The very turf is hallowed. It is a sacred place that waits to embrace those who truly wish to find it. But only those with pure hearts can feel it. Only those with a clear vision and firm mind can see it. Only they can hear soft voices on the wind and see into the hearts of the rocks and flowers of Enlli'.

His words had set something on fire in Catrin. It was as if someone had held a glowing taper to her so that a brilliant conflagration of light had streamed through her veins like quicksilver. No words were necessary. They fell away like discarded leaves in the cleansing winds of an autumnal equinox. Only certainty remained, like one of the great blue-green crags that rose from the ever-moving surf. She was a pilgrim!

'You can't get to Enlli without a boat', said the ever-practical Ifan.

They looked at him, thunderstruck!

'We haven't got a boat', he said, emphasising again the unpalatable truth of the situation.

It was devastation! To Catrin, it was like a physical blow in the solar plexus.

'What shall we do?', asked Rose.

'Think! Think hard!', answered Ifan, taking the initiative by adopting a posture that did justice to Rodin in the intensity of clenched fist applied to purposeful brow.

They thought and thought and thought. Ideas squirrelled through the labyrinthine branches of their collective minds. Suggestions enthused past the obstacles and snares of rationality. Aspirations soared above the convolutions of cortex and cerebellum, but to no avail. They had no boat!

'Can we go to Enlli, Mam?'

Catrin's request as she dried the supper dishes brought a rueful, sad little smile to her mother's face.

'I don't know, cariad. I haven't been there for years. I suppose so, as long as the coastguard says it's alright. But there'd have to be a boat going ...'

Her voice trailed away, thinking back to the green days when the earth sang and the handsome boy who was now a man, forging the grey convoys of a brutal Atlantic, had taken her hand in his as they stood on Enlli's headland.

'Marry me, Bethan!', he had whispered, with the breath of the surf surging through their veins. And she had tasted the salt of his lips and the fire of his blood as they pledged themselves to each other, on Enlli.

'But is there a boat going?', asked Winnie, stacking the dishes away in the corner cupboard. 'Can't we ask someone with a boat to take us?'

'Oh please, Mam', said Catrin. 'And can Ifan and Rose come too?'

The cousins kept up a relentless campaign until bedtime. Why couldn't they go? It wouldn't matter if they missed a day from school. The school would understand if it was a trip to Enlli. Everyone had to go three times and they hadn't even been once. Who could possibly object? Auntie Mari had thought it was a good idea. She'd said so. Yes, she would, had been Bethan's inner response to that comment, already feeling her resistance beginning to crumble.

Nain thought so, too, Winnie had added. This was not strictly true. Nain had indeed praised the holy island, but then commented that there was a fair chance of drowning on the way to Enlli. If a successful landing were to be made, it was easy to fall and break your neck on the rocks. Then there was always the likelihood of being marooned on the island for weeks if the weather deteriorated, and wouldn't there be a lot of wishing to be safe home in Llanwrtan if that happened?

Bethan thought again of her husband Richard but dared not dwell too much on her feelings for him. To do so was to face the rawness of what she would do if he did not return. The cruel Atlantic had taken so many victims; brave men who did not deserve to perish in its unforgiving depths.

She shook herself slightly. Richard was coming home. Of course he was coming home. He'd promised her he was coming home. There was a lot to do before then. She still hadn't finished painting the washhouse. She should be able to do some special cooking before he came, as well as finishing the weeding in the vegetable garden. If only she could get all the mending done as well. Then, she would ....

Surface thoughts busied themselves with the needs of

of the present. They were effective barriers against the deeper regions where pain and fear reside.

'I'll tell you what! Dad's coming home for a few days when his ship arrives in Liverpool next week. I'll ask him if we can arrange to go to Enlli. It may not be for a while, though. We'll have to choose the time carefully. Those tides in the Sound can be treacherous. We can only go if it's calm. High winds can cut off the island from the mainland. I'm not making any promises. Is that understood? Now go and clean your teeth!'

It was understood. They had prevailed against all odds. It was a triumph of the sweetest kind. Tomorrow they would tell Ifan and Rose. On Sunday they would have something special to tell the German. Tomorrow they would make their plans. Tomorrow and tomorrow and tomorrow . . .

They settled down to sleep secure in the knowledge that they were now well on the path towards becoming true pilgrims.

7.

Werner hesitated before knocking at Pant Uchaf's door. He could see that it was ajar but had forgotten the phrase used by the villagers before they went into each other's houses. Perhaps it wasn't appropriate for him to just walk in anyway. He was an outsider and an enemy prisoner of war, after all.

He had spent longer than usual getting ready, making sure that his best trousers and jacket were pressed, that his best cream shirt was clean and that his face was closely shaven. His blonde hair had been slicked back with a damp comb and his green and brown tie carefully knotted. Yes, he didn't look too bad, he had told himself, as he studied his image in the cracked mirror at the annexe. There was nothing that Mari's family could object to as far as he could see, except for the fact that he was German, of course.

When Peter had discovered where he was going, he had subjected Werner to a considerable amount of good-natured ribaldry, but Hans had merely walked away, muttering something about there being no substitute for a real family back home.

Werner was just about to knock at the door when he noticed four young faces peering at him through the window. When they saw that he had spotted them, they withdrew quickly behind the curtains. Once again, he raised his hand to knock, but this time an elderly woman pulled the door fully open before his knuckles could connect with the wood.

Dressed in her Sunday best, Nain was a dignified figure in a black skirt and high necked white blouse with a
gold brooch at her throat. On every other day of the week,
a wrap-around pinafore over more utility clothing was
the norm, but Sunday was different. Sunday was a day of
rest when, apart from essentials such as milking, feeding
the animals and cooking, no work of any description was
done. She had had a moment's soul searching about the
clock being mended on the Sabbath, but reasoned that as
this was the only time available for the German, the Almighty would understand.

She gazed at Werner sternly and unsmilingly.

'Iw are the Cherman, yes? Iw come in!'

He held out his hand in greeting and prepared to give
a slight bow, but she had already turned away and was
hobbling back inside. She obviously expected him to follow her so he entered the house and found himself in a
large comfortable kitchen with a gleaming black range
and a glowing fire at one end.

'Hisht, Pero!', she shouted at the dog which had been
asleep in front of the fire, but was now barking fiercely at
the intruder. It was an effective admonishment because
he promptly lay down and fell asleep again.

'Clock, you mend, yes?', said Nain, fixing him with
another stern look, obviously wanting to establish his
aims and credentials for the task ahead.

'Ja ... yes ... fix clock, I do', answered Werner. 'Show
him and I fix!'

He suddenly remembered what Mari had said about
the old lady being deaf, so he nodded enthusiastically.

She stared at him for another moment, then gestured for him to follow her into the parlour. Giggles and the sound of running feet preceded him, but by the time he entered the room, the children had vanished again.

The stately grandfather clock stood proud and mute in the corner. Nain looked at him, then at the clock and back again, as if measuring one against the other.

'Is beauty', said Werner, running his hands over the polished oak surface, and gazing in admiration at the clock face with its brass hands and depiction of the phases of the moon. 'He go for you soon', he said, turning to smile at the old lady.

'Humph!', said Nain, going back into the kitchen. She could see that he was enthusiastic in a way that met with her approval, but she was not going to say so. He probably knew what he was doing, but she would reserve judgement until the clock was ticking again.

'There you are!', said a voice. 'I didn't hear you.'

This was quite untrue! As soon as she had seen him coming through the gate, Mari had rushed upstairs to have a final look at herself in the mirror. She had dressed carefully in her best frock with the paisley pattern and short sleeves, and brushed her dark hair until it gleamed. She had saved the best bits until last, however. From the inside pocket of her shoulder bag she had drawn out the lipstick and the *Evening in Paris* perfume she had bought on a recent visit to Pwllheli. Nain would not approve, of course, but it would be a fait accompli now, for she was not likely to say anything in front of a visitor.

Bethan had been horrified when she saw what Mari

was doing. It reinforced her suspicions about a possible and developing relationship between Mari and Werner. What was she thinking about?

'Don't put too much on!', she had said, in a half-hearted attempt at restraint, but Mari had merely given her a grin and told her generously that she could borrow the lipstick and perfume if she liked.

'I'm glad you could come', she said, aware that Werner was looking at her in admiration. He had only ever seen her in her Land Army uniform and could hardly believe her transformation into an even greater vision of delight. Walking up to her, he gave a slight bow and kissed her hand gravely.

'I come to see clock and clock is beauty but you much more beauty have', he said, smiling into her eyes.

'Get away with you!', laughed Mari. 'I bet you say that to all the frauleins at home. Come on out here, you little urchins!', she added, as more giggles came from the doorway that led from the parlour into a small lobby. 'Come on and I'll introduce you. He won't bite you'.

Slowly the four children emerged and stood in a nervous line in front of Werner.

Catrin, Winnie, Ifan and Rose had been ready to salute, click their heels, goose step and do 'ch' spits, but Bethan had caught them doing their final practice behind the barn before they all went to chapel that morning. She had been horrified and warned them that on no account were they to do any of these dreadful things.

So, they stood tongue-tied in front of the tall German who smiled at them and then stepped forward to shake hands with each of them in turn. They were really surprised. No one had ever shaken hands with them before. He must think that they were as good as grown-ups. Ifan decided there and then that, in future, he would do the same.

The children settled themselves down to watch proceedings as Werner produced a small bag of tools.

'Now, I do magic on big clock', he said, giving them a wink. 'You help vith hand me tools, OK?'

It was more than OK. They watched intently as the clock case was opened and its inner workings revealed. They took it in turns to hand Werner the appropriate tool when it was requested, and brought him a cloth on which to wipe his hands after he had cleaned and oiled the parts.

'Now is even more magic moment', said Werner. 'I vind up clock then all count one, two, three and pendulum he goes. You ready?'

They all nodded and waited breathlessly as the clock was wound up with the old brass key that was kept on a ledge inside the case. Gravely, Werner looked at his watch and then set the clock's hands to half-past four.

'One, two, three!' The pendulum was released and everyone held their breath expectantly. Yes! The clock was ticking, its familiar sound falling on their ears like the echo of a friend's laughter. It was fixed!

Everyone cheered and Mari ran out into the kitchen to tell Nain. Just at that moment, Bethan entered the room. She had been reading upstairs but curiosity had finally got the better of her.

'I'm Bethan, Mari's older sister and Catrin's mother',

she said. 'I'm pleased to meet you. Nain will be glad that you've fixed the clock.'

Werner bowed and kissed her hand, causing her much confusion, but she was spared further embarrassment when Nain and Mari entered the parlour.

Everyone went quiet. Nain stood in front of the clock and gazed at it intently. Then, she turned to Werner, smiled and held out her hand to him.

'Diolch yn fawr - thank you very much. It pleases me to have my old friend again.'

'It is much please for me to see you be happy', said Werner, gallantly raising her hand to his lips, a gesture that pleased Nain enormously.

'A real gentleman, he is', she was later to report to all the neighbours. 'He's nothing like Hitler and his gang. He's a real gentleman.'

'Come on, it's time for tea!', said Mari. 'And there's cake too, thanks to Bethan.'

Butter and eggs had not been a problem, for the small-holding produced its own supply of these commodities. It was sugar that was in short supply, but Bethan, in a moment of inspiration, had taken some carrots and shredded them finely, then mixed them with a little honey and melted butter. After leaving the mixture to marinate for a while it was ready for the cake.

She had whisked her way cheerfully through cake making the previous day, with her keen assistants Catrin and Winnie who were helping to break the eggs for her in the hope that they would be allowed to lick the empty bowl and the spoon at the end. When the cake emerged from the oven, it was a triumph of culinary skill, well risen and just the right degree of light, warmish brown for a home-made sponge. They all gazed at it in admiration. It was truly worthy of the occasion. Surely no German household could have produced such a fine cake? What would Lord Haw Haw have to say about that, they wondered.

They went through to the kitchen where Nain had been busy at the big table. The four children sat on the settle, while Mari and Bethan sat opposite them. At one end of the table, was Nain, with Werner facing her at the other.

After grace was said, small bowls of tinned peaches were handed out, together with thinly sliced bread and butter. The cake sat magnificently on the sideboard, ready to be cut. Nain poured the tea, which was served in the second best tea service, and looked about in satisfaction.

'Is it true that you and your friends have joined the choir?', asked Bethan.

'Ja ... yes ... ve are in choir and ve are to be singing in the Velsh', said Werner proudly. Ve go to practise vith Herr Jones at his house and next Sunday ve sing Velsh hymns in church.'

'Do you mean the church or the chapel?', asked Bethan, casting a slightly worried glance in Nain's direction.

Werner was unsure about this distinction and looked to Mari for guidance.

'He means the chapel, of course', said Mari. 'There's hardly anyone goes to the church, except a few toffs, or when it's funerals, and that's only because they own the churchyard', she explained to him. 'Most people in Wales go to chapel.'

'Ja, chapel it is, not church vith steep on top', agreed Werner. 'In Germany too, most peoples go to chapel'.

There was a brief silence as everyone considered this statement. How could Germans be chapel-goers when they had started a world war? No one voiced this however. It was deemed to be impolite and a breach of hospitality to speak of such things, especially on a Sunday.

'We're pilgrims', announced Catrin suddenly. She'd been wondering how to introduce the subject.

'Yes, and we're going to Enlli when Uncle Richard comes home on leave', said Winnie.

'It has to be in a boat because it's an island', said Rose.

'And you have to go there three times instead of going to Rome once', added Ifan.

Werner looked at the children in total bewilderment and then laughed before turning once more to Mari for an explanation. 'Sounds good, but to explain please.'

'They mean the holy island of Enlli or Bardsey', said Mari. 'It's just off Aberdaron at the end of the peninsula. There's an old ruined abbey there and it's reputed to be where Merlin is buried. In medieval times, pilgrims would go there and it's said that 20,000 of them are buried on the island. Local people ploughing have often unearthed skulls and bones so there must be something to it.'

'Das is wunderbar story', said Werner. 'Me, I vould vish to go too, but Germans they not allowed in boat I think, in case they escape to try. But who vish to go from this willage? Not me. I vould like to stay here for ever to live, not back to Germany go.'

As he spoke, his eyes rested fondly on Mari. He is keen on her, thought Bethan, I knew it!

Nain, too, had picked up the unmistakeable signals, despite her inability to hear the conversation. She looked at him critically. He was a good-looking man, but that wasn't necessarily a good thing. Good looking men were often more trouble than they were worth. They sometimes had too high an opinion of themselves to the detriment of anyone and everything else. She studied him again. Yes, he was good looking but he had a kind face too. He was a prisoner of war, but the war couldn't last much longer, could it? Did he have any money? He couldn't have much in his state, but he had skills that would enable him to earn his living when peace returned.

He seemed to be the sort of man who would be a good provider, and he could sing, and in Welsh, too! That was a major factor in his favour. He would have to stay in Llanwrtan, of course. There was no question of taking her Mari to a place like England or Germany. Winnie was a Welsh girl, too, despite having an English father. No, if he was really keen on Mari he would have to accept Winnie as his own daughter and be prepared to stay in Llanwrtan. Yes, that was the best thing. That there might be official complications was not an aspect to be considered. When it came to matters of the heart and of the family, all things were possible as far as Nain was concerned.

'I have idea', said Werner to the children.

'Me, I cannot go to island, but you for me take offering! Always on pilgrimage, offering necessary. Look, you

71

take this and leave on island for me!'

He rummaged in his pocket and produced a small tin that rattled. Inside were a few small brass screws.

'These are of my trade', he explained. 'Always offering should be special for own trade.'

He placed the tin on the table in front of the children. They gazed at it in wonder and then looked at him searchingly and with a sense of gravity. They had been given a sacred task. They were to be the bearers of a special offering. Enlli would surely receive them as true pilgrims.

'Get down, Llwydyn!', shouted Mari suddenly, leaping up from the table to where the old grey cat was about to take a bite out of the cake on the sideboard.

Everyone joined in the laughter, then they all tucked into a generous slice of Bethan's cake.

8.

Lowry Morgan was where she always was, in the creaking fastness of her outhouse at Nant, a small cottage on the outskirts of the village, where she lived with her brother Griffith.

Dark of skirt and pinafore, she hovered beakily over her pots, pails and jugs of patient toil. Here were secrets, dark and powerful, sharp tangs of the green earth, fruited aromas of captured sunlight and, over all, a yeasted mystery of barm permeated by paraffin.

In her mid-sixties, Lowry looked older. Steely threads of hair drawn back into a bun emphasised the stark lines of her careworn face. Yet, these could not quite conceal the fine bone structure beneath. Thick, dark eyebrows twitched above keen eyes that missed little.

'What is it then, Catrin? Paraffin or yeast? No, it can't be paraffin. Your Mam came by for some the day before yesterday'.

'Mam says please can she have two pennyworth of yeast because Dad is coming home on leave and she wants to bake barm cakes for him', said Catrin without a pause.

'Barm cakes is it? Well that should please him. He won't have had cooking like your Mam's where he's been.'

A shadow of pain momentarily touched her features, like the dark wing of a passing raven. She saw again, through the long uncompromising years, the tall figure of her handsome Idris, vigorous, young and confident in the uniform of an earlier conflict, shattered in the mud, blood and pulp of Passchendale.

She shuffled to the great slate slabs that gave their coolness to the air, sighing her momentary tribute to a past, that lay still green within the confines of her heart.

Opening the door of a wire-meshed meat safe, she extracted a large bowl covered with cheesecloth. Catrin, following close behind, watched fascinated as it was placed on the table and the cloth removed. She held out her jam jar as Lowry scooped out two large spoonfuls of the mysterious grey-brown mass and plopped them into it. They slid into the jar, leaving a glutinous trail down the side, like soft slugs with trains in their wake. Lowry took the jar, wiped the sides dry carefully and replaced the lid.

'There you are. All ready for your Mam's baking. And you'll be helping too, I shouldn't wonder?'

'Yes, Winnie and me, both. We'll be doing the mixing and then cleaning the bowl and spoon afterwards. We're allowed to lick them first, of course.'

She handed over the two pennies but was reluctant to go just yet. There was so much here to see and wonder at.

The Aloe plant in the window was a great spider with spiked legs, crouching over the pots and pails. If you touched it you could easily cut your finger on its thick serrated leaves but those very extrusions were a source of miraculous healing powers. When she'd scalded herself with boiling water two years before, Mam had rushed her over to Lowry, while she and the agony-racked leg screamed their anguish to the winds. Ignoring the clamour, Lowry poured boiling water over a blend of herbs and left it to infuse with a teaspoonful of precious sugar, then turned her attention to the Aloe plant. While Catrin's mother sat hugging her blanket-wrapped, screaming child, rocking her backwards and forwards and murmuring comforts, Lowry carefully cut a long tentacle from the plant. Slicing the knife downwards, she removed the serrations then peeled away the cuticle from one side of the fleshy pulp. Squeezing the rest of the leaf until the sap ran freely, she gently applied it to the scalded leg. So gentle was her touch that Catrin barely noticed, but as the sap covered the wound it gradually formed a gelatinous, protective skin that soothed the hurt.

'Drink this now, cariad, and you'll soon feel better.'

The herbal tea tasted of earth, greenery and sweet blackcurrants. As it warmed, it calmed and comforted. Catrin drank it all down, sobbed a few times then burrowed her face against her mother's breast. In two weeks the leg had healed!

She turned her attention back to the yeast in the jar.

'How do you make it? How do you make yeast?'

'Well, cariad ...'

Yeast was alive, lots of little cells, Lowry had said, all clustered together in chains. It didn't look like chains, though, just a thick brownish grey liquid with blobs and a smell that intrigued the nose. It wasn't a particularly nice smell, but not one that you disliked either. She had tasted some a few months before, on her way home from Lowry's. A little bit at first, then some more and finally a large gulp.

'It'll grow in your insides now', said Martha Roberts, coming up unexpectedly in the lane. 'It'll make you swell up like a Hot Cross Bun and you won't be able to fart it away. It clings to your insides and won't let go, and then it grows and grows and grows. People have died of eating yeast and not being able to fart.'

Martha's one visible eye behind the steel-framed spectacles with sticking plaster over one lens gleamed with satisfaction.

Catrin ran home all the way, clutching the hateful jar.

'I told you not to run!', scolded her mother, tut-tutting her way to the pantry. 'Now go and make your bed properly! You haven't tucked in the blankets.'

Catrin watched her retreating back miserably. She wanted to call out, Mam I'm going to die because I've eaten yeast, but the words refused to come. They were gummed up in her insides with the invidious yeast, incapable of being belched or farted.

For the rest of that Thursday evening Catrin accepted the inevitable. Speaking to no one, she had inwardly and outwardly prepared herself to meet her Maker.

'Jesus Christ, son of God, have mercy. Make me fart, but if it is your will for me to die, please make it quick and take me to your bosom in heaven.'

Outwardly, she set out to make reparations for misdeeds, actual or imagined, and to demonstrate Christian charity in order to enhance her chances of achieving the kingdom of heaven.

'I'm sorry I told on you when you broke the parlour window that time', she confessed to an incredulous and suspicious Winnie. 'Will you forgive me?'

The unexpectedness of the question made Winnie run

to her Auntie Bethan with the news that Catrin was sickening for something serious because she had gone mad.

'It must be leprosy or TB', she said breathlessly. 'Or something worse!'

'Yes, cariad, but I'm sure she'll get over it', murmured a harassed Bethan, preoccupied with the ironing and trying to remember what else she had to do before nightfall.

One of Catrin's most treasured possessions, a large multi-coloured glass marble, was solemnly presented to Harri, the witless boy in the village, because she'd once laughed at him to his face.

'I want you to have this Harri. If you hold it up to your eye like this, and twiddle it about a bit, you can see into the heart of the rainbow. That's what my Uncle Dafydd told me when he gave it to me. He said that he found it at the end of the rainbow'.

Uncle Dafydd had neglected to reveal that the end of the rainbow had been a ditch outside the Red Lion. After coming perilously close to falling into the ditch after a leave celebration, his wavering eye had alighted on a winking pearl of perfection in the mire.

'It's the eye of the Tylwyth Teg, sure enough', he belched, and placed it in his greatcoat pocket.

'Whenever you look into it, think of me', said Catrin, pressing the marble into Harri's hand. 'And remember that I was really your friend'.

Harri's wide open velvet eyes gazed earnestly into her face, while his undeveloped mind struggled to comprehend. The significance of her words was lost upon him, but he appreciated that something momentous was under discussion. Taking a deep breath, he strove to control his meandering thoughts.

'Pretty rainbow!', he pronounced solemnly.

It had been a surprise to Catrin when she had awoken to a new day the following morning. God had not seen fit to take her to his bosom, which is where children scheduled to enter the gates of Paradise went, according to Mr Elis Jones, the Minister. Perhaps she was going to the other place. Perhaps she was already there and this was only a dream! But no! How could it be? There was Winnie lying on her back with those irritating little snores because Auntie Mari said she didn't blow her nose properly and got catarrh.

The tumult of small birds in the apple tree outside the window was not sufficiently tuneful to be a choir of angels. William Jones, Choirmaster, said the angelic host was a mighty harmony of ethereal music and that Llanwrtan's choir, even at its most inspired moments, could aspire to be but a pale reflection of its divinity. No, she was still alive, but for how long?

Carefully she examined herself for signs of ballooning. There was nothing to detect but that didn't mean she wasn't already blowing up inside. Jumping out of bed, she ran to the mirror. She looked alright, but you never know! Slowly she puffed out her cheeks, watching the reflection as it indicated what she would probably look like eventually.

Breakfast was a solemn affair. Bravely she tried to eat some porridge, but only managed a couple of spoonfuls.

'You're not sickening for something are you?', said a

slightly worried Bethan, placing her hand on her daughter's forehead, remembering Winnie's remarks of the previous day.

Tears came into Catrin's eyes and she felt an overwhelming urge to tell her mother the awful truth, that her only daughter had but a short time to skip the lanes of the living, before creeping the solemn paths of the dead.

'Mam, I'm going to ...'

'I think you need a dose of asafoetida', said her mother, striding purposefully to the medicine cupboard.

'No Mam! I ...'

She watched, ashen-faced and transfixed with horror. Not asafoetida! Not that bitter, foul-tasting venom that racked the human frame, the bane of rural Welsh youth!

As if caught in a nightmare in which she was powerless to intervene while fate moved remorselessly on well-oiled wheels, she watched as Mam's left hand closed on the dark green medicine tumbler. As if in slow motion her right hand grasped the brown ridged bottle containing the baleful fluid. Slowly she turned, the erstwhile gentle mother transformed into a malevolent witch who advanced towards her doomed victim with the relish of a Bili Ffegor with ever open, devouring jaws.

> *Gwelais y Bili Ffegor*
> *Ai gêg ar haner agor...*

The old rhyme, about the ancient Brythonic god of destruction with his jaws ever agape, echoed in the caverns of Catrin's mind like latent thunder. The destroyer was coming for her!

A little cold water in the glass and it was ready to receive the maliciously poured drops of poison. Catrin could see it all in her mind's eye without needing now to look. The coils of brown eddied and swirled into the water, faster and faster to the clink of the stirring spoon, until it was ready; a cauldron of milky white venom.

'Open your mouth and pinch your nose', gloated the witch, holding the vial of torture at the ready.

One earth heaving, ear popping gulp and it was gone, but that was only the start of it! The bitterness welled in her stomach at the same instant that the aftertaste struck. It produced such an involuntary shaking of the head and protestation of the limbs that Catrin thought she would never be able to keep still again.

'It'll serve you right if I get St. Vitus Dance', she gasped at last, tears running like rivulets across mouth and chin and a hoarseness of voice indicating the depths of torture she had endured.

Winnie for once was silent. She knew too well the trauma that Catrin was experiencing. A sympathetic bond between fellow sufferers was manifest in the solemn, understanding look she gave her cousin, but she made no sound. There was always the possibility that Auntie Bethan would take it into her head to dose her as well! She could never understand how such a kindly person could become a terrible, tyrannical force when she wielded the asafoetida. It was as if some evil genie emerged from the bottle and took over the familiar figure in the blue and white wrap-over pinafore. Discretion was definitely the better part of valour.

'Come on girls! Hurry up or you'll be late for school', said Bethan, wiping Catrin's face gently with a comforting handkerchief.

All the way up the lane, past the church and the chapel, to the village school, the taste of asafoetida was with Catrin. In assembly she tried to concentrate on her private missive to the Almighty, rather than on the headmaster's public utterances of allegiance to creator, family, school, village, king and country, but the foul taste kept bubbling up.

At registration her name had to be called three times before she could answer, such was her preoccupation.

Arithmetic came next! Pencils scrawled laboriously recording the mysteries of long division. Catrin had never been able to establish why long division was harder than long multiplication where you could put a nought down first to make it easy then do a series of little sums. With long division you had to make a wild guess at how many times a number went into another, put a total down, take away and carry the remainder to something else. If you were lucky, it came out right, but most times you had to guess again, while Mavis Davis with her neat plaits and tidy socks always got it right first time.

She stared at the starkness of it. Seven hundred and twenty three divided by twenty six. The unfairness of it! The silliness of it! Why must she waste her time on earthly trifles when divine judgment waited around the corner?

Why indeed? The subtle touch of inspiration moved through her like a thread of fine silver. She would soon be beyond earthly trivia. God did not care if you were good at long division. He required only that you loved him and that you blew your nose and said your verses clearly on Sunday mornings. He did not expect you to know about remainders, but to love your neighbours as yourself and to make your bed and clean your shoes. He did not mind if you had crosses instead of ticks, only that you did not steal, kill or lust in your heart after Hendy's donkey, which is called adultery. The last commandment was an easy one anyway. The donkey was an unpleasant, smelly creature that bit people, but adults were apparently prone to such temptations.

She laid down her pencil and folded her arms. She took a long, deep breath and felt it permeate through her body. She closed her eyes and put aside the imponderable aberrations of adults and long division, to concentrate again on her inner meditation.

'Catrin Hebon! For the third time, come here!'

It was not the voice of God calling her to his bosom. It was a sharp, irate voice, full of jagged inflections and barbed threats. It was the voice of temporal authority. It was the voice of Mrs Myfanwy Humphries, School.

'How dare you be so insolent! Come here at once!'

Catrin opened her eyes. Inspiration vanished, melted away like the intricate delicacy of hoar frost when the angry sun confronts it. She was being summoned, not to the golden gates of Paradise, but to the polished oak desk of scholastic judgement. A pang of fear struck her, like a movement in the bowels and a bile of asafoetida in the throat. Slowly she rose and made her way to the front, eyes downcast like a penitent, between the rows of desks.

Icy faced, Mrs Myfanwy Humphries waited. The insolence of the child! What was she doing? It was the second time she had refused to answer. At registration she had made allowances. Sometimes a child could still be a little sleepy first thing in the morning, but not, definitely not, after the commencement of lessons! This was different! A deliberate downing of tools followed by that defiant fold-arms gesture and then, most insulting of all, the child had pretended to be asleep! Mrs Humphries was not a woman to tolerate incipient revolt. It had to be nipped in the bud before the tendrils of radical insolence grew into the tangled jungle of social rebellion.

Ashen-faced, Catrin stood before her, gazing at the teacher's neat brown shoes with tassels on the ends of the laces.

'Well, I'm waiting', said Mrs Humphries, 'What do you have to say for yourself?'

It was then that fate intervened in that way which is inexplicable to mortals. The lack of breakfast, the tension, the sudden physical movement following a sedentary period, and the asafoetida, all conspired to produce a massive build-up of metabolic gas in Catrin, gas that needed an outlet urgently. It emerged with a sudden explosive force that echoed through the schoolroom like a gun battery.

Never had there been such a fart! It was a fart of epic proportions! It was a fart that Ifan was to describe later, as one that would have made even old Hitler turn and run. For a moment time stood still, then Ifan sniggered. A chuckle came in response from the other side of the room, then another and another! Like the first pattering of an April shower, the chuckles coalesced into a thunderous outpouring of laughter that seemingly would never stop.

A deep tide of crimson rose up the teacher's neck and suffused her face until she resembled an impotent turkey that has forgotten how to gobble.

'Silence!', she screamed at last. 'Silence!'

Slowly the merriment subsided but Mrs Humphries knew that the psychological advantage now lay with the class. There was only one course of action if face were to be saved. It was essential to regain control and then change the subject without delay.

'We are going to recite tables', she announced, 'Starting with the two times table and going up to the twelve times. Catrin Hebon, go back to your place. You will stay in at playtime and write out twenty times the sentence, "I must learn to behave in a seemly fashion". All together, one two is two, two twos are four, three twos are six ...'

Catrin walked back to her place with head held high and a spring in her step. She felt the admiration of the chanting class reaching out and embracing her like the mantle of a conquering hero. Life was sweet! She was not about to enter the vale of shadows. She was alive! Life was to be lived to the full. Wholeheartedly she threw herself into the continuing recitation as she sat down at her desk.

Walking back down the lane from Lowry's house, she smiled as she remembered the sublime experience. Yeast held no terrors for her now. She'd got her own back on

Martha, too. Catching her unawares, tripping her up and pushing her face into a fresh cowpat had been well worth the thunderous smack she'd later received in return. The sight of Martha roaring home, vainly trying to clear cow muck from her one clear lens as she ran, was vengeance of the sweetest kind. She hadn't got the marble back from Harri though! Try as she might she could not get him to remember what she was talking about.

As she approached Pant Uchaf's gate, she suddenly saw a vision! A far-off figure, carrying a case in one hand and a canvas bag on the other shoulder, was wending its way down the lane from the bus stop at the post office. Catching sight of her, the figure threw down its burdens and held out both arms. She raced towards him and launched herself into his arms.

'Dad, dad, you're home!

9.

Damn this bloody country! If he'd realised it would be like this, he would never have volunteered, not that he'd had much choice. Why couldn't it have been somewhere near a city? Why did it have to be this hole in the back of beyond? A remote spot, that's what they'd said, then make your way as quickly as you can to the contact point. Thank God that was in the city!

Why the hell hadn't they told him that they spoke some strange dialect in this part of England? Maybe they didn't know. No-one seemed to know anything that really bloody mattered. It had been sheer luck that he'd found out before blundering into what could have been a disastrous situation.

Surreal, that was the only word for it! Sitting on a rock on the beach, whispering in German about his wife and kid, his informant was obviously a bit touched, but he'd told him some useful things. He'd bring some food in secret, he'd said. It was just as well because he'd managed to lose most of his supplies on the way. Just a short while now and he'd be out of here and not before bloody time either. Even his bloody socks were wet!

• • •

Richard looked around the homely kitchen with warm gratitude and satisfaction. He could hear the steady ticking of the old clock from the parlour, welcoming him back from the hell of the Atlantic convoy crossing. Last night he had slept soundly for the first time in weeks. Secure in

Bethan's arms, there were no klaxon horns, shouts and the horror of oil-fired seas that engulfed men and stricken ships before they vanished in the unrelenting waves.

He had woken up some time during the night and listened to the silence punctuated only by Bethan's gentle breathing and the friendly ticking downstairs. A whole week's leave stretched before him like Nirvana. The ship had suffered some damage that required attention in the dry dock before it was ready to face the submarine packs again. They were like grey, predatory wolves that circled their prey before moving in for their remorseless kill.

At least, the convoys had proper escort protection now, as well as more air cover that was capable of hunting down and destroying the U-boats. In the initial stages of the war, zig-zagging techniques had been the only option open to the vulnerable tankers, but now the tide was at last beginning to turn against the submarine packs.

As he drifted off to sleep again, his last thought had been of the welcome he'd received when he opened the door of the cottage and Bethan had flung herself into his arms, tears of relief flowing down her cheeks.

'A cup of tea for you Richard?', asked Nain, coming into the kitchen with a basket of eggs from the hen-house.

'I'll make it', he said, getting up from the fireside chair and pointing to himself, in deference to her deafness.

'You will not! You sit there and I'll make it', she said firmly. As far as she was concerned, Richard was a battle-scarred hero who deserved to be waited on hand and foot while he was home.

'Alright, Nain', he laughed, sitting down again, realising that protests were futile.

The whole family had embraced him in a warm canopy of welcome the previous day. Their delight was infectious and he had waltzed around the kitchen with each of them in turn. Catrin and Winnie had been so keen to tell him all their news that they were both talking at once at the tops of their voices. Eventually, he had to ask them to take it in turns while he heard all about barm cakes, Werner the German, the fixing of the clock, a trip to Enlli and offerings that were to be taken there. When they had both recounted their stories, they sat back and looked at him expectantly.

'Well, I think all that deserves something special', he said. 'Perhaps I'll have a look in my kitbag.'

The kitbag was always a source of interest and delight and the children felt their excitement growing. Bethan, Nain and Mari were also affected by their sense of anticipation and gazed at Richard fondly as he unlaced the bag and rummaged amongst its contents.

'Well, would you believe it? There are some special things in here. Let's have a look!'

There was a tin of strawberry jam and one of apricot jam, five tins of corned beef and four bars of soap that were wrapped up and had a fragrant smell, not like the carbolic ones from the village shop. That was not all! A couple of American magazines came next, followed by several pairs of stockings, so fine that the women gasped when they saw the shimmering quality. The finale however, was when he withdrew six bars of chocolate and placed them triumphantly on the table.

They were all stunned. Chocolate!

'Can we have some now?', pleaded Catrin and Winnie almost in unison. 'Just a little piece to taste, and can we give some to Ifan and Rose as well?'

'Go on, then!', said Richard. 'Bethan, you'd better do the doling out, I think.'

'Not too much at a time, otherwise it won't last', said Bethan. She took one of the bars and broke it in half. 'There', she said. 'You can share that.'

The cousins raced next door to get Ifan and the three of them ran down the lane to fetch Rose. In a short while, the four of them were sitting in the tree-house. In their haste, Catrin, Winnie and Ifan had forgotten about the buttermilk drinking ceremony. Rose, who had not, made no effort to remind them of it, assuming hopefully and correctly that the chocolate took precedence.

Carefully, Catrin opened the foil and broke the bar into four equal portions that were solemnly distributed. In unison they proclaimed the sacred phrase after the password 'Rommel' and then proceeded to eat the chocolate.

As they chewed, it was like a smooth caress on the tongue and palate that filled their mouths with a heavenly taste and sweetness that remained even after the chocolate had been swallowed. No words were spoken until every bit of the blissful product had been consumed.

They sighed and looked at each other in satisfaction.

'That was the best thing I've ever tasted', said Winnie, a comment that was swiftly endorsed by the others.

'And I don't have to go to Liverpool and Australia', said Rose happily. 'Mrs Prys says so.'

• • •

John and Megan Prys and Eluned Thomas looked expectantly at Mr Elis Jones, the Minister while he considered what they had told him.

'So you're all agreed that Rose should be adopted by you?', said Mr Elis Jones, nodding towards John and Megan. 'Is that what Rose wants, too? And is that acceptable to you, as well, Eluned?'

They all nodded readily and the Minister went back to his perusals, running his hand across his face as if that would in some way increase his understanding.

'It won't be easy, mind, but with the Lord's guidance, I will do everything I can to help you. There are few hearths better than that of Ty Fron to offer a home to an orphan child, and few who would make such good parents as you, John and Megan. It's convincing the authorities that will be the problem. You'll need to go to Bangor and probably to Liverpool as well. Are you prepared to do that?'

'Of course', said John. 'We'll do anything we have to.'

'I will give you a letter of recommendation as well as a character reference, of course', said Mr Jones. 'I will also speak to Edwin Humphries at the school because you'll need his help, too. He will know whom to contact in Bangor and will probably make an appointment for you.'

Edwin Humphries was the headmaster of the village school and was one of the few people in the village to have a telephone in the house. A character reference from him would also be invaluable.

'I'll call in at the school tomorrow and also ask to speak to Rose while I'm there', continued the Minister. 'I'll come and see you as soon as I have any news. Meanwhile, let us bow our heads in prayer for a moment or two.'

• • •

'When can we go to Enlli, Dad', asked Catrin. 'Will we be able to go before you go back to your ship?'

The 'go to Enlli' campaign had been transferred from Bethan to Richard since his arrival and the cousins had kept up their relentless barrage of requests ever since they had come home from school.

'Alright, I give up', laughed Richard. 'I'll go down to the harbour and enquire this evening. No promises, mind! It depends on a lot of things, so don't be disappointed if we can't go.'

They ran off to rendezvous with Ifan and Rose in Ifan's house next door. It was raining slightly and it was a more congenial place in which to meet than it would be in the tree-house.

Rose was already there, holding a skein of wool across her arms, while Ifan's grandmother wound the wool into a ball. Ifan was normally given the task but he was glad that Rose had offered to do it instead.

Catrin and Winnie imparted the exciting news that a trip to Enlli was now truly in the offing.

'But we need to decide on our offerings', added Catrin.

'What can we take to Enlli as an offering, Nain?' asked Ifan, turning to his grandmother. 'Werner says that it has

91

to be something from our trades.'

'You haven't got a trade', she replied. 'Although you're scholars, I suppose. You could take something to do with your studies. Perhaps you could do a piece of writing, a poem maybe, or a special picture. Or what about giving up something that means a lot to you? Not that you've got much, come to think of it. Don't forget that if you take an offering, you can also take a wish.'

The wool came to an end and Ifan's grandmother rose to go and help his mother who was cleaning the pantry and checking the provisions on the shelves. As she left, she turned and added, 'Not any old wish, of course. It has to be a wish of the heart, a real wish for Enlli.'

A wish of the heart! A real wish! The children looked at each other seriously and considered the implications. What was a wish of the heart?

'It's not like asking for a new football or something like that, I suppose', said Ifan, whose heart had been set on that particular wish for some time.

'No, I think it has to be more serious than that', said Winnie. 'It's to do with things like being kind, thinking of other people and . . . '

'We can each think about our special wish and write it on a piece of paper', said Catrin who knew precisely what her wish was going to be. 'Maybe we should keep them secret, too, and not tell each other', she added, thinking that this was the advice given when the Christmas pudding was stirred and everyone present made a wish.

' That's right', said Rose, who also knew what her wish of the heart would be. 'A special wish should be secret.'

General agreement was reached on this point and the discussion moved on to the question of offerings. Even paper was in short supply, although used envelopes that were opened out and trimmed could be used for writing or drawing. All their households kept used envelopes as well as newspapers, the latter having a role as wrapping paper or for even more utilitarian purposes when cut into squares and suspended on a hook in the ty bach, or outside lavatory.

'I'll take my catapult', said Ifan determinedly, adopting a saintly expression that would have done justice to the early Christian martyrs.

The others looked at him in shocked amazement and admiration. The catapult was one of Ifan's most prized possessions. Then they remembered that one side of it was developing a split and he had said he was going to ask Gruffydd Morgan, Nant, to make him another one. No one had the heart or the affrontery to mention this, however. Such a comment would be unworthy when grave issues were under discussion. Winnie had been about to blurt out the truth but the serious faces of those around her had stopped her just in time.

'I'm going to write a poem and draw a picture on the piece of paper with my wish', said Winnie. 'And I'll take one of my special beads as well.'

Winnie's beads were her pride and joy. She had been collecting them for over a year and several of the villagers had added to her collection. Kept in a small wooden box that Nain had given her, they were in a variety of shapes and colours, including three imitation pearl buttons taken from an old blouse that could no longer be worn or cut up into something serviceable.

'I'll take one of my pearl buttons', she said gravely.

The others gasped. It was a magnificent offering. They all knew how Winnie treasured her beads, especially the pearls which she'd told them came from a distant ocean where magic shells grew them for hundreds of years before they were collected. They looked at her with respect. The offering was truly worthy of a pilgrim.

'I'll do a poem and picture as well, and I'll take my next piece of chocolate', said Catrin. She immediately wondered whether she had been too rash when the others gasped again. There was no going back, however. Her friends were deeply impressed and she would lose face if she were to withdraw the statement.

'I can do a poem and a picture, but I haven't got anything to give', said Rose miserably. 'I mean, I've got my clothes but I need them, don't I? I haven't got anything really special.'

'Could you make something?', asked Ifan.

'I don't know how to make things', she began, then brightened. 'I could knit a square', she said happily.

Knitting or crocheting squares to stitch together for making blankets was an activity that most of the village women undertook, either for their own use or for the Red Cross to send to soldiers and prisoners of war. Eluned Thomas had taught Rose how to knit and several squares had been produced as a result. That one or two had slipped stitches was not important. Eluned had made sure that the errant stitches were caught and secured before the squares were handed over.

'You'll need wool', said Catrin. 'Have you got any?'

'No, but I could ask Mrs Thomas and Mrs Prys if they have any spare bits', she replied.

'My Nain will let you have some, as well', said Ifan, certain that Rose's unselfish action in holding the skein of wool while it was wound into a ball would be rewarded.

'Let's go and make a start', said Catrin, remembering that she had seen a crayon stub in the dresser drawer.

No bard or medieval monk toiling over an illustrated manuscript could have matched the zeal shown by those four earnest pilgrims as they prepared their offerings for the forthcoming pilgrimage to the holy island of Enlli.

10.

With sleeves rolled up, Werner and Mari were working in Hendy's greenhouse, thinning out the late-sown cabbages that were to be planted out in the harvested potato field, once that was cleared, harrowed and limed. The weather was in a forgiving mood after the recent showers, and it was so warm and humid that all the greenhouse vents and doors had to be left open. We should be doing this in the coolness of the orchard, thought Mari, but the task was nearly done now, so it was hardly worth moving everything.

In the distance the voices of Hans and Peter could be heard, interspersed with the occasional firing up and roaring of the tractor in the farmyard. The engine had been coughing recently and had even died several times in the last few days. With their employer's approval, they had decided to take it apart for a proper service. Jacob was not convinced that they knew what they were doing, but after watching them critically for a while, muttering darkly to himself that no good would come of it, he had gone to repair a section of fencing where the sheep had broken through.

Lass and Ben, the farm's sheepdogs, had soon rounded up the wandering sheep so that they could be penned temporarily until their escape route was blocked. Now, they loped forward in response to Jacob's instruction - 'Tyd yma!' - and padded obediently at his heels as he went to collect the necessary tools. You know where you are with dogs, thought Jacob. Not like bloody Chermans!

That bout of depression has certainly lifted, thought Peter as he and Hans delved into the tractor's innards. Hans was whistling cheerfully to himself as he worked, and every so often would pause and look towards the headland with a smile on his face. He suddenly realised that Peter was looking at him rather quizically and ducked his head down. I must be careful, he thought. The others will not understand. They must not find out!

Over in the greenhouse, Werner paused for a moment and looked across at Mari.

'Old clock, she still OK?', he asked. 'Tea vith you vas special nice and your family vas velcome to me, a stranger in the willage.'

'Yes, it's fine, ticking away as if it had never stopped, thanks to you', said Mari. 'By the way, the clock is an *it* not a *she*, and a *w* sound is not pronounced as a *v*. A *v* sound is not pronounced as a *w*, either. *With* and *village*, not *vith* and *willage*. Do you remember?'

Werner had asked her to correct him every time he made a mistake with his English. After some hesitation at the beginning, when she thought she might be hurting his feelings, he had assured her that this was not the case, and that he welcomed corrections at all times.

'The clock, *it* is going now and I had tea *with* you. I am also living in a w .. *village*.' he said triumphantly.

'Well done', said Mari. 'As for the welcome, think nothing of it. We're supposed to welcome strangers who come to the door. It's the tradition. But I ... I mean we wanted you to come anyway', she added, in case he thought that he had been asked merely out of duty.

The warm, peaty smells of earth and vegetation were strong in their nostrils. Mari felt a warm trickle of perspiration at the side of her forehead. We really should have been outside, she thought, wiping her hand over her forehead, oblivious of the fact that there was now a muddy mark on her face.

Werner stopped again and looked at her fondly. She was undoubtedly a very pretty girl with one of the most beautiful smiles he had ever seen. It curved her lips and made little dimples at the sides of her mouth. The mud on her face was oddly touching.

'What are you looking at?', said Mari, 'We're not going to finish this if you stop every few minutes.'

He took out a not too clean handkerchief from his pocket and wiped the mud from her face.

'You have the dirty face. If I vere ... were not a prisoner, you I would ask to come out with me to the picture house', he said. 'But only if you have a clean face. I do not go out with girls who have dirty faces', he added with a chuckle.

'Thanks for nothing', laughed Mari, swatting away his hand. 'There's no pictures here. Pwllheli's the nearest place for that. And you can't leave the village. Maybe you wouldn't like it anyway, I mean, seeing all those newsreels about the war, and so on.'

'Fighting is far away here', he said looking about him as he spoke, absorbing the green tranquility and thinking back to the insane conflicts of war. He had hated the whole business, although he had been loyal to his country. It had been traumatic and almost a relief to be captured and taken prisoner during the desert war. It had also been a surprise to find that the hated enemy they had been told about, had treated them well and humanely. The young corporal who had approached with rifle at the ready had actually given him a cigarette once Werner had held up his hands in surrender and allowed himself to be taken to a fenced enclosure.

'Perhaps on Sunday, we go for a walk along cliffs after chapel', he said, turning to look at Mari again. He smiled as he saw the slight confusion on her face. 'I be good and hold hands only.'

She laughed and then nodded. 'Alright, then. Just a little walk'.

'Das is gut ... good', he announced to the cabbages. Me I take prettiest girl in village for a walk on Sunday. Every man in village jealous will be ...'

He broke off when he saw that she was looking slightly concerned.

'Is not good?', he enquired anxiously.

'I don't know. I mean, they may think that as you're a prisoner of war, we shouldn't be going out together ... alone I mean. Maybe we ... Oh damn this silly war!'

She concentrated again on the plant thinnings, trying to think what she wanted to say. He waited patiently, his eyes fixed on her face.

'Let's just go for a walk. We don't have to tell everyone we're going. Let's just take things slowly and see how things develop.'

'Slowly we go and not tell no one', he said then leaned forward and kissed her gently on the lips.

'Oh no!', she exclaimed, drawing away and looking over his shoulder through the greenhouse door. In the distance she could see a cyclist making his way slowly towards the farmhouse. 'Oh please, no, not a telegram!'

• • •

The news that Gethyn, Samuel and Beti's son, had been lost at sea spread through the village like an unrelenting spring tide that rushes ruthlessly into every crevice. In a conflict where thousands died daily, the reality of war came home starkly and cruelly to the small community when it was one of their own who had perished.

Beti, initially stunned, took some time to assimilate the reality of the news. However, once the stark truth had wormed its way into her reluctant consciousness, she was inconsolable. She took to her bedroom, sobbing pitifully against her husband's strong shoulder as they clung together, trying to come to terms with their aching loss.

Hefina, one of Beti's sisters came immediately to look after the house, making preparations for the many callers she knew would come to Hendy to pay their respects. There must be plenty of cups and saucers at the ready. The day-to-day farming and dairying activities, as well as catering for the farm workers must also continue. Life, however painful, inevitably took precedence over death.

Samuel's brother Ishmael arrived to oversee the farm activities until Samuel felt able to resume his duties. A quiet, taciturn man who was blind in one eye, he was nevertheless well-versed in the practicalities of farm management and maintenance.

A steady trickle of callers came to pay their respects and express their condolences, each bringing a contribution to the grieving household. A packet of tea, a small cake, a pie, each symbolising the shared sorrow and solidarity of family, friends and neighbours at a time of grief.

'Bloody Chermans! Murderers!', muttered Jacob as he went past the subdued prisoners as they stood uncertainly by the barn.

'Stay inside for a while', advised Mari. 'Go to your dormitory and keep out of sight while the visitors are calling. I'll bring your food out to you later on. It's best that way for now.'

It was good advice and the three Germans went inside and closed the door discreetly. After a moment's hesitation, Hans turned the key and locked the door, casting a slightly hunted look at the others.

They were just as shocked as everyone else, but knew that it was too soon for them to express sympathy. Let the initial rawness pass! Let the healing touch of time pass over those who grieved! They did not know Gethyn, but Mari had told them that he was a cheerful lad who had been at school with her and had never had a bad word to say about anyone.

Werner stretched himself out on his bed and thought again of the futility of war. When would it all end? When would the world come to its senses?

Hans reached for the book that he was reading. It was a German novel, one of several books provided by the Red Cross. He tried hard to concentrate but found that he was having to re-read the same passage over and over again. What if they found out? What if the villagers took it out on them? The three of them were innocent bystanders now, but they were still the hated enemy to some. He shivered and pulled his blankets up around him. He would give anything to be home again with his wife and child in Dresden: going to the park, feeding the ducks, simple, ordinary things. But, soon, soon, all would be well. He would be out of here. Until then ...

Peter shared some of these fears but felt that problems with the villagers were unlikely. His days as a schoolteacher in Berlin seemed far away, but he never doubted that one day, he would return when the war was over. And it must end before too long! They were able to listen to the news on the wireless, with some help from Mari or Beti when it came to translation. The combined might of America, the British Empire and Russia was insuperable, he thought. The days of the Third Reich were numbered. Whatever the outcome, there would surely always be a place for teachers of mathematics? He had been a good schoolmaster before the army claimed him. Would she still be waiting for him, Helga with her fair hair and laughing eyes? He and Helga on a picnic with the warm sun, the smell of grass and the rippling of the nearby river. Helga's hair brushing against his face as she leaned towards him. It was a shock like a kick in the stomach when he suddenly realised that he could no longer recall and visualise her face!

Werner sat up and reached for his penknife and the piece of wood that he was carving into a horse's head. The grain of the wood had suggested the head before he had even begun. Michaelangelo had been right in his view that a sculpture is already there, in the wood, stone or marble, just waiting to be released, he thought.

The sudden tap on the door made them all jump.

'Who's that?', asked Hans, throwing back his covers and jumping to his feet so that his book went careering across the floor.

'It's only me', said Mari. 'I've brought your food.'

They took the food gratefully, a pie, bread, cheese and apples, while Mari returned to the farmhouse kitchen to get a tray of drinks.

'You'd best keep your heads down for a few days', she said as she poured out the tea on her return. 'Everyone is upset at the moment, but I think most people don't blame you personally. It's just this awful war. There are one or two hotheads in the village, though, so it's best to stay in and around the farm and not go into the village at all for a while.'

'But we are to sing in chapel on Sunday', said Werner.

'I'd forgotten that. I'll ask the Minister and the Choirmaster what they think about you attending. Whatever they decide, I'm sure the villagers will agree to it. I'd better go now. Don't worry. Good night!'

She threw them a sad little smile and hurried out. Hans got up and locked the door again. The others noticed that he was white and shaking.

'Is that necessary?', said Peter.

'I don't know but it's better to be safe than sorry. They could come when we're asleep.'

'Of course they won't', scoffed Werner. 'They all know

us in the village. They know that this tragedy is not our fault. They've been very kind to us.'

'Well I'm not taking any chances', said Hans. 'You heard what Mari said. There are a few hotheads in the village and I don't know about you, but I'm scared.'

He was still shaking as he took up his book again. The other two looked at him in concern but decided to let the matter rest. He'd been so much better after his earlier odd behaviour. Now, it looked as if he might be heading for another bout of depression where he was in his own world a lot of the time. Poor Hans, thought Werner, remembering that his companion had been a bank clerk in Dresden before being called up into the army. Anyone less suited to military life would be hard to find. Werner knew that he had a wife and small son at home. He must be missing them, too, poor bastard.

Werner was grateful now for the fact that he had no close relatives left in Hamburg. His mother had died when he was a boy and his father had been killed in an industrial accident at the factory where he worked. He'd been an only child. Apart from two cousins, there was no one.

As the three prepared for bed, Werner thought again of Mari. She was unlike any girl he'd ever met before, and there had been quite a few. He knew that she had a child, but what of it? She was a pleasant little girl. He was still thinking of Mari when Peter put out the oil lamp and he drifted off to sleep.

There were shouts, smoke, the smell of burning and someone shaking him in a frenzy.

'Get up, Werner. The bloody place is on fire!'

To Peter's relief, Werner leapt up and took in the situation in an instant. The broken window through which the fiery missile had come, the curtains and an old armchair blazing, while more flames licked their way towards the wooden table and chairs.

'Come on! We have to get out', said Peter, but where the hell is Hans?'

The door was closed but unlocked and the two rushed out into the farmyard. There was no one there, apart from Samuel Jones and his brother Ishmael who were running towards them, coats thrown hastily over night attire.

'You alright?', shouted Samuel. 'What happened?'

'Someone break window to start fire', said Peter, as the four of them rushed towards the water pump.'

'Where's Hans?', said the farmer as he worked the pump handle to fill the buckets that the others were holding at the ready.

'He is not there', answered Werner over his shoulder as he ran towards the annexe to throw water onto the advancing flames.

'Diawl!', muttered Samuel, pumping even harder. 'But first things first. Let's get this bloody fire out!'

It did not take too long to get the fire under control, but the annexe was a mess. Blackened wood, charred materials and pools of dirty water everywhere. An acrid smell filled the whole area, catching in their throats and making everyone cough.

'We sleep in the hay barn tonight?', asked Peter. 'We'll need some blankets. Tomorrow Hans maybe he come back. If not, we help you find.'

'I'll get you some blankets but then I'll have to go down to the village to telephone the police. They'll need to know about a missing prisoner and find the idiots who did this.' He looked in a rather apologetic fashion at the two Germans and added, 'I'm sorry. I know Gethyn's death is nothing to do with you, but feelings are running high.'

He stumped off to the farmhouse from which Beti and her sister were just emerging, with feet hastily thrust into slippers and shawls thrown over nightgowns.

'Go back inside, cariad, and you too Hefina! Everything's under control now. Can you just get a couple of blankets for the lads so that they can sleep in the hay barn tonight? Hans has gone somewhere, but we'll sort him out in the morning. I'm going to the village to telephone the police now.'

Peter and Werner had just settled themselves down with their blankets in the surprisingly comfortable hay when Beti appeared again, this time holding out two mugs of strong, sweet tea.

'Here you are', she said. 'These will help to keep you warm.'

11.

The Enlli offerings were nearly complete. Catrin had drawn a posy of flowers on the back of an envelope. There were rays of warm sunshine playing on the bright red petals, while some rather large and pregnant looking skylarks flew above. Her wish, carefully written under the picture, was that her father would be safe at sea, and that all her family, friends and neighbours would be safe in the village, too. Arguably, this was stretching the wish a bit, but she didn't think that was an issue likely to be haggled over by the blessed saints of Enlli.

She had also composed a poem about the flowers. It began in a burst of descriptive eloquence but after the third line, the elusive quality of inspiration that the muse Erato guards with jealous zeal, had deserted her. She had reasoned, however, that the saints would not hold it against her, especially as she was taking chocolate. That offering had originally been three squares of the precious commodity but the human frame by its very nature is subject to perfidious temptation, and now only one square was left to be wrapped in silver paper, with the whole offering placed in a tobacco tin.

Ifan had drawn a fearsome looking Spitfire. The girls secretly wondered whether this was a suitable subject, but declined to say anything in view of the effort that had gone into its creation. His poem also seemed to have rather an excess of 'bangs', 'crashes' and 'woomphs', but again it was decided that discretion was the order of the day. His secret wish was that, with the help of Spitfires, the war would soon end triumphantly for the Allies. His offerings, together with the precious catapult, were placed reverently in a tin that had once contained apricots, with newspaper secured by an elastic band for a lid.

Another empty tin had been drafted into service for Rose's offering. Her by-now, not-so-secret wish was to live at Ty Fron with Megan and John Prys for ever and ever, Amen.

She had nearly finished knitting her square, a task that had taken much patience and lip-biting. Strictly speaking, it was more a parallelogram than a square, and had one or two dropped stitches, but as she explained: 'If you pull it a bit like this, it's alright.'

Her picture was of an angel with wings that would have been worthy of one of Eryri's great eagles, while her poem extolled the virtues of skipping. The connection between the two was not quite clear to the others, but who were they to question inspired creativity when its mystic mantle descended upon artistic shoulders?

Winnie's pearl bead was placed in a matchbox with a folded picture of the gigantic oyster that, for hundreds of years, had incubated it in the lagoon of a mystic island in a faraway ocean. Her poem reflected this theme while introducing a thoughtful comparison between the ugliness of the oyster and the unparalleled beauty of its pearl. It was an impressive poem that the others felt to be worthy of the local eisteddfod, but Winnie was steadfast in the view that it would be cheating to use it for any non-divine purpose.

Her secret wish was far more prosaic, however, in wanting her mother to have more clothing coupons.

Together with Werner's tin, the offerings were stored carefully in the cupboard under the stairs at Pant Uchaf, ready for the pilgrimage to Enlli.

• • •

Morning came stealthily with a dim light that gradually revealed the fields, hedges and secret places of the landscape. Dew lay heavily like a silver shroud on the grass until trudging boots displaced it in a shower of droplets.

'Duw, it's bloody cold this morning', said Sergeant Thomas, banging his arms against his body, still grumbling at having to be up at such an hour.

The line of police, regular soldiers and home guard had fanned out across the fields and cliff tops in an effort to trace the missing prisoner. Every house in the village had been contacted, and all the outbuildings searched but so far there was no trace of Hans.

There were roadblocks on all the lanes leading out of the village, as well as on the main roads farther afield. He could not have gone far in a short time, especially at night. Alerted by the telephone call to the police, the authorities had reacted quickly in sending out a military search party while it was still dark. Being used to night manoeuvres, the regular soldiers were well organised and thorough. Just before dawn, they had been reinforced by the Home Guard and the police who had also arranged for two detectives to visit Hendy.

The two Germans were questioned closely as they sat

in Hendy's kitchen. The police obviously suspected all three Germans of having tried to escape, but Samuel Jones was adamant in his defence of Werner and Peter.

'They could have run off but they didn't. They stayed to help me put out the fire. And come to that, when are you going to look for the ones who started the fire?', he asked belligerently.

'How can you sure that it wasn't started by the prisoners themselves?', asked one of the detectives.

'Don't talk daft, man! Of course, they didn't start the fire. Why should they? If they wanted to escape, they could have done that anytime.' He paused, remembering that, contrary to regulations, the prisoners weren't locked up at night, but fortunately, the policemen did not pursue that avenue of investigation.

'It was probably a young fool in the village', he continued. 'Some silly and misguided revenge for my son's ... my son's ... '

He paused, sighed heavily and continued in a quiet voice. 'You see, my son Gethyn, he's just been reported lost at sea. The telegram to tell us came yesterday.'

'We're very sorry to hear that, sir', said Inspector Pugh, the senior of the two detectives. 'We'll continue our investigations, of course, including asking questions in the village. But now, we'll leave you to carry on. If there's anything else that occurs to you, please get in touch.'

Handing Samuel a card, he and his colleague went back to their car and drove out of the farmyard. Samuel and the two Germans followed them outside then stood watching until the car had gone out of sight.

Jacob and Mari emerged rather nervously from the barn and came to join the others.

'Jacob wants me to tell you that he's sorry about the fire, but it wasn't him', said Mari.

The three men looked at her incredulously.

'Of course, it wasn't Jacob', said Samuel irritably, while the Germans continued to look in a bemused fashion. Then, recognising the olive branch that was being extended, Werner stepped forward and held out his hand to Jacob. 'Diolch. Thank you', he said gravely, bowing his head briefly as he did so. They shook hands and then Peter stepped forward to do the same.

Jacob nodded to them both in a manner that embodied both relief and embarrassment, before going off to see to his pigs.

'We help you find Hans now?', asked Peter, but Samuel shook his head. 'No, you have to stay on the farm. I've no choice, I'm afraid. Look, my brother will tell you what needs to be done now. I have things I have to see to.'

He turned wearily and went into the farmhouse where the Minister was waiting to see him.

They had still to learn that, not long after dawn, Ron Harris, the Englishman, had been scouring the beach from the headland with his binoculars. Instead of the seals that he expected to see, he saw what at first appeared to be some clothing washed up by the tide. Closer inspection revealed a pathetic and crumbled body that lay where it had fallen from the cliff edge. Hans would never return to Dresden now, to see his wife and small son.

12.

The chapel was packed to the doors that Sunday when the whole village came to pay their respects to the memory of Gethyn. His body could not be laid to rest in the churchyard where his forefathers lay. It would lie for ever in the depths of the wide Atlantic where his ship now rested, countless fathoms in the deep.

The atmosphere was subdued as the congregation waited for the service to begin. As the organ played softly in the background, everyone sat with their own thoughts, quietly considering, remembering. Hushed remembrances were of happier times: the first steps of a beaming toddler, the youthful pranks of a grinning schoolboy and the ready laughter of a confident young man in his naval uniform. Grief was raw and painful despite these reminiscences from a green time of peace.

Catrin looked across the aisle to where Ifan was sitting and then turned round to exchange glances with Rose. Face-pulling, normally a pleasant way of passing the time, was out of the question today given the gravity of the situation, so she confined herself to a sad little half smile that seemed more appropriate. She thought back to what her mother had said:

'Dad says we can go to Enlli, but it will have to be delayed until after Gethyn's funeral. It wouldn't be respectful to go before then.'

'But Dad won't be able to come with us', had been her response. 'He'll be back on his ship by then.'

'I know, cariad, but it can't be helped. Mr Beynon will

take us in his boat next week, if the weather is fine.'

'Dad won't be lost at sea like Gethyn will he Mam?'

'Of course not! He'll come back to us safe and sound with his kitbag full of surprises as he always does.'

As Bethan sat in the family pew with Richard, Nain, Mari and the girls, she remembered Catrin's question with a sudden and agonising lurch in her stomach. She reached out and grasped Richard's hand and held it close. Please God, watch over him! Please don't let anything happen to him! Richard, knowing what she was thinking, squeezed her hand gently in return.

Bethan glanced to where the two German prisoners of war, heads bowed, sat on a pew to one side of the chapel. As Samuel and Beti and the rest of the grieving family entered with the Minister, the Choirmaster and the Vicar from the nearby church, they stood up with the rest of the congregation, their tall stature towering above those around them.

The third prisoner's death had shocked everyone in the village. It had brought home to them the shared grief and reality of a war that affected all sides. Who could have done such a thing? Whoever it was must be sorry for what had happened. Perhaps the fiery missile was not meant to harm, but just to shock. It was a sobering experience for all concerned, but the general consensus was that the matter should now be laid decently to rest.

The same could not be said of poor Hans. His body had been taken to Bangor for a post-mortem. Internment could not take place until the authorities had completed their enquiries and a coroner's report issued. It was a state of limbo that distressed both Werner and Peter, although the officer in charge of the investigation had assured them that Hans would eventually be accorded full military honours at his funeral.

As Samuel and Beti took their place in the front pew, they could feel the sympathy and solidarity of the congregation surrounding them like a protective mantle. If only their other son Bleddyn could be here with them, but he was far away in the Mediterranean war. There were many other families in the village who also had loved ones in the various theatres of war, and who felt their absence like unseen presences in the quiet chapel.

It was a simple yet dignified service of remembrance. As one who had known Gethyn all his life, the Minister spoke movingly of the young man's generous nature and the many positive aspects he had brought to village life, observations that brought murmurs of agreement from many in the congregation as well as from the important, throat-clearing chapel elders at the front.

The Minister sat down and old Jacob came forward, hardly recognisable to the two Germans, in his Sunday best. This was not the shabby, shuffling farmhand that they normally saw. This was an upright and distinguished man with the gravitas of one who commands immediate attention. His dark suit was old and shiny, but it was clean and well-pressed. He was freshly shaved with the old cutthroat razor he espoused as being the only tool capable of doing the job properly, and his grey hair was combed back so that his broad forehead was revealed.

This was a noble figure. This was the village bard come to deliver an eulegy to one of their own.

Speaking in his native tongue, Jacob's voice was clear and resonant, as if it came from some deep and inner wellspring within. Not a sound disrupted his oration as the form, colour and music of his poetry took life and meaning, and flowed through the atmosphere to move the feelings of his listeners. An appreciative sigh passed through the congregation as his recitation came to an end. Many wiped away tears as Jacob went forward to hand a copy of the poem to Samuel and Beti before returning to his seat.

The congregation gave of their best when the hymns were sung, their voices in four-part harmony resounding to the very roof under the whole-hearted direction of the Choirmaster. Werner and Peter joined in the soulful Welsh hymns, their tenor and baritone voices raised in unison with those of the congregation. There was no divisiveness in death.

• • •

Later that evening Mari and Werner went for a walk along the clifftops. The residual warmth of the day rose up in fragrance from the headland as their feet trod the wild thyme, while the surf below breathed in steady motion. It was a time of quiet and of reflection, made even more poignant by the events of the day.

Werner held her hand as they walked, appreciating the splendour of the view and the calm of the evening light. Every now and again he looked at her and smiled but words did not seem to be necessary. For a long time they walked in silent companionship until they came to the highest point of the headland.

'Look!', said Mari suddenly, pointing out to sea where dark shapes were looping out of the waves as they emerged and submerged in sequence. 'Porpoises! They're beautiful aren't they? We often get schools of them around the coast here. They must be after a shoal of mackerel.'

They watched the graceful sea creatures until they were lost to view around the headland.

'The old people here say that porpoises and seals can change their shape and come ashore when no one is looking', continued Mari. 'The females become beautiful girls with long flowing hair, but the men have green faces and red noses. Don't ask me why! The sea women used to go to Pwllheli market, apparently, but you could always tell who they were because their aprons were damp. I don't know what they would have been buying there. It can't have been fish', she laughed.

Werner joined in with her laughter, bending down to pick some thyme flowers and then throwing them at her.

'Me, I leave you now because I go instead to look for beautiful sea porpoise with flowing hair.' He made as if to run off then, changing his mind, came back and added: 'But maybe not! Already there is beautiful sea girl here.'

He drew her gently towards him. 'In Hamburg, too, there are Rheinmaidens that come from great river, but none like you. You, Mari, I think of all time I am at work. Even in sleep you come to my dream.'

He bent down and kissed her then looking into her

116

eyes said: 'I think maybe I am begin to fall in love with you sea girl. I think maybe I wish to stay here with you for always. Is it possible that you love me also a little, an enemy prisoner?'.

Mari was touched yet flustered at the same time. What were her feelings for this tall, handsome man from an enemy country? Was it possible that she loved him? She was certainly attracted to him. Who wouldn't be, with his looks and his manner? But what kind of future would there be for them if she did love him? Would her family and the rest of the village accept him? There was Winnie to consider, too. Was he prepared to accept her as his daughter and to live in a country that was foreign to him?

There were so many questions and she was confused.

' I don't know. Well, maybe just a little bit', she grinned. 'Come on! It's time to go home now. I'll race you back.'

13.

Catrin sat with her back pressed against the hard seat support of the motorboat as it chugged and ploughed its way through the truculent waves of the Sound. Next to her sat her mother, with Winnie on the other side. In front of them were Ifan, his mother Enid and Rose. Placed carefully in front of them were all the bags with the picnics and the offerings. Every so often Ifan rested a proprietorial hand on them in case they needed some protection against any marauding sea creatures that might come their way.

The children were well acquainted with stories of creatures of the deep. There were whales, great leviathans whose booming calls echoed around the oceans of the world. There were huge sharks that could swallow the unwary in an instant, leaving only a few bubbles to show where they had been. There were giant squids with tentacles so huge that they could wrap themselves around a ship and drag it down to the bottomless depths of Davy Jones's locker. So graphic had been Ifan's descriptions to them the day before that the girls had begun to have second thoughts about the sea trip, but he had hastened to reassure them that there was nothing to fear.

'You see, Davy Jones is Welsh', he said. 'So he'd look after us. He'd probably ask us to tea in his Locker and then just send us back again.'

'But we'd drown', said Rose, not at all convinced by his reasoning. 'We're not fish!'

'No', agreed Ifan. 'Of course not, but mermen and

mermaids change themselves into people to come ashore in Wales so it stands to reason that we can turn into them if we need to.'

The girls had considered this statement carefully. There certainly were seals, porpoises, mermen and mermaids who lived in Neptune's caverns amidst brilliant corals, pearls and shells. They were known to go on land from time to time, even visiting Pwllheli market, according to Ifan's Nain. They were alright apparently, but you couldn't always trust them, she had said, because they were full of trickery. How could they be sure that they would be safe in their slippery hands?

Finally, it was Catrin's argument that had saved the day. 'It stands to reason', she said. 'If we're going to Enlli as pilgrims, we can't come to any harm because Myrddin and all the saints will be looking after us. I expect that Davy Jones, the merpeople and all the sea creatures would listen to them.'

The bags had been packed carefully with the picnics and the offerings placed on top. Hard boiled egg sandwiches had been made by Nain, but she had had to be restrained from making too many - 'in case you get caught on the island'- because Ifan's mother had already made a considerable quantity of paste sandwiches.

'For heavens sake, Mam, we're only going for the day, not for a week', protested Bethan. 'There's enough there to feed an army. And we've got lots of apples, too.'

'Well don't blame me if the Sound gets angry', said Nain. 'If it does, you'll wish that you'd gone well prepared. I remember once ...'

But Bethan had changed the subject quickly because they had heard many times before the story of how Enlli had once been cut off from the mainland by great storms that roared about the island without let up for several weeks. Although the islanders grew many crops, they were dependent upon the mainland for many of their supplies and necessities, including flour.

'The storms went on so long that their food supplies dwindled to almost nothing', Nain would never tire of telling them. 'It got so bad and they were so hungry that there was only one thing to do. They all gathered in the chapel to pray for divine help. They prayed as they had never prayed before, or since I shouldn't wonder. All night they prayed without ceasing. They prayed until dawn light came through the chapel windows and then they wended their weary way back to their homes.'

'But what do you think?', Nain would ask dramatically at this point in the narrative. 'What do you think they found on the shore? There on the sands was a great wooden cask. When they broke it open it was full of flour. It was a bit spoilt on the outside where seawater had got in, but the inside was perfect. They all rejoiced and straightaway set to making loaves of unleavened bread. They survived on those until the storms abated and the supplies boat was able to come from the Tir Mawr again.'

'But the cask was probably just washed off the deck of a ship somewhere and it was a lucky coincidence that it came ashore at Enlli', Mari had once volunteered, but after Nain's furious reaction she had never done so again.

'Coincidence indeed! It was the saints of Enlli looking

after their own, and don't you forget it my girl!'

'Not far to go now', said Edward Beynon. 'You'll be able to stay until the last tide. That should give you enough time on Enlli. I've got a cousin there. I've been promising to get him some new fish hooks and he's made me some lobster pots in return, although I'm not sure how good they'll be. They're long ones like the ones they use in Brittany, not like the round ones we have here.'

Edward Beynon was a fisherman and a member of the local lifeboat crew. He had one leg twisted and slightly shorter than the other, a defect that had effectively kept him out of the armed services, but he made up for it in many ways, including taking a stint on coastguard watch as well as piloting the regular mail boat to Enlli.

'Just let them try and get ashore at Llŷn from their U-boats! Just let them try! They're not going to take anyone by surprise on my watch. There won't be any Nazi spies coming ashore here, I can tell you', he would proclaim.

'It's very good of you to take us, Mr Beynon', said Ifan's mother, having heard from Bethan that there would be no charge for doing so. He had been adamant about that.

'I'm going anyway, with the post and any other bits and pieces that are needed', he had laughed. 'So why should I charge you? Anyway, there may be a time when you can do me a favour. Who knows?'

It was a viewpoint that was shared by most in the small communities of Llŷn. They relied on each other in a way that was relatively unknown, or had been forgotten, in larger conurbations, although the war had generally brought people closer together, even in the cities.

It was a relatively short crossing to the island, around two miles as the crow flies, taking just under an hour in all, but there were many dangers for the unwary. Safe crossings could only take place at the appropriate time in relation to the tides. The north-west going tide splits into two streams as it hits Enlli, one going along the northern side, the other flowing along its southern side. The streams unite about a mile and half beyond the island, with a strong eddy then setting back towards Enlli. The ebb tide behaves in a similar fashion, with split streams passing along the eastern and western sides, followed by a boiling eddy swirling into the Sound. Spring tides and high winds bring added dangers. It is no wonder that the medieval pilgrims used to pray for a safe crossing at the ancient church of Mary at Aberdaron.

'It used to take longer when we had to row across the Sound before we had a motorboat', Edward Beynon continued. 'But this little boat, she skims along like a seagull, and I've been making this crossing more times than I can remember. It's not like carrying that old ram, though, I can tell you.'

The said ram had long taken its place in the realms of local mythology, with the narrative gaining more detail with every telling. It had been transported from the mainland some years before, to one of the islanders who wanted to improve his sheep breeding stock. All had gone well during the first part of the journey, for the ram's legs were securely bound together. At least, they had been securely bound when they started, but this particular ram was endowed with the devilish cunning more frequently found in goats than in the more staid realms of sheep. Two thirds of the way across the Sound, the confining ropes gave way and the ram, which had been lying in a prone position on its side, suddenly found its feet. Tossing his magnificent horns to the winds, he faced the two oarsmen with contempt, bleating in ovine derision.

During the ensuing struggle, swaying and thrashing about, the ram's feet went through the bottom of the boat and water began to pour in. All might have ended there and then, with everyone at the bottom of the channel, but ovine cunning is no match for that of humans when in dire straits. As quick as the slithered turn of an eel, Edward Beynon had pushed the ram down until its legs were wedged into the hole, and then he sat on him. The waterlogged fleece was an effective plug.

'There, you bugger! Get out of that!', he had proclaimed in satisfaction. In this fashion, with his colleague rowing at a speed previously unmatched, the boat had arrived safely on the island. The recalcitrant ram was then thrown into the shallows from where it was hauled to land with a crook, while the boat sank to the bottom with a gentle gurgle, until it could be retrieved when the tide went out.

'Two days we had to stay on the island while the boat was mended', he would recount, 'But that old ram he stayed there for ever. He sired many a good lamb, it seems, despite his dunking.'

'Here we are', said Mr Beynon as they approached the Cafn, the island's small landing bay. 'But we don't have to have royal permission to land these days.'

There had once been a king on the island! It had come

about because in the late nineteenth century, Lord Newborough, who owned the island, had insisted that there should be a spokesman for island affairs. The response from the elected representative had been: 'If I'm to be the King, I need a crown'.

Lord Newborough had entered into the spirit of the occasion and commissioned the making of a gilt crown worthy of the position. There had even been a coronation carried out with due solemnity that had included the firing of a gun salute from one of the boats at anchor.

Several incumbents had occupied the position of monarch, including one who had been deposed by the islanders and subsequently went to live on the mainland. Unfortunately he took the crown with him, which was a bad mistake on his part because a boatload of irate island men had followed him and demanded the immediate return of the crown. The crown, they said, was of the island not of the mainland!

One king had even started an ingenious enterprise so that whenever a boatload of visitors arrived, they had to obtain landing permission from him before they could set foot on the sacred sands. After the required permission had been granted, visitors were carried in piggy-back fashion from their boat by the King's official 'Carrier'. It was only a few feet in distance to dry land, but each one had been charged a shilling for the service that ensured they did not get their feet wet. With only one landing place where a boat could gain access, visitors had no choice but to pay up. Fortunately, the charge had been waived for Llŷn people.

'I'll see you here before the last tide turns', said Edward Beynon, after he had helped each of his passengers ashore and secured the boat. Ifan had been ready to emulate him and stride through the surf but Edward in his waders, had scooped him up before he could get his feet wet.

'Don't be late or you'll have to swim', he added as he walked to the boathouse with the bundle of letters that had been entrusted to him for delivery. There were only a few people living on the island now, a mere fraction of the busy community that had once existed on this westernmost tip of Llŷn. Three families still worked the land and went fishing for mackerel and herring. The school and chapel still functioned, but only with tiny congregations. At the southern end was a lighthouse manned by resident keepers who took it in turns to ensure that the beam warned ships of the treacherous rocks that had claimed so many in the past.

'Right where do we start then?', said Ifan's mother, looking round in pleasure. It had been a long time since she had visited the island, at least ten years. At that time a relative had lived on one of the small farms, but that branch of the family was now living in one of the mainland villages. Bethan too, had fond memories of Enlli, although she had no family connections there.

The island was only about two miles long and a mile or so wide. Its buildings included thirteen houses - many now empty - the chapel, school and lighthouse, as well as the ruins of the ancient abbey. The dwellings were situated in the lee of the mountain that stood on the eastern side, with the houses having the benefit of looking down on the flat land that faced the western ocean.

'Oh, can we have something to eat please?', said Winnie. 'I'm starving.'

'Me too', said Catrin, Ifan and Rose in unison.

'We've only just arrived', protested Bethan, but Enid, realising that the belly protests would only continue, said: 'Why don't we go to the abbey first and have a picnic there? Then we can explore a bit more afterwards.' She neglected to tell them that it was a mile's walk to the abbey, but felt that after the confinement of the boat, it was a good thing for them to exercise their legs.

A general consensus having been arrived at, they set off up the winding path from the landing bay until they reached the first of the houses. Two of the islanders gave them friendly smiles as they passed, realising that they were mainland locals, not some outlandish visitors to be regarded with suspicion.

'I know you. Your aunt used to live here, didn't she?' said one of the women to Enid. 'How is she liking it on the Tir Mawr?'

'She's fine, thank you, but she still misses Enlli', said Enid diplomatically. Although her aunt had initially reacted against the iniquity of having to pay mainland taxes after leaving the tax-free island, she had however commented favourably on the many conveniences, such as that of having a horse-drawn delivery service from the local butcher. Meat was officially only available with the requisite number of points from wartime ration books, and these were collected with due solemnity by the butcher, but who was to know if, from time to time, there was a little extra and unofficial pork or lamb that did not require points?

'We're going to have a picnic up near the abbey', said Bethan. It's so beautiful here.'

'You've chosen a good day', said the other woman. 'You wouldn't want to be here when the wind and the sea are angry. Then we just keep our heads down at home. You be sure to keep away from the cliffs', she added, addressing the children. 'They're very steep and if you fall from there, it's hard and cruel rocks you'll be landing on.'

The children nodded solemnly and the group continued up the path to the abbey. All around them was the soft sibilance of the sea, with the calls of seagulls, choughs and shearwaters resounding like a symphonic poem laid on for them by Nature in one of her more gentle moods.

The sunlight shone on the golden gorse and the purple wealth of wild fuschias and foxgloves that greeted them on every side. Tall fronds of bracken waved at them in the light breeze, but there was no danger of hidden adders or other venomous creatures here on this sacred island. Even frogs and toads were absent.

'Look! There's the abbey', said Bethan, pointing ahead to where the looming shape of a ruined tower beckoned near the nineteenth century chapel and mission house that catered for the religious needs of the present community. The tower was all that was left of the monastic settlement of St Mary, apart from a few ancient inscribed stones, some mounds in the ground, a graveyard and a well from which the monks had drawn their water.

The children ran ahead towards a great Celtic cross

that had been erected in Victorian times to commemorate the 20,000 saints buried near the spot. *"In hoc loco Requiescant in pace"*, read the inscription.

'It means, *"In this place, rest in peace"*, written in Latin', said Bethan. 'It's written in Latin because that would have been the language they used for prayers.'

'Didn't they say their prayers in Welsh?', asked Catrin, aware that her personal supplications to the Almighty were invariably couched in her native tongue. Perhaps the fact that they were not always heeded was because of her lack of Latin.

'I'm sure they did, because they all spoke Welsh, of course. Even St David himself spent time here and you don't get more Welsh than that.'

But further metaphysical discussions came to an end when the children again realised how hungry they were.

'Come on! Let's sit over here,' said Enid, walking towards the base of the tower and beginning to unpack the bags. 'We'll have our picnic and then you can decide where to leave your offerings.'

Despite the informality of the picnic, there was tacit understanding that, out of respect for any listening saints, grace would be said before they started eating. The egg and the bloater paste sandwiches were soon consumed with relish. Bethan realised with a pang of conscience, that Nain had not over estimated their combined eating capacities after all. As Rose crunched her apple, she was relieved to see that buttermilk had not followed her to the island, and that watered down orange juice was the drink of the day. Hurray!

There followed much discussion amongst the children as to where they should leave their offerings, but it was finally decided that somewhere on the side of the hill above the abbey would be an appropriate spot. It would be facing the glittering western sea where great Atlantic ships passed along the horizon, on their way to and from far-off Liverpool.

'That's the way Dad's ship goes', said Catrin. 'He'll be able to see Enlli on his way out and on his way back. He'll know that our special offerings are here.'

'Don't go too far away or to the top of the cliff! Stay where we can see you', said Bethan, as she and Enid settled themselves down for a brief siesta after the meal.

It was not long before the children found a suitable place. There was a slight depression in the ground that was just big enough to take all the offerings. They laid them down reverently then went to gather stones to make a small cairn over them. The large stones were laid around them first, followed by smaller ones until the cairn was complete.

Catrin placed a small bouquet of wild fuschia flowers on top then they stood around the cairn, each with his or her own private wish and thoughts as they looked solemnly at the sheltering stones. Were they true pilgrims now? Were they like the travellers John Prys had described? *"Only they can hear soft voices on the wind and see into the hearts of the rocks and flowers of Enlli."*

Then Catrin became aware that the others had now transferred their attention from the cairn to her. They were all looking at her in expectation. She remembered that it had been her idea to come. They were waiting for her to say something. What should she say? It had to be something that was appropriate to the gravity of the situation. Then, taking a deep breath, she addressed the cairn:

'Myrddin and the saints of Enlli, we have come here as pilgrims and we have brought you offerings from our trades. Well, we haven't got trades really, but Werner has, so we hope that's alright. We've brought you pictures and poems, too. We hope you like them.'

'Don't forget wishes of the heart', whispered Winnie.

'I was coming to that', Catrin whispered back, slightly irritated that her oration had been interrupted. 'If you like the offerings, we've got wishes of the heart, too', she continued. 'We won't say those out loud because they're like Christmas puddings so we'll just think them now, although we have written them down as well. Thank you very much. Amen'.

'Amen', echoed the others.

All in all, it was an impressive performance and the others felt that Catrin had done full justice to the occasion. With a last look at the cairn, they ran down the hill, imitating aeroplanes, with their arms outstretched as each tried to outdo the other in speed and manoeuvrability. None of the girls could compete with Ifan on this front, but he told them generously that this was only because he'd had more practice, and anyway girls couldn't be expected to know exactly how Spitfires flew.

The game continued for quite some time, while Bethan and Enid snoozed gently in the sunshine by the abbey tower. They opened their eyes somewhat reluctantly when the children returned, but soon entered into the spirit of things and walked up to see the cairn.

'That's lovely', they said, touched and impressed by the children's efforts.

The rest of the day was spent in exploration, with visits to the chapel, the sacred well and the only accessible sandy bay on the west side of the island. Here, they met up with some of the island children and made impressive sand castles until they were invited to one of the houses for a cup of tea. Then it was time to go.

It was as they walked down towards the landing bay to meet up with Edward Beynon that the miracle occurred. Turning back for a final look towards the hill, the children were astounded to see a bright light emanating from where they had built the cairn. As they stood, breathless and awe-struck by the steady gleam, they heard some plaintive, minor-chord cries of the kind that they had never heard before. The calls echoed and re-echoed for a moment until they gradually receded, leaving only the trace of a whispered memory.

'Come on!', called Bethan turning round to look at the children who were still standing in a small group farther up the path, like figures frozen in a timeless landscape.

'Come on, stop dawdling! We'll miss the tide if you don't hurry up.'

'Mam, did you see the light up there', said Catrin, pointing up to the side of the hill. 'And the voices ...'

'What light? I can't see anything.'

Like the calls, the light had gone, just as the ephemeral gleam of a glow-worm disappears when examined too closely. The children looked at each other and realised that further discussion on the matter was fruitless. They ran down the path to join Bethan and Enid and they all made their way down to the harbour.

The children were quiet on the journey back but their hearts were full. Myrddin and the saints had heard them! Their offerings had been accepted! Their wishes of the heart would now be heeded. They were amongst the sacred ranks of the privileged for they had seen into the heart of the rocks and flowers of Enlli! They had heard soft voices on the wind. They were now true pilgrims!

The children were not to know that the sun slanting towards the western sea had caught the edge of one of the reflective tins that was not quite covered by the cairn. Nor did they know that the basking seals on the quiet stretch of rocks near the lighthouse were calling plaintively to each other. Well does Enlli keep her secrets.

14

The bus from Pwllheli drew to a halt outside the post office at Llanwrtan with a screech of brakes followed by a heavy sigh, as if relieved to have arrived at last. Against the sound of the engine ticking over, it disgorged its passengers. Amongst them was a tall, brown-haired and pleasant young man with a walking stick. He descended from the bus carefully, then stood looking about him with pleasure.

'Thank you very much', he said, smiling at the bus conductor who was depositing his case on the ground. 'That's jolly decent of you.'

'That's alright, sir. Mind how you go now', answered the conductor before getting back onto the bus and ringing the bell with a gusto that was at odds with the prowess of the ancient vehicle.

Martin Taylor watched the bus as it wended its way down the lane until it was out of sight, but leaving behind a familiar smell of oil, metal and exhaust fumes. He nodded politely in response to that from the friendly couple who had also travelled on the bus, and who were now turning to walk away. He noticed with interest that they were walking arm in arm and were deep in conversation.

He looked around to get his bearings. Yes, he had remembered correctly. There was the inn, the Red Lion, only a few yards away.

'I'll take that for you', said one of his fellow passengers who, unlike the others, had not yet left the bus stop.

He picked up Martin's case. 'I expect you're going to the Red Lion. Is that right?'

'Yes, that's right', said the young man. 'But you don't need to worry. I can manage.'

'It's no trouble', said the man, and before Martin could protest, proceeded to make his way to the inn, humming tunefully and resolutely to match his vigorous stride.

' Here you are John! It's a customer for you', he said in Welsh to the middle-aged barman who was standing behind the bar polishing some glasses. He put the case down then held out his hand to the young man following in his wake and addressed him in English.

'I'm William Jones. I take it that you'll be staying here for a while?'

'Pleased to meet you Mr Jones. My name is Martin Taylor. Yes, I'll be here for a while. Thank you very much for your help.' He turned to the barman and said: 'I have a room booked here in the name of Martin Taylor.'

'Oh yes, sir. You'll be the English gentleman. Would you sign in, sir?'

He turned the register round on the bar so that Martin could sign. Both men watched him as he wrote, craning forward in order to read the details.

'Are you on holiday then?', asked William Jones, showing no inclination to leave.

'Yes. I am actually.'

'Are you staying long?'

'Well, I'm not too sure yet. It's just a brief holiday', replied Martin, beginning to feel a little irritated.

'Nice to be able to have a holiday in wartime', said Mr

Jones. 'Very nice indeed.'

'Yes it is. I hope I'll be able to have some peace and quiet without disruptions', said Martin, his irritation growing apace. However, the irony implicit in his comment appeared to be completely lost on his companion.

'I don't suppose you'll be in the forces, what with your leg and all', continued Mr Jones earnestly, gazing with interest at the said limb.

'Yes, I am actually, or at least I was until a short time ago', retorted Martin sharply, a note of bitterness entering his voice. 'Look, I might as well tell you, it's ... it's a kind of convalescent holiday really'. He gestured at his leg with distaste. 'I'm a bit of a crock at present. Came down without any wheels, you see. Bit shot up on the way back'.

'Oh, you're in the RAF then', gasped William Jones as realisation dawned. He gripped Martin's hand again and proceeded to pump it up and down as if he would never stop. 'It's an honour to meet you, Mr Taylor. I mean that, truly. It takes great courage to do your job and we all appreciate the heroism of the boys in the RAF, although none of us likes having to wage war. Welcome to Llanwrtan. I'm the Choirmaster here, and if you want to join us in the chapel on Sunday, we'd be delighted to see you. You'd be a tenor, right?'

'Well, I'm not sure. Yes, I suppose so, but I'm not what you'd call a singer. Thank you very much for your invitation anyway, Mr Jones. I'll certainly bear it in mind. I'd better get going now and see my room, get unpacked and so on. I expect I'll see you around the village. I came here with my parents once, quite a few years ago now, when I was on holiday from school. I've never forgotten it and I thought it would be just the place to relax and recuperate for a while. I'm supposed to be convalescing.'

'You couldn't have come to a better place than Llanwrtan, that's for sure. The sea air in your lungs will certainly do you good and there's plenty of nice level walks to get that leg of yours going. Well, I'll bid you good day now, Mr Taylor, and I hope that you'll enjoy your stay with us. Let me know if there's anything I can do for you. I live in Ty Gwyn, the white-washed house, three doors down from the post office. Just call anytime you're passing. My door is always open.'

With that, William Jones went on his sonorous way. It would not be long before the news had spread throughout the village, that an RAF hero who was a tenor was staying in their midst.

John and Megan Prys, walking arm-in-arm down the lane from the bus stop, were deep in conversation. It had been a full day in Bangor, with meetings and discussions with innumerable people. The Minister and the Headmaster had done a good job in making appointments for them, furnishing character references and generally smoothing their path towards their aim of adopting Rose. There had been so many questions to answer and forms to fill, and even then, they were none the wiser. How long would it all take?

'It's just a matter of being patient', said John. 'There's bound to be a lot of waiting. They said it would take time, and we have to go to Liverpool as well, don't forget!'

'But what do you think they thought of us, John? Do you think they liked us?'

'Who could look at you and not like you, cariad', said John, squeezing her arm against his side. 'Everything will turn out fine in the end. You just wait and see.'

In his room at the Red Lion, Martin lay down on the bed and looked about him. It was good to be here. It was incredibly quiet. He'd forgotten how quiet the country-side could be. In the distance he could hear the sound of a sheep calling its lamb, then a cockerel somewhere re-minding its listeners of his territorial rights. It was so far removed from the stress of waiting, then scrambling to take off when the word came, the roar of the engine, the acceleration and the take-off into the blue that was so beautiful yet so threatening. The sheep called its lamb again and somewhere, far away a seagull seemed to an-swer as if it knew where the frolicking lamb had strayed. It was so quiet here. So quiet ...

He started awake and looked at his watch. Good God, he'd been asleep for nearly two hours.

'Who is it?', he called in response to the knock at the door that had awakened him.

'I've brought you some extra towels, sir.'

'Come in!' He rose up but was still sitting on the edge of the bed when the maid came in with a couple of large bath towels. He struggled to his feet and smiled at her.

Normally, guests staying at the Red Lion would be given one large towel, one small one and a flannel. He was not to know that an exception was being made in his case. RAF heroes, especially those with beautiful tenor voices, were in a special category.

'The evening meal will be served at seven o-clock, sir, but you can get a cup of tea anytime.'

'Thank you very much.'

When Ceri went down to the bar, it was to report that Mr Taylor, the much decorated RAF hero with the famous tenor voice, was tall and brown-haired. His eyes were a lovely shade of grey and he was ever so good-looking.

'He's got lovely manners too', added Ceri. 'Not at all like a Welshman. He was sitting on the bed when I went into his room with the towels, but he stood up straight away, even though he's got a bad leg. He knows that it's only polite to get up when a lady comes in.'

If the listeners were dubious about Ceri's qualifications to be a lady, they kept a discreet silence as they listened, in case they were deprived of further nuggets of information. Ceri was a great devotee of films and spent many a happy hour in the picture house at Pwllheli. Her perception of the ideal male was a compound mixture of the swashbuckling bravado of Errol Flynn, the romantic manners of Leslie Howard and the devastating wit of Noel Coward. It was a continuing source of disappointment to her that her boyfriend Rhys, who was in the reserved occupation of farmer and therefore exempt from call-up to the armed services, did not measure up to these impossible ideals. Rhys, however, was of a philosophic turn of mind and reasoned that she would settle for him one of these days. She was his girl. She just had a bit of growing up to do. Once married, all would be well. In the meantime, he was content to take her to the pictures every week and for her to dream.

Martin put down his cutlery, sighed in satisfaction and announced in all truthfulness: 'That was the best meal I've had in years, Mrs Rowlands.'

'Are you sure you wouldn't like a second helping of pudding? It's no trouble', said the cherubic Mrs Rowlands, beaming at him with pleasure. Despite the shortages of war, she took her culinary responsibilities as hostess of the Red Lion seriously. Her husband John was the proprietor and with the help of their daughter Ceri, the couple ran the inn with wardroom efficiency.

'I couldn't find space for another crumb, but it was absolutely delicious', said Martin. He had dined splendidly on home-made rabbit pie with mashed potatoes, carrots and onion gravy, followed by apple dumpling and the best custard he had ever tasted. There were certainly advantages to living in the countryside in wartime. That rabbit had no doubt been caught locally and he had spotted the inn's large kitchen garden where the proprietor grew a lavish selection of fruit and vegetables. There were also chickens pecking around contentedly in a large enclosure, no doubt the source of the eggs for the magical custard. Yes, he'd made the right choice in coming here.

The doctors had been adamant. There was no question of Martin returning to his unit until the leg was completely healed and that would take some time. It was still questionable whether he would ever return to active service. It was more likely that his future role would be in training, preparing those who were scarcely more than boys for the aerial combat that would have many plummeting to their deaths.

'I think I need a short walk after that feast', he said, getting to his feet and reaching for his walking stick. 'I'm supposed to exercise this leg as much as I can but I'm going to need even more with your excellent cooking, Mrs Rowlands.'

'Oh get on with you. It's just plain home cooking, that's all. Nothing special.'

The evening air was soft and balm-like as he walked along the High Street. House martins chattered in flight as they flitted around the roof tops. Soon they would be replaced by bats. *"The bat that flits at close of eve has left the brain that won't believe"*, he recited to himself. His nostrils caught the sudden fragrance of honeysuckle from one of the cottage gardens and he stopped to savour it.

'Good evening to you', said a gentle voice and he turned to see an elderly clergyman with snow-white hair emerging from a side turning in the lane. 'Permit me to introduce myself. I'm Roger Walters, the Vicar of this parish. You'll be Mr Taylor who's staying at the inn, I think?' He shook hands with Martin and continued. 'News soon gets around the village and there won't be anyone who doesn't know that you're here. That's the way of small villages, I'm afraid, but we're all very pleased to have you with us. A warm welcome to Llanwrtan.'

'Thank you, Reverend', said Martin, touched by the

vicar's quiet simplicity. 'If I remember correctly, the church is quite old, isn't it?' I stayed here once when I was a boy.'

'Ah, you've been here before? Yes indeed, it is an old church. All these ancient Llŷn churches are the legacy of Celtic Christianity, you know, not the later Roman foundations that came with Augustine. Our church here has one of the earliest fonts in the area. We're also very proud of the Tudor stalls with misericords in the chancel. The village is on the old pilgrim's route to Bardsey, and the spring near the church would have been one of their stopping places. The local people will have it that Merlin is buried on Bardsey and there's no changing their minds on that. There must have been some reason why it was so important as a site of pilgrimage, of course, and three pilgrimages to the island were said to be equivalent to one to Rome, but history is tantalisingly short of clues. What we do know is that the survivors of the great Celtic foundation at Bangor Iscoed escaped to Bardsey for sanctuary when their monastery was sacked by King Aethelfrith of Bernicia in AD613. Just a few escaped the Saxon massacre, but enough to ensure that the hallowed status of the island is remembered even to this day.'

The Vicar nodded to himself then, perhaps realising that he had moved into an overtly didactic mode, said:

'I'd be very happy to show you around the church during your stay, Mr Taylor. Most of the villagers are chapel, of course, but my friend, the Minister Mr Elis Jones, and I often have shared services. Since the disestablishment of the Church of England in Wales, we've all got on very well.' He laughed and then, replacing his hat, continued:

'But I mustn't keep you from your evening stroll. I look forward to seeing you again soon.'

Several more villagers stopped to greet Martin on his walk, each anxious to welcome him and, it must be said, curious to see the wounded and much decorated hero with the glorious tenor voice who had come to stay in their village.

As Martin made his way back to the inn, he felt a sense of contentment that had eluded him for a long time. The stress that had become his shadow during the months of combat, followed by the enveloping bitterness inflicted by his disability, seemed somehow less burdensome now. He could almost believe that ...

He stopped suddenly at the sight of an extraordinarily pretty girl who had just come out of one of the cottages by the chapel. Dark curly hair framed her face and her large brown eyes seemed to smile with a life of their own. She walked away rapidly, but not before she had given him a friendly nod and a smile.

He cursed his inability to walk fast. She had already disappeared around the bend in the lane. He could never catch up with her now. Who was she? She must live in the village. He must find out. It wouldn't be too difficult. It was only a small place, after all. He was bound to see her again.

As he turned into the doorway of the inn, he told himself yet again that he had made the right decision in coming to stay in Llanwrtan.

'Come in, Mr Taylor', said John Rowlands gesturing

him towards the bar. There are several people here who want to buy you a drink.'

• • •

Catrin was already in bed while Winnie, in turn, was having her hair brushed vigorously.

'Ninety eight, ninety nine, a hundred. There, That'll do!', said Mari, laying aside the hairbrush.

'Why does it have to be a hundred?', asked Winnie. 'Why not fifty or ninety nine?'

'Because that's what works if you want lovely hair', answered her mother. 'It wouldn't do for such beautiful girls to have untidy hair, would it now?'

She leaned down and gave her a kiss, then did the same to Catrin. 'Your Mam will be up to say goodnight and tell you a story', she smiled at her niece. 'Then it's off to sleep the pair of you, and no chatting and giggling once the candle is out.'

Mari and Bethan took it in turns to brush the girls' hair and tell them a story at bedtime. It was a routine that they all enjoyed, although it was sometimes difficult to think of new stories. It was just as well that the old ones were perennially popular.

'Mam, do you like Werner?', asked Winnie unexpectedly, causing Mari to pause as she went to the bedroom door. 'Because he likes you a lot, doesn't he?'

'What on earth do you mean? How do you know he likes me? He likes a lot of people and a lot of people like him. Settle down now while I go and tell Auntie Bethan that you're ready for your story.'

'But he does like you, Mam', persisted Winnie. 'He looks at you much more than anybody else and he's kissed you special on the lips, not on the cheek hasn't he? '

'How do you know that?', gasped Mari, coming back to the bed. 'What nonsense have you been listening to?'

But Winnie merely smiled and snuggled down more comfortably. 'It's alright, we like him too, don't we Catrin?'

Her cousin nodded vigorously and then added, 'Will we be bridesmaids when you get married, Auntie Mari?'

Mari looked open-mouthed from one to the other.

'I don't know where you're getting these ideas from. Who said anything about getting married?'

'But he kissed you on the lips and that means you have to get married', said Winnie. 'It's alright, Mam, we think it's a good idea. He'll be my Dad and he'll be Catrin's Uncle Werner won't he? Will he live here after you get married?'

'Well, you two are the limit. There's nothing like that going on. He's just a friend, that's all, someone I work with. You just put that nonsense out of your heads. Good night, now.'

Mari closed the door behind her and then paused on the landing. The innocent questions had shaken her. Was it so obvious? What was the relationship between her and Werner? Was he in love with her? Did she care for him in that way? She shook herself slightly and went down the stairs to the kitchen. It was all nonsense, of course, but the memory and taste of his lips on hers was suddenly real and present.

15.

Bethan closed the gate on the two cows in the field and went back to the milking parlour to retrieve the pails of milk that would supply the household with their milk, butter and cheese. Llwydyn, the old grey household cat and the four outdoor cats that slept in the barn were fully occupied, lapping up the foremilk that was put out for them in the yard at each milking. Although Llwydyn was in the privileged position of being fed household scraps, the outdoor cats were only given milk so that they would be encouraged to hunt for their food. It was an effective way of controlling rodents.

She glanced in the direction of the sea to see what the weather was going to do that day, then wished she hadn't for it immediately brought an image of Richard on board his ship. Oh God, keep him safe! Watch over him and don't let the U-boats prowl near him. Let me concentrate on what I'm doing, while you keep him safe, Lord. Don't spill the milk! Bring some potatoes, carrots and peas from the kitchen garden! Don't forget to darn Catrin's spare cardigan this evening! Oh please keep him safe, Lord!

Nain was busy black-leading the range in the kitchen , singing and humming snatches of various hymns and lyrical ballads, including one of her favourites that told the story of an unhappy maiden who had drowned herself in the torrent of the Dee after being deserted by her treacherous lover.

> *'Gan ddistaw sisial wrthi ei hun*
> *Gadawyd fi un unig ...'*

Despite her earlier fears, Bethan smiled. The sound of Nain singing was as much part of Pant Uchaf as the house itself. Her deafness did not seem to affect her musical ability. Perhaps the sounds were already there inside her head, requiring only a remembered echo to bring them back to life. Bethan's late father had often said that he had heard Nain singing before he ever set eyes on her.

'It was the voice of an angel and I knew straightaway that she was the girl for me', he would declare grandly, while the secretly pleased Nain then made a great show of casting disparaging looks up at the ceiling.

Nain broke off her singing and went to wash her hands before helping Mari deal with the milk in the buttery. Pero the dog, who had been despatched outside while she was cleaning, took the opportunity of sneaking back to his favourite place on the rag mat in front of the fire.

Winnie and Catrin had already left for the mile and a half walk to school, while Mari had made an even earlier start at Hendy. A sense of quiet reigned in the house, punctuated only by the occasional crackle from the fireplace, the clock ticking in the parlour and the muffled voices from the buttery. Llwydyn, having finished her milk in the yard and disdainfully ignoring the lower caste outdoor cats, came in and jumped up onto her favourite cushion on the armchair by the fire.

The call 'Oes yna bobl?', following an unexpected knock at the door had both animals awake immediately.

'Hisht, Pero!', said Megan Prys, coming in and stroking the dog's head so that he immediately stopped barking and resumed his interrupted sleep. 'I'm on my way to the post office. Is there anything I can get for you from the village?' she asked as Nain and Bethan emerged from the buttery.

'I don't think so, thank you', said Nain. 'Griffith, Nant, called by and left us a rabbit he'd caught, so it will be rabbit pie today. Would you like a cup of tea, Megan?'

'No, thank you. I'd better get going. I've got a lot to do when I get back, and I've left the lob scouse to cook slowly while I'm out. John might forget to check it for me.'

'Any news from the adoption people yet?', asked Bethan.

'No, we're still waiting. We've been to Bangor but we have to go to Liverpool as well. I've never been there. Have you?'

Both women shook their heads. Bethan had been to Chester and to Shrewsbury but, as far as Nain was concerned, England was a faraway place that might as well have been on the other side of the moon.

'You be sure to look after your purse when you go to Lloegr', said Nain. 'You can't be too careful in a place like that.'

Bethan, who was standing behind Nain, gave Megan a conspiratorial wink. They were well aware of the old lady's view that crime began outside the confines of Llŷn.

'Mari came by yesterday to tell us that Samuel Jones will do the milking while we're away', said Megan. That was kind of him, wasn't it? Everyone is being so helpful to us with regard to little Rose's adoption.'

'It's no more than you deserve, cariad', said Nain, pushing an indignant Llwydyn off the chair so that she could sit down. 'We all wish you well in that.'

'The tall German - Werner is it? He seems keen on Mari, doesn't he?', ventured Megan. 'How does she feel about him? I thought that ... ' She broke off when she saw the sudden change of expression on Bethan's face. 'Oh, I'm sorry. Have I spoken out of turn?'

'No, of course not', said Bethan. 'But I don't know ...'

'I don't know either but if it's meant to be, it will be', interrupted Nain. 'If it does come to anything, it's alright as long as he looks after my Mari and Winnie, and stays in the village, of course. That's all one can say, isn't it?'

'Did you mean that, Mam?', asked Bethan after Megan had gone.

'Mean what?'

'What you said about Mari and Werner. Would you be in favour of them marrying?'

'Of course, I would, as long as he does marry her', responded the old lady, thinking back to the philandering English sailor who had fathered Winnie. 'But let's have a cup of tea and then I'll skin that rabbit.'

• • •

Mari, unaware that she was the topic of conversation at home, tightened the screws on the cheese press in the dairy at Hendy. More of the whey oozed out from the compressed curds, in a bluish white trickle. Another day in the press and it would be ready for removing before being wrapped then set to ripen on the wide wooden slats at the side of the room. It would be several months before it was ready to eat, but there were other large truckles at different stages of maturity that would supply the dinner table before then.

She looked out of the window and saw the Germans going across the yard to the barn. They had quite different walks. Werner had a long stride that was almost a lope at times, while Peter moved in a more precise way. They were both handsome men, tall and confident. What were they thinking about? Were they thinking about poor Hans and their homeland? Did they feel diminished by being prisoners? What was Werner thinking about at this moment? Was he thinking of her?

She remembered the feel of his embrace. His arms had been strong, but his touch was gentle. The male smell of him suddenly came back to her and she recalled again the touch of his lips on hers when they had walked on the headland.

'Jacob wants to know if you'll help him dose the sheep when you've finished here', said Samuel Jones, looking into the dairy from the doorway, but reluctant to come in with his muddy boots. 'He wants you, not the Germans, silly diawl, but I said it would be alright.'

'That's alright, Mr Jones, I've nearly finished here. I'll join him in a few minutes.'

'That's alright, then.'

It had been a busy morning. They had finally planted out all the winter brassicas at Hendy, a back-breaking task that had had to be fitted in around the regular routine of the farm. It had been a sombre morning, too, with thoughts of Hans and his untimely death hanging heavily on all of them. The arrival of letters for him from the

Red Cross was an unbearably poignant postscript to the tragedy. The realisation that they were letters from his wife in Germany had reduced Mari to tears.

'If only they'd come a few days earlier', she sobbed against Werner's shoulder. 'Damn the censors, and damn everyone else who delayed them. Now he'll never know that she was thinking of him.'

Jacob was rather out of his depth in the situation, but felt compelled to offer help with the brassicas, although his lumbago normally precluded planting. Even so, he had nearly blotted his copybook again, after insisting that the right way to plant winter cabbages was to heel them in firmly, then to go back and loosen a few rows so that they would take longer to establish.

'Tell them it's the only way to have some later cabbages', he instructed Mari. 'You don't want the whole crop ready at the same time.'

'But Samuel Jones wants the crop ready for harvesting at the same time, Jacob', insisted Mari. 'It's not like a kitchen garden where it's a few lifted every now and again when it's time for greens, not just carrots for dinner. The whole crop will be lifted and sold at the same time.'

'Have it your own way then. You usually do. It doesn't matter what I say. No one wants to listen to the voice of experience these days.'

He shambled off in his usual fashion, much to the relief of Werner and Peter, but they resisted the temptation of making it obvious. They still remembered the remarkable transformation they had witnessed when the shabby old man had blossomed into a noble bard. They were also aware that it must have cost Jacob something to come and shake hands with them after the fireball incident.

The culprit had still not been found, despite a thorough and on-going police investigation. It was as if all traces had been erased by a landscape reluctant to give up its secrets. It was the same old story, thought Inspector Pugh. No one knew anything. Even if they did, would they tell him? They were all the same in these little villages, reluctant to tell on their neighbours. Perhaps that wasn't a bad thing most of the time, but it was a damn nuisance in an investigation like this.

Anyone could have done it. Someone with a grievance, who had lost a loved one in the war, perhaps? Was it just some silly prank that had gone wrong or was there some deeper motive that drove the culprit in a spirit of dark venom? It was more likely to be a crime committed by a man than by a woman, he thought. Women tended to be more subtle in their choice of weapon and mode of attack. Anonymous letters, poison, that was more their style. Fiery missiles were somehow more overtly male. Still, anyone could have done it. Paraffin-soaked rags, intertwined with newspaper around a stone, were easy enough to make into missiles. It was the sort of thing that young men fired up by too much drink and a sense of injustice might resort too, but enquiries at the Red Lion had also drawn a blank: No, there hadn't been anyone who was the worse for wear for drink. No, there hadn't been anyone making threats. No, there was no one who had made disparaging remarks about the Germans.

Inspector Pugh sighed as he got back into his car to

return to the police station. Hopefully it might just be a one-off incident if the culprit had had a fright. He probably hadn't forseen that one of the POWs would die as a result. It was likely that they would never know who did it and the whole incident would be relegated to some case notes in a dusty file. Maybe that's just as well, he thought. There are more serious things to attend to. What mattered was understanding and being able to act on the bigger picture.

Ceri Rowlands, wiping down the bar, glanced through the window as the police car drew away from the Red Lion. The inspector had been been quite pleasant, but he wasn't the type to spend the time of day in friendly chat. So many questions, he'd asked, too. He seemed to think that someone from the village was responsible for the fire, but it could have been an outsider. Anyone could have done it, although it would have to be a very determined person to have driven, cycled or walked to Hendy late at night.

Motive, that was the thing they always considered first in films. There had to be a reason. It could be anything, and it was often the most unlikely person who had done it. She mused on the intricacies of the various plots and motives that she had enjoyed, courtesy of the Pwllheli picture house. There always seemed to be complications, but perhaps it was simpler than that. It could be that ...

She paused suddenly and considered. What if ... ? No, that wasn't likely, was it? What was it he'd said? Something about ... Should she have mentioned that?   It ...

But fate, as was its wont, suddenly intervened to provide a diversion in the (to Ceri) comely figure of their English guest coming into the bar. His arrival was effective in driving away away her random perusals.

'Hello, Mr Taylor', she said. 'Are you going for a walk?'

The question was perhaps superfluous, given that Martin was wearing a sports jacket and was heading towards the outer door with his walking stick, but it was a friendly query that was part of what Ceri considered to be good customer relations.

'Yes, I thought I'd wander around a bit after I've posted these letters. See you later.'

'Bye Mr Taylor. Enjoy yourself. Mam's got a boiling fowl today so it'll be chicken broth and bread pudding when you come back.'

Martin had spent a good part of the morning writing letters. It wasn't an activity that he normally gave much time to, but friends and relatives had been unstinting with their correspondence after his accident, and it was the least he could do. To his surprise, he had quite enjoyed it. There was an art to writing letters that he had never appreciated before. Each could be tailored to its recipient in a way that encompassed individual interest as well as general news to impart and queries to make. He had a friendly, informal style that once embarked upon, flowed effortlessly across the pages.

The initial greyness of the morning had now lifted in favour of a warm sunshine that was irresistible. After posting his letters and chatting to the postmistress, Martin set off down the High Street towards a cow-patted lane that wandered down towards the sea. The earth-banked hedges were tall and secretive here, with briar roses and old man's beard twining sinuously towards the light, wherever they could gain hold. A blackbird suddenly flew from cover at his approach, its warbled cry of warning alerting other denizens of the hedgerow that danger was near. Martin smiled, picturing in his mind the little wrens, voles and lizards that would now lie low until he had passed. He imagined small, keen eyes noting his every step. He wondered if they could smell him as well. They probably could. Each creature has its own scent, after all. The lane had a smell of passing cows, with here and there, a beguiling scent of honeysuckle in the hedgerow, but human sense of smell is pretty crude by comparison with the creatures of the wild, he thought.

It was no coincidence that Martin had chosen to go down this lane, that led to some of the outlying farms. His queries at the inn the previous evening had proved fruitful, although he had been careful to couch his queries in a roundabout way. His general comment that Welsh girls were surely amongst the prettiest in Britain, had produced a warm response to the affirmative. It was the combination of shining brown eyes and expressive faces that made them so attractive, he had continued. There were bound to be some who looked just like that in Llanwrtan. It was such a pretty village that inevitably, it would have its quota of equally pretty girls, he had opined.

It had not taken too long for Martin to establish that his vision of the previous evening was one Mari Evans who lived in Pant Uchaf but who worked as a Land Army girl at Hendy. The news that she had a daughter had been a slight shock, but that was allayed by the revelation that her man was dead; killed in the war. So, she was a young widow, like so many others in this bloody war, he thought, then pondered on the absurdity of human emotions that could simultaneously experience sadness and gladness over the same event.

'Mr Taylor! Good morning to you, although it's not far off mid-day is it?'

It was the Vicar, beaming brightly as he appeared at the bend of the lane. 'I'm just going back to the church now. Let me accompany you. I'd be delighted to show you around, as I promised yesterday.'

The fact that Martin was going in the opposite direction appeared to be lost on the Vicar, and before the young man could protest, he found himself retracing his footsteps, while the Reverend Walters enthused about the ancient bell that hung in the church tower.

'It's thought that it came from the monastic foundation at Bardsey. Of course we weren't able to peal it during the early years of the war, not until the victory at El Alamein when Mr Churchill gave permission for all church bells to be sounded. What a lift that gave everyone when those peals rang out across the countryside.'

Oh well, I might as well give in gracefully, thought Martin. There'll be plenty of other opportunities, I hope.

He listened attentively as his companion spoke about the early foundations of the church. Despite himself, he found it interesting, for the Vicar undoubtedly had the gift of imbuing his descriptions with life and colour.

'So many of our rituals are based on ancient, pre-Christian practices, you see, although we're not supposed to say so officially. Take the spring by the church, for example! It was there before there ever was a church. It was a holy site where for untold generations people came to worship and to ask favours of their pagan divinities. One of my predecessors in Victorian times apparently tried to cover up the little well that had been made at the spring, but his parishioners weren't having that, I can tell you. Despite his efforts, and his condemnation of heathen practices, they just kept uncovering it and placing little posies of flowers there. They still do, you know.'

'Well, here we are', continued the Vicar as they reached the church gate which he thoughtfully held open for Martin. 'You'll see that the tower is ...'

He stopped when he saw that he no longer had Martin's attention for the latter was looking in rapture at a figure who was just emerging from the church.

'Mrs Jones, Hendy, asked me to leave some extra flowers in the church, Reverend', said Mari. 'The roses at Hendy have been exceptionally good this year, and that old cabbage rose from the orchard wall is so fragrant, too. Its scent is filling the church already. I've left some in the chapel as well. That's only fair, isn't it?'

She smiled as she spoke, then looked at Martin who was gazing at her in open admiration. The Vicar, realising that they had not met, made the introductions.

'Mari, this is Mr Martin Taylor who is staying at the Red Lion. Mr Taylor, this is Mari Evans of Pant Uchaf.'

'Pleased to meet you', said Martin, taking her outstretched hand. I saw you in the lane last night didn't I?'

'That's right', said Mari, gently retrieving the hand that Martin seemed reluctant to release. 'You're in the RAF, aren't you? I've got a cousin in the RAF too, but he's with the ground maintenance staff. You fly, I believe?'

'Well, I did until I had a bit of a prang. I have to wait until this leg heals before they'll let me go back.'

Martin could not believe his good fortune in running into Mari so soon. His first impression of her had not been mistaken. She was indeed the prettiest girl he had ever met, and her voice, with its melodious up and down intonation, charmed him. It was quite different from the cultured yet flat monotones that he was used to in the Home Counties.

'The Vicar is going to show me around the church. Would you like to come as well?', he asked hopefully.

'I'm sorry. I have to get home for dinner and then go back to work at Hendy', said Mari, then noting his crestfallen expression, added: 'Not that I wouldn't if I could, of course. Perhaps another time, but you must excuse me now. It's been a pleasure to meet you, Mr Taylor. I expect I'll see you around the village.'

With that tantalising half-promise, Mari smiled and nodded at them both then went out of the gate, leaving Martin gazing after her with a mixture compounded of fantasy, admiration and disappointment.

An hour later, his head full of ecclesiastical and architectural details, but with the memory of Mari's shining eyes and lilting voice, Martin went back to the Red Lion for lunch. All in all, it had been a good morning.

16.

The post-mortem results had finally arrived, but they had not revealed anything that was not known already, thought Inspector Pugh. There was nothing to show that the German had not met his death other than by an unfortunate accident in falling over the cliff.

The body could now be released for burial. It was to take place in the churchyard at Llanwrtan. There had initially been some queries raised about that, but recognition had been given to the wishes of his two friends who had requested it. They were the nearest thing he had to a family outside Germany, after all, and the church authorities had also given the necessary permission.

As for the fire, the military authorities seemed to have lost interest, presumably seeing it as a purely local matter, an incidental that had no real bearing on the case.

They were probably right, thought the Inspector, but something bothered him. He disliked loose ends. Why had the German taken off like that? Where did he think he was going? Why not stay to help his friends? There was no evidence that more than one person had been responsible for the fire. Three able-bodied men, and trained soldiers at that, could easily have dealt with an intruder. There was no reason for Hans to have fled in fear of his life. But, wait a minute! The dormitory had been locked. Neither he nor the others could have got out.

He paused and frowned, then cursed under his breath. They had all assumed that Samuel Jones had released the prisoners and that one had escaped under cover of darkness and the chaos resulting from the fire. What if the prisoners had not been locked up? What if Hans had gone earlier? Damn it! Why hadn't he pursued that line of enquiry? Then he recalled that the farmer had just been informed of the loss of his son at sea. Further questioning then had seemed intrusive.

Inspector Pugh determined that this last avenue should be explored. He would speak to Samuel Jones again, and also Ron Harris, the Englishman who had found the body. If nothing came of it he would just have to accept that there were some ends that stubbornly refused to be tied. He decided to go to the funeral in his official capacity and then ask a few more questions. At least, his presence in the church would be one more in a small turnout. There wouldn't be many to grieve for the poor chap.

It was with considerable surprise that the Inspector viewed the large number of people who had gathered for the funeral at the Anglican church of St Mary in Llanwrtan. A large proportion of the village was there, although he had understood that they were mainly chapel-goers.

Sitting in a side pew that gave him a clear view of the mourners, he watched as the Vicar and the Minister came in together. They obviously cooperated in these matters, then. The organ began to play a piece that he recognised as being from Tannhauser, an appropriate Germanic choice. The congregation rose to its feet as the coffin was borne in on the shoulders of Werner, Peter and four members of the local Home Guard. Behind them came half a dozen regular soldiers who made up a guard of honour. Full military honours were to be accorded to the German by the same British soldiers who had hunted him but a short while before.

The Inspector found the service oddly moving. It was conducted with great dignity by the Vicar, with a thoughtful reading from the Minister. Peter gave a brief eulogy in German which Werner then translated into English. The congregation, under the keen-eyed direction of the Choirmaster, sang in their usual whole-hearted manner, the baritones and altos harmonising magnificently with the tenors and sopranos, so that their voices seemed to reach into every corner of the ancient roof timbers.

He was surprised to see that the Germans sang the Welsh hymns as well as the solitary English rendition of 'The Lord is my Shepherd.' They had obviously blended well into village life here. What a curious thing was war; enemies killing each other one minute, the next moment, respect and friendship developing in unlikely places.

Outside, the timeless rendition of 'ashes to ashes' reverberated amongst the tombstones, while solemn faces paid their last respects to the earthly remains of a foreign soldier. As the first of the soil was sprinkled onto the coffin, Mari took hold of Werner's hand as they stood amongst the mourners, and squeezed it gently. The guard of honour fired a salute into the air, the salvo disturbing a nearby rookery, sending the great black birds cawing and wheeling above their heads, as if they too were adding their tribute to the dead.

The Inspector looked about him as the gathering began to disperse, each person shaking hands with Werner and Peter, expressing their condolences before departing. He noticed a young man with a walking stick shaking hands with them before turning to speak to an attractive girl who stood nearby. Surely she was the one who'd been holding hands with one of the Germans a few minutes earlier? He remembered her now. She worked at Hendy where the POWs were based. One of them had a good reason for not trying to escape, then.

He walked over to where the Germans were standing. Guarded expressions appeared on their faces as they recognised the bastion of the law approaching, but they acknowledged his condolences with grave courtesy.

'We're no nearer to finding out who started that fire, I'm afraid, but I don't think you'll have any more trouble now', he said. 'But if either of you should think of something, anything at all that might have a bearing on the case, just let me know. Speak to Mr Jones at the farm and he'll get in touch with me.'

They nodded and he turned to where Mari was still speaking to the young man with the walking stick.

'Oh, Inspector, this is Pilot Officer Martin Taylor. He's staying at the Red Lion. Martin, this is Inspector Pugh. He's investigating a case of arson that we had at the farm.'

'Yes, I heard about that at the inn. It doesn't seem a likely scenario for a peaceful place like this, does it Inspector?'

'Thankfully no', said Pugh, 'But we take these things seriously. Are you staying long, sir?'

'A few weeks, I expect, until this leg of mine is fighting fit again. Until then I'm grounded, I'm afraid.'

'At least he knows you didn't do it', whispered Mari as they watched the Inspector's retreating back. 'He will have checked up on you at the inn.'

'Definitely not guilty', smiled Martin in return, aware that their heads were now close together in an intimately conspiratorial way. 'I say', he said, 'You wouldn't like to join me for ... '

'Come on Mari, we have to get back. There's work to do', called Samuel Jones.

'Sorry, I have to go now', said Mari, giving him one of her radiant smiles before running towards the lych gate where Samuel and Beti, Jacob and the two Germans were waiting.

Martin cursed under his breath as he followed them and watched them climb into the old lorry. Werner, who was the last to get in, turned to look at him coldly before climbing into the back of the vehicle. What's got into him?, wondered Martin.

He walked through the gate and down the lane, then turned for one final look at the lorry. To his surprise, Samuel Jones had got out again and was speaking to Inspector Pugh some distance from the vehicle. The police were never off duty, it seemed, not even when there was a funeral. He made his way slowly back to the Red Lion. It was time for a drink.

'What'll it be?' asked Ron Harris as Martin entered the bar. Ron had had his caravan parked on the headland in one of Hendy's fields since before the war. He still had his house in Bootle, but seemed to spend most of his time in the caravan since his wife was killed in an air raid. How he managed to obtain petrol for his journeys to and from England was a source of mild curiosity, but the local people were too polite to ask. It was not their business.

'Half of bitter, please Ron', said Martin, joining him at the corner table by the fire where the flames flickered their reflections on the old brasses on the wall. It was a congenial spot, with the wooden farmhouse chair providing just the right degree of support for his back. He eased himself down gratefully, hooked his walking stick on the dado and rested his arms on the chair's armrests. They were just at the right height, too, a tribute to the long-dead carpenter who had made the chair.

'You went to the funeral, then?', asked Ron coming back to the table with two full glasses slopping slightly as he set them down. 'I did think of going but since losing my Dorothy in the Blitz I can't face going to funerals, I'm afraid. At least not just yet. Many people there?'

'Seemed like most of the village. Cheers!', replied Martin drinking his beer gratefully.

'That's the Welsh for you. Funerals, weddings, anything to do with a bit of hymn-singing, and they're there. Strange people in many ways, but I must admit, I have a lot of time for them. Cheers!'

A few more people wandered into the bar, each giving Ron and Martin a nod and a few words of convivial greeting in English before reverting to their native language as they settled themselves into companionable groups around the room.

'Are you a bird-watcher?', asked Martin, nodding towards the large binoculars on the back of Ron's chair.

'Yes, I spend a lot of time watching them. There's a good variety in the area; cormorants, curlews and other seabirds, birds of prey and all the usual small species like finches, warblers and so on. We get some rare visitors, like shearwaters and choughs to these shores, as well. There are also good colonies of seals and porpoises. Mind you, I do a regular stint of coastguard watch, too. When the authorities realised that I had a caravan on the headland and some powerful binoculars, it was natural enough for them to draft me in. It's not likely that an enemy submarine would nose around these parts, but you never know.'

'I've brought my binoculars with me. Would you mind if I joined you sometime?', asked Martin, remembering that Ron's caravan was on the headland of the farm where Mari worked. 'I'm afraid I'm not up to scrambling over rocks just yet, but I'm fine on relatively flat areas.'

'That would be a pleasure', said Ron enthusiastically. 'When would you like to come?'

It was not long before they had agreed a time, a few days hence.

'If it rains, we can always dodge into the caravan', said Ron. 'I've still got some carefully-hoarded Scotch as well', he added with a wink.

17.

The small, end-of-terrace house looked empty, but it was definitely the right place. It had to be! Yet the building had a forlorn appearance, although it was relatively undamaged. That was more than could be said for the terrace opposite, where large gaps separated many of the houses, each with a ruinous pile of masonry, all that was left of what had once been family homes.

Wooden boards had been nailed across the windows, an indication perhaps, that the glass had been blown out by the explosion that had demolished the houses opposite. He peered through the gaps between them but could see virtually nothing, except for the dim outline of some heavy furniture.

What had once been a tiny front garden was now a patch of scrub, with the remains of a straggling privet hedge bordering dog-fouled grass, dandelions and a few tall rosebay willow herb plants. Splinters of glass, caught between the cobbles of the side street, winked in response to the sun's glance, as if mocking the efforts of the elderly woman on her hands and knees, scrubbing clean the steps of the house next door.

'There's nobody there now love', she called to him as, once again, he went to knock at the front door. 'Mr O'Connell left about a week ago.'

'Do you know where he went?'

'No love. He never said. Any road he always kept himself to himself.'

'Do you think he will be back soon?'

'I don't know love. Is he a friend of yours?'

'Er, yes, but from quite a long time ago.'

The woman sat back on her heels and wiped her hands on her apron. She pushed back the straggling bits of hair that were escaping from the curlers under her head scarf and looked at him curiously.

'You're not from around here, are you love?'

'No, but I am on leave and thought I would just call and see him.'

'Well, I don't think he's coming back love, because I heard that the council is going to use the place for re-housing people. You know, for people who haven't got anywhere to live. I hope they won't be a load of scallies. We have enough of them around here already.'

'But where could he have gone to?', he asked, rather desperately. 'He can't just have gone without telling any-one.'

'Well he did, as far as I know, and you're not the only ones asking about him. There were a couple of rozzers here wanting to know the same thing. You're not one of them plain clothes rozzers are you?'

'No, no, of course not. I'm just a friend and I haven't seen him for years.' He could feel coldness beginning to move in the area of his midriff. He had to get out of here quickly.

'Thank you for your help', he said hastily and backed away from the front door. He walked quickly down the street, but not too quickly as to arouse suspicion.

'Bye love', called the woman after him and resumed

her scrubbing. No one could accuse her of not having clean steps. She hoped the new tenants would be better than the last one in that respect. It wasn't much to expect people to clean their steps. There were enough dirty scallies around here already.

He had to get away! There might be someone watching the house. Was there anyone following him? He couldn't see anyone, but you never know. Even now there could be eyes watching through any of these windows. There was the main road at last. Not too quickly now! Which way? Look casual! Stop and light a cigarette! There's a tram! Quick, jump on!

The clanking green conveyance was a temporary haven, despite the smell of stale beer, cigarettes and urine. He drew deeply on his cigarette as he fished in his pocket for the appropriate fare.

'Thanks', he mumbled to the conductor and pocketed his ticket. Stay for a couple of stops then get off again, that was the best ploy. He tried to avoid meeting the gaze of the old man sitting next to the 'No Spitting' sign, who was looking at him with undisguised interest.

'Are yer alright der, la?' said the old man.

'Yes, I'm fine thank you', he responded reluctantly and then turned away in order to avoid further conversation. The old man spat in disgust and looked out of the grimy window.

A fat woman wearing a lacy black woollen shawl around her shoulders, moved her enormous bundle of washing slightly, to make room for him.

'Der yar love. Good job you're only thin.'

He mumbled his thanks again and tried to look about him without appearing to do so. At the third stop he got up and nearly tripped over the old woman's feet. Apologising hastily he got off and walked towards some shops. Look in the windows! Is there anything suspicious to be seen in their reflections? No, everything seemed normal. Lose yourself in the streets and shops for a while! Cross and re-cross, in and out, and backwards and forwards!

The discipline of training quickly re-established itself as he took further measures to lose any tails. He felt calmer now. His breathing was nearly back to normal. There didn't seem to be anyone following him. Now what? A place to lie low for a bit until he could consider his next move, that was the thing. Surely there would be another contact, but even if there was, how would he know where to find him? Perhaps the whole operation would need to be cancelled now. The best thing was probably to head for Ireland. He had the necessary documentation. He would be safe in a neutral country. He could contact the German consulate there. Thank God he had ample funds. At least he hadn't lost his wallet. He could find a room somewhere. Yes, that was it. If he was quick he'd ...

But here his training let him down, for in his eagerness, he forgot momentarily that British traffic drove on the left side of the road. He failed to see the taxi until it was upon him. A blare of horn, a squeal of brakes, and he knew no more.

• • •

It was years since Martin had sent thin, wave-smoothed pebbles skimming and ricocheting across the surface of the water. They were like mayflies teasing the fragile meniscus only to reconsider, over and over again, before finally succumbing to the waiting depths.

He steadied his feet, wide apart, so that his centre of gravity was well-established before his next throw. The first one had nearly made him topple over, but he was now well-used to making such adjustments.

The tide was well in, but the day was so still that barely a ripple stirred the sea's tranquil surface. Only a slight movement of the seaweed's fronds, backwards and forwards, swaying gently beneath the clear water, betrayed the presence of a tide.

It was a perfect day, in a perfect place, he thought, taking in the vista of soft green headland, golden sand and blue-grey rocks like static seals in the whispering surf. He had been agreeably surprised to find that there was no restriction on beach access. So much of Britain's coastline still had obstacles, barbed wire and concrete tank traps for the invasion that fortunately had never come. On a recent visit to Hastings, he had observed the enormous anti-aircraft guns above the promenade and the acres of lethal barbed wire that kept all visitors off the beach, whichever side they happened to come from. He had assumed that it was like that everywhere. Still, this was not exactly the first line of defence, as was the case with the south coast resorts. Here was a small world far removed from the noise, fears and conflicts of war.

A pebble flashed across the water, striking it five times before sinking. That was a good one!

He turned to see that a small group of children had approached and were now standing watching him.

'Hello there', he called. 'That was a good throw. Which one of you is the dab hand?'

'Dat was me,' said a burly young lad with a grey pullover and a pronounced Liverpool accent. He bent down nonchalantly, then made a great performance of selecting an appropriate stone before sending it skimming effortlessly to touch down five times again before sinking.

'Oh bravo!', enthused Martin, and before long they were all at it, searching, selecting, aiming and then hurling, with shouts of delight when particularly good shots were apparent. The girls in the group were just as good as the boys. They were obviously all well practised in the timeless art of ducks and drakes.

'Please, sir, are you a squadron leader?', asked a boy with a Welsh accent, when there was a natural pause in the proceedings. Ifan had told the girls that he would instigate a conversation with the stranger, for they would not have the requisite experience and knowledge of Royal Air Force matters to do so.

'No, I'm afraid not. I'm just an ordinary pilot officer', said Martin.

'Do you fly a Spitfire, sir?'

'Yes, I do actually.'

There was a deep collective sigh that betokened both appreciation and admiration.

'Does your leg still hurt, sir?', asked a little fair-haired girl rather anxiously.

'No, it's not too bad now, thank you. I hope to be able to chuck this away before too long', he said, holding up his walking stick and smiling at Rose.

'Have you killed lots of Germans, sir?', asked Winnie breathlessly, remembering that Ifan's many descriptions of aerial dog-fights invariably had Spitfires sending Messerschmitts and Heinkels down to a watery grave-yard called The Drink.

'Well, I suppose so', answered Martin rather reluc-tantly. It seemed wrong to be talking of death in this beau-tiful place, especially to impressionable young children.

'You won't kill Werner and Peter will you, sir?', asked Catrin anxiously.

'Who are they?', he asked, mystified.

'They're Germans working at Hendy. My Mam works there, too', said Winnie. 'Werner is our friend. Well, they're both our friends really, but Werner is our special friend because he fixed our clock.'

Of course! German prisoners of war. Martin remem-bered some of the conversations he'd had in the bar at the Red Lion.

'No, I wouldn't dream of harming your friends', he smiled reassuringly in answer to Catrin's question. 'Did you say that your mother works at Hendy?', he added, turning to Winnie and seeing the strong family resem-blance even as he spoke.

'Yes, sir. She's called Mari and I'm Winnie. This is my cousin Catrin and these are my friends Ifan, Rose and George.

'Pleased to make all your acquaintances, I'm sure', he said, giving them each a token salute with his free hand.

They immediately responded in kind and then stood looking at him expectantly.

'Well, I'd better be getting along now. It's been a pleasure meeting you. I expect we'll flick stones again some other time. TTFN.'

'TTFN', responded George and Rose in unison, while the others, to whom this communication was a mystery, saluted again or waved as they saw fit.

'It means Ta Ta For Now', said Rose later, with all the authority of the worldly urban-born. 'It's a kind of special thing you say to people in England, but I don't know whether you're allowed to say it if you're Welsh.'

'Why not?', asked Winnie indignantly. 'We let English people say Welsh special things if they want to.'

'Like what?', challenged Rose, but the question flummoxed Winnie, who was quite unable to think of a pertinent example. Ifan came to the rescue, however.

'We let them say Llanfair PG instead of the long name, Llanfairpwllgwyngyllgogerychwyrndrobwllllantysiliogogogoch. So they should let us say their special things, too. It's only fair, isn't it?'

Rose, aware that she had inadvertently strayed into deep waters, nodded hastily in agreement. She knew of the extraordinarily long name of the village in Anglesey but did not relish the possibility of being challenged to say it. Tact was obviously of the essence.

'Yes, you're right. English people can say Llanfair P.G.

so I expect it's alright for Welsh people to say TTFN', she said diplomatically.

'I know another one', said George, determined not to be left out.

'What is it?', asked Winnie.

'SWALK. People put that on envelopes when they write letters.'

'What does it mean?', asked Catrin.

'It means Sealed With A Loving Kiss - SWALK. D'you gerrit?'

There was a shocked silence.

'Ugh! Ach y fi! that's disgusting', said Ifan. 'I'm going. TTFN.'

'TTFN', they all chorused, then followed him up the path to Ty Fron's barn.

Megan Prys, glancing out of the window, saw the children trooping into the barn, then turned back to resume her conversation with Lowry.

'It isn't for the lack of trying, Lowry. We've seen so many officials in Pwllheli and Bangor. Two of them came to inspect the house the other day. They asked to see every room and wanted to know where it is that we have a bath and how we do the washing. They even opened the oven door and had a look inside. I don't know what they expected to find there. We have to go to Liverpool next week, to the offices of the Adoption Society. It's a Mr ...'

She stopped and consulted the letter that lay on the table in front of her.

'It's a Mr Edmunds that we have to see apparently. Every time it's someone different. I hope they all know what they're doing.'

Lowry nodded sympathetically. She was fond of Megan, as she had been of her late mother who, in years gone by, had been her greatest friend. She was so like her mother, too. There were the same hazel eyes, light brown hair and serious, hard-working approach to life. It was a tragedy that she and John were unable to have children of their own, but adoption was a sensible option for them.

'But how are things with you, Lowry? I've done nothing but talk about me. How is Griffith keeping?'

'He's well, thank you, Megan, at least as well as can be expected of Griffith. You know how he is.'

Griffith was two years older than his sister. A silent, taciturn man, he had sustained terrible head injuries in the trenches during the first world war. As a result, coherent thought patterns were beyond him. It was as if an erasing cloth had wiped part of the slate that was his mind, leaving behind only those areas that enabled simple everyday tasks to be carried out. He was able to look after himself and, thanks to Lowry's unmitigating care, had improved dramatically from the broken wreckage that had been transported back from the carnage of the front. But despite everything, he was mentally a child.

'Good. I'm glad to hear it. We were all very grateful to him over that fox business', said Megan with a smile.

'Hisht, Megan!', said Lowry nervously, glancing towards the door in case any sharp ears should hear details that were of a confidential nature. The incident of the fox was one of those events in the category of 'it never happened'. It was acknowledged but never discussed.

Foxes were always a problem for those with poultry or early lambing ewes, but one particular marauder had recently appeared to cause more than the usual level of carnage. His guile and determination were matchless. He could slip by even the most keen-eyed watcher without detection. The toll of victims mounted steadily. Few households had escaped his depredations.

Keeping a determined fox out of livestock ranging areas was nigh on impossible, given the ban on erecting high fences that had been imposed by some of the big landowners. To them, a fox was there to be hunted for pleasure. High fences that would impede the progress of horses during the hunt were not tolerated. The killing of a fox by a smallholder was a cardinal offence that carried the threat of eviction.

It was against this background that Griffith had emerged as an unlikely hero. Despite the brain damage that he had sustained, he had the shrewd cunning and dexterity of a natural hunter. His ability to move swiftly and silently through the darkening copses was enviable. Like a wavering shadow that might have been, but one was never sure, he flitted here and there about his nefarious business.

One of the ways in which he was able to contribute to the domestic economy at Nant was to catch rabbits for his sister to turn into delicious pies and casseroles. The Ministry of Agriculture also paid a levy for each rabbit scut, a small income that was a welcome addition to

Lowry's paraffin and herbal sales. The occasional pheasant that crossed his path also had a habit of disappearing into one of his capacious pockets, only to reappear as a resplendent Sunday dinner at Nant. There was never a feather left to excite the attention of the gamekeeper.

Lowry's casual and unguarded remark: 'If someone doesn't stop that fox soon, none of us will have any chickens left', had sounded and echoed in the vacant caverns of Griffith's mind. His beloved sister was upset. Why was she sad? It was the fox. If there was no fox, Lowry would be happy. The fox must be caught. Who would catch it? He, Griffith would catch the fox.

With aim and purpose thus clarified, Griffith slipped silently into the shadows of evening in search of his prey. The fox was cunning and resourceful, he was quick and he was sly, but he was no match for Griffith.

The first hint that Lowry had was when she came in from the outhouse where she had been restocking some of the shelves. There was an unmistakeable reek of fox in the house. She rushed into the kitchen and there, an astounding tableau met her eyes. An enormous dog fox lay stretched out on the table, its eyes half-closed and with teeth bared in a last rictus of death. The reddish brown coat still gleamed in the lamp light, while its long brush of a tail curved almost defiantly over the edge of the table. It was a savage creature, but with all the nobility of the wild that death could not quite conceal.

Griffith, standing by the table, turned as she came in and gave her one of his rare smiles. 'Fox for you', he said simply, pointing at his prize.

Lowry was horrified. 'Did you kill it, Griffith? Tell me the truth, now. Did you kill the fox?'

'He was a bad fox. He made you sad. I killed him for you Lowry.'

'Oh, Griffith, cariad, what am I going to do with you?'

Lowry thought rapidly. They must get rid of the fox before anyone saw it. If the landowner found out, he had the power to evict them from their cottage. Was that likely? Yes, it was a real possibility. Similar things had happened. A distant cousin had even been evicted for voting against the wishes of his landlord before the war. In years past, the landowners of the time had successfully annexed many of the small farms in the area, under the auspices of the Enclosures Act. It had been blatant theft legitimised by the tawdry actions of a self-serving government of privilege. The first that her ancestors and their neighbours had known, was when the bailiff had delivered 'notices to quit', unless rent was paid to the landowners. There was little the protesters could do. Most could not even speak English, and Welsh had no legal recognition. When a squad of Dragoons was sent from England to keep the peace, the protestors went back to their homes and agreed to pay rent. It was the early nineteenth century, but power then, as now, lay with the strong.

No, she couldn't take a chance. They would have to bury the fox. Yes, that was it. Bury it! Bury it deep where it could not be unearthed by scavengers.

'Griffith, did anyone see you, cariad? Did you meet anyone while you were out? Did anyone see you carry-ing it back?'

'No', he said, giving her another smile and shaking his head in an exaggerated way, as if to emphasise the silliness of the question.

It was probably true. He did have the ability to melt into the landscape. Perhaps things weren't so bad after all, but they must make haste.

'Griffith, I want you to dig a big hole by the hedge in the kitchen garden. I'll show you where. Then we're going to put the fox in the hole and cover him up so that no-one knows he's there. We have to do it', she emphasised, sensing that he was about to protest. 'He'll just be our fox that no-one else knows about. It'll be our secret. You must not tell anyone about this. You promise me now, that you won't tell anyone.'

'I promise', he said reluctantly, but was cheered when Lowry continued: 'I know you did it for me, Griffith, cariad. He was a bad fox and now he won't catch any more hens.'

The deed was safely accomplished and Griffith was true to his word in not saying a word to anyone, but inevitably word of the fox's demise soon went around the grateful village. How this happened is anyone's guess. It was as though some natural process of osmosis were at work, with both the story and the need for confidentiality being absorbed simultaneously. No-one said a word, but a series of callers came to Nant, each bearing a gift: an oven-ready chicken here, a quarter pound of tea or a packet of Woodbines there. Nothing was said. It was just that the callers happened to have a surplus of items that might as well be shared as go to waste.

No whisper ever reached the landowner. What he doesn't know, he won't worry about, Lowry had told herself, before finally putting the matter to rest.

'We saw that young Mr Taylor from England when we came back from Bangor the other day,' said Megan. 'He was on the 'bus with us. He seems to have had a very lucky escape when his plane crashed. Lovely manners he has, and he's made himself popular with quite a few people in the village.'

'Yes, he was lucky, but there have been so many who weren't. It's such a waste, Megan. So many fine young men with their lives before them, reduced to dust. When will the world realise that war is just an evil game where bullies run rampage over other people's lives? Will there ever be a time when people are content with what they have and live in peace, without interfering with others?'

Lowry gazed sadly at the fire and Megan, knowing whose image she was seeing in the flickering flames, said gently, 'Yes, indeed, it's a terrible madness.'

Lowry gave a sigh then looked away from the fire, as if to draw herself away from an aching past to the needs of the present.

'He's a good-looking young chap, too', she said with a faint smile. 'He'll already have set a few hearts fluttering in the village, just like one or two others, I can think of.

'I'm sure you're right', said Megan. 'But let's hope it doesn't lead to a declaration of war in Llanwrtan!'

18.

Immediately after breakfast Martin made his way towards Hendy farm, but his well-laid plan for inadvertently bumping into Mari was not to reach fruition. The only person he could see was an elderly man who appeared to be talking to himself. The two sheepdogs that were dancing about his heels suddenly spotted Martin and raced over to investigate, their barking making him retreat hastily behind the farmyard gate.

'I say, can you tell me where the caravan is?', he called over to the old man, but his request was ignored. After glancing at him scathingly and calling the dogs to heel, Jacob continued on his way.

Perhaps he's deaf, thought Martin charitably, then saw that a burly figure was coming towards him from the farmhouse.

'Can I help you? You're Pilot Officer Taylor, aren't you? I'm Samuel Jones, the farmer here.'

'Pleased to meet you Mr Jones. I was looking for Ron Harris's caravan. We're going to do some bird-watching, as well as coastguarding, of course.'

'That's alright then. You just go back to the lane and take the little track on your left. That will bring you to the headland.'

'Thank you very much Mr Jones'.

If Martin had harboured the idea of asking him about Mari, the opportunity had gone for the farmer was already returning to the farmhouse after a final 'That's alright, then', accompanied by a slight gesture of his hand.

Turning back the way he had come, Martin soon found the little track to the headland. Mari, glancing out of the dairy window where she was dealing with the morning's milk, saw him just as he moved away from the gate. Where was he off to, then?

It wasn't long before Martin reached the caravan. It was far bigger than he had imagined. Ron must have done well in business to have afforded something this size.

'Hello there! Glad you could make it. Do you want to dump your gear inside?' The said gear didn't amount to much. It was a shopping bag with a picnic and a thermos flask that Mrs Rowlands had prepared for him before he left the inn. She had been somewhat surprised to hear that he would be out for the day and therefore would not require a cooked meal until the evening. Grown men, in her experience, needed a cooked meal in the middle of the day, but he was a customer and his wishes must be adhered to, regardless of eccentric leanings.

The caravan was spick and span inside and Ron was obviously very proud of it. Every drawer and cupboard was opened for Martin's inspection.

'You must be really comfortable here. You've got virtually everything you need. What about water and so on?'

'There's a spring along the headland with the purest water you could find anywhere. I'm allowed to use the earth closets at Hendy, and once a week I pay to have a bath at the inn, so I'm always presentable to the world', he laughed. 'Now, I was going to suggest that we go a little farther along to where I've set up a hide. We can get a good view of the cove as well as the cliffs from there, and you won't have to do any scrambling.'

There were rock pippits busily investigating the rock pools for unwary shellfish when Martin first trained his binoculars on the beach below. At first they were almost impossible to detect, so well camouflaged were they against the sheltering rocks. It was only when some of them took to the air, with their characteristic 'parachuting' flight and *'seeep'* calls, that he spotted them. The cormorants on the rocks farther out to sea stood with wings outstretched, like watchful sentinels of the deep, while overhead, black-headed gulls wheeled about scolding all and sundry with their harsh *'karr'* cries.

'We won't see any Manx shearwaters until the evening', explained Ron. 'They breed on the islands around the coast, at Bardsey and St. Tudwal's, but they can only be seen out at sea from here. They go fishing in the late afternoon and then you can see them flying down and shearing through the waves, hence the name.'

Ron was an agreeable and well-informed companion, without being too talkative or over-bearing, thought Martin. He was glad to be in his company.

'You're lucky to have a little spot of paradise like this', said Martin as they drank some of the coffee from his flask. 'It's so beautiful here and that has to be one of the most perfect little coves I've ever seen.'

'It is that', agreed Ron. 'But even the most beautiful and perfect of places can still harbour tragedy, you know. It was down there on the rocks that I found him, the German POW, after he'd fallen off the cliff. I spotted the poor sod early in the morning. He wouldn't have stood a chance, landing on those rocks.'

Martin looked down at the blue-grey crags that reared menacingly below and gave a slight shiver. No, there was no chance, but at least it would have been quick. He suddenly thought of friends he had lost, blasted out of the air by enemy fighters. Theirs would have been a quick ending, too, although who could tell how long those remaining few seconds might have seemed in the last downward spiral to destruction? He shivered again and tried to thrust the thought out of his mind.

'Anyone at home', called an unexpected voice outside the hide. 'Sorry to disturb you. Just a few questions.'

'Damn, there goes our bird-watching', whispered Ron. 'It's that bloody detective again.'

'Good morning, sir', said Inspector Pugh, as Ron emerged from the hide. 'Oh hello again, sir', he added, as Martin followed him outside. 'I didn't know you were here as well. I'm really sorry to disturb you both, but I just wondered if you could spare me a few minutes, Mr Harris? It won't take long.'

He paused and looked at Martin who said hurriedly: 'I'll wait for you by the caravan, if you like, Ron'.

'There's no need to do that. You can stay. That's alright, isn't it Inspector? But perhaps we should all go back and sit down in the caravan.'

'Thank you very much, sir, that's an excellent idea.'

'I wonder if you could tell me again about finding the German?', said the Inspector when they were back in the caravan. He had accepted gratefully Ron's offer of fresh tea and now looked rather apologetically at his host.

'But I've already told you everything', said Ron. 'I saw him on the rocks through my binoculars and then I went down to the beach so I could climb up from there to where he was lying. You couldn't get to him from the cliff-top. I just wanted to be sure that he was dead, not that there was much likelihood of him being alive. But you know how it is, I had to be certain? Then I went back up and ran to the farm, but I met a group of soldiers on the way and reported it to them. The rest you know.'

'What time was this?'

'I don't know exactly, to the minute that is, but it was just after dawn.'

'Are you normally up that early, sir?'

'No, not as a rule. I'm usually an early riser, but that would be around seven.'

'Why were you up so early that day?'

'I don't know. I was just awake, that's all. Sometimes it happens doesn't it? I didn't feel like going back to sleep, so I thought I'd go and have a look at the cove before breakfast. I'd seen a couple of seals the previous week and I thought I might be lucky again.'

'Did you see anyone on your way there?'

'No, of course not. It was much too early.'

'Did you hear or see anything unusual during the night? Did you get up and look out of the window, for example'

'No, I didn't. I know what you're thinking. If I'd looked out of the window, I'd have seen the glow of the fire at Hendy, but I didn't.'

'Were you asleep right through the night, sir?'

'Yes, of course, although ...' He paused and frowned.

'Yes, I did wake up, come to think of it, but I went back to sleep very quickly.'

'What was it that woke you up?'

'Well, I don't know. I just did that's all.'

'Did you hear anything at all? Please try and think, sir. It could be important.'

Ron frowned as he tried to recall. 'No, I can't think of anything, unless ... Wait a minute! Yes, there was a fox or perhaps a screech owl. Yes, that was it, but then it was all quiet again and I fell asleep.'

'What time was this, sir?', asked the Inspector eagerly.

'I've no idea. I didn't look at my watch, but it was quite dark still, so it was the middle of the night.'

'Have you heard foxes or screech owls on other nights?'

'No, I haven't actually, but they are around of course.'

'You've been very helpful, sir. Now, if I can trespass on your time still further, can I ask you if you have seen anyone about at night on other occasions?'

'No, of course not.'

'What about during the day?'

'No, there have just been the people from the farm.'

'So there's been nothing at all unusual?'

'No, not really. There was someone from the village going for a walk, but ...'

'Who was it?' said the Inspector sharply.

'I don't know.'

'How do you know it was a villager?'

'Well, he was wearing an old jacket and a cap, so it's not likely that he was a visitor.'

'When was this, sir?'

'It was the previous day, and I saw him in the distance. He was quite a long way along the path. I only caught a brief glimpse and then he was gone.'

'What time was it when you saw him?'

Ron frowned for a moment as he considered. 'Let's see now ... It must have been around quarter past seven, I suppose, because I hadn't been up all that long.'

'Didn't you think that was rather early for someone to be out walking?'

'Not really. The villagers tend to get up early and, as far as I knew, he could have been going fishing or catching crabs.'

'Was he carrying any fishing tackle?'

Ron frowned again. 'I can't be sure. He was quite a distance away.'

'Where did he go?'

'I suppose he must have continued along the cliff path.'

'But you would have seen him, if he'd done that. It's a fairly long, straight path, isn't it?'

'Yes, that's right. I suppose he must have gone down to the beach then.'

'Why should he do that?'

'I don't know, do I?', said Ron rather irritably.

'Can you show me exactly where he was when you saw him sir? It would be really helpful, and then perhaps we can see where it was that he went down to the sea.'

'I suppose so', said Ron rather wearily. 'You'd better stay here, Martin, because you won't be able to cope with the slope going down to that particular stretch. Just make yourself at home. I won't be long.'

Martin watched them as they set off towards the cliff path then settled himself more comfortably in a corner seat. He lit a cigarette and drained the last of his, by now, cold tea. His gaze wandered idly over the interior of the caravan until it settled on a bookshelf to his right. There ought to be something there to keep him occupied until Ron came back. He got up and browsed through the shelves but the selection was a disappointing one. There were a couple of novels which he'd read already, and some that didn't look particularly interesting. There were bird books, a dry looking volume on British history and a few magazines. Then he spotted a book on the wildlife of the area. That was more like it! He reached down but found that it was wedged in some way. He frowned and pulled again before realising that something was caught above and behind the book. That was what was causing the problem. He gradually worked to free the obstruction and then looked at it in surprise. It was a Morse Code manual.

• • •

'It would have been down here', said Ron, gesturing towards a narrow sheep track that led precipitously down to the rocky beach. 'It's the only place he could have left the path.'

Inspector Pugh looked around him. Yes, it had to be the spot. Forwards or backwards along the cliff path, or down. There was no other way.

They negotiated their way down carefully to a rather

narrow and uninviting stretch of beach. There was nothing there but seaweed strewn rocks.

'Why would he come down here?', mused Pugh. 'It doesn't seem a likely spot for fishing, or for crabbing come to that.'

Here, the Inspector spoke from experience, for in his all-too brief leisure time, he was fond of both activities.

'What's farther along?', he asked, pointing towards the ragged outcrop of cliff at the end of the beach.

'I don't know', said Ron. 'I've never been along there. It's just the cliff and the sea, I expect.'

'Let's take a look', said the Inspector, to Ron's dismay. At this rate, he would never get back to his bird watching.

It was a difficult scramble to get round the crag that rose steeply to the cliff. Several times they almost lost their footing on the slippery rocks but at last they succeeded. Breathing heavily, Inspector Pugh looked up at the sheer cliff face and realised that this section of strand could not be seen from the top of the cliff, for the rock face was at an angle towards the sea.

'Well, there's nothing here', said Ron rather peevishly, anxious to get back to the caravan, but not relishing the prospect of scrambling back along the treacherous rocks.

'Wait a minute! There's a crack here', said the Inspector, moving up to the cliff face. 'I think it leads to a cave. Come on! Let's have a look.' He turned to look at Ron who was looking rather shaken. 'Are you alright?'

'Yes, I'm fine. I could just do with a breather before we go back. I'll be there now.'

It was just possible to squeeze behind the projecting section of rock and through the crack into a cave that lay behind it.

'I had no idea this was here', said Ron, looking about him. Light filtered dimly from a crack somewhere high above their heads, revealing an area about the size of a garden shed. Even without the Inspector's torch it was possible to see the cave's interior fairly clearly. 'I shouldn't think anyone else knows it's here either.'

'Someone does', said Inspector Pugh softly, bending down to retrieve something from the ground and holding it up to examine carefully. It was a cigarette end.

19.

Edwin Humphries took seriously his duties as head master of the village school. A small man in stature, he nevertheless had a natural authority that overcame his lack of height. After an initial meeting, people would forget that he was relatively small, and if asked to describe him, would have said things like: a nice man; diligent at his job; obviously a good headmaster.

A well-educated man, he came from Cardiganshire and still retained the accent of that county. Despite initial amusement at the southman's precise tones, Llanwrtan had soon accepted him as a worthy headmaster, if just a trifle conceited, but it is arguably necessary to have at least one small fault in order to leaven perfection.

He saw himself, perhaps, as Oliver Goldsmith's school-master in *The Deserted Village*:

"There in his noisy mansion skilled to rule,
The village master taught his little school."

It is also possible that the local inhabitants were to him like those of *"Sweet Auburn, loveliest village of the plain"*:

"Amazed the gazing rustics ranged around
And still they gazed, and still the wonder grew
That one small head could carry all he knew."

He took his responsibilities seriously, not only towards the children in his care, but also towards the villagers generally. The fact that John and Megan Prys needed help in their goal of adopting one of his evacuee pupils had spurred him to immediate action. Appropriate letters and telephone calls had been made. Character references had been provided and every encouragement given to them in their quest. As far as he could tell, there was nothing likely to hinder them now. It was a satisfying situation.

Edwin was a great lover of poetry, both English and Welsh. He regarded Matthew Arnold's description of the tide in *Dover Beach* as a masterly depiction of a natural phenomenon that was evocative of the human condition:

> *"Listen! You have heard the grating roar*
> *Of pebbles which the waves draw back and fling*
> *At their return, up the high strand.*
> *Begin, and cease, and then begin again*
> *With tremulous cadence slow and bring*
> *The eternal note of sadness in."*

It was a source of sadness to him to ponder on the fact that this was the same man who, as a schools inspector and subsequently Professor of Poetry at Oxford, had declared: *"The sooner the Welsh language disappears, the better for England."*

Why? Surely the ability to speak two languages was an asset? One did not interfere with the other. It had to be fear, of course. It was a matter of political expediency. The ancient language as a living tongue was a continual reminder of the presence of an older race that pre-dated England. What was it that the Bishop of Avila had said to Queen Isabella of Spain when she asked why the first book on Spanish grammar had been necessary?

"Language is the perfect instrument of empire."

His musings came to an abrupt end as the bell sounded for the end of the afternoon session. He got up from his desk to go and to join his wife in the main schoolroom.

Myfanwy Humphries was glad to see the end of school. The children had been more boisterous than usual, but she put that down to the fact that it had been windy during the night, although it was calm again now. It was extraordinary how weather had an unsettling effect on children, just as it did on animals. Children were like small animals. Both needed a firm hand. Discipline was essential from the first.

Husband and wife differed greatly in their approach to discipline. To Edwin, the attention and respect of the children came naturally. He rarely had to raise his voice and even walking into a classroom had the immediate effect of bringing silence, apart from the scraping of chairs as the children rose to their feet. He invariably had a smile for them. With Myfanwy it was different. She was unrelentingly stern, with a demeanour that did not endear her to her pupils. Many of the younger ones were afraid of her. She was undoubtedly effective as a teacher, but it was a regime based on fear rather than on respect.

They had no children of their own. At one time there might have been, but as the years went by the possibility grew more remote. When did the grave smiles that had occasionally illumined Myfanwy's face cease to be? When did the lines of disapproval that were etched into her face appear, rarely to be lifted now even by a shadow of amusement? When had the disapproving pursing of her lips begun, or the stiff walk and the precise enunciation that all too often carried overtones of sarcasm appear?

Myfanwy Humphries was not an overtly unhappy woman, and it would be difficult to deny that she was, in her own way, content. Vocation, duty, discipline and respectability were the cornerstones of her world. They were the moral foundations of society that she sought to inculcate into her all-too-often reluctant pupils.

Edwin and Myfanwy had met when they were students, initially seeing each other at lectures and then more frequently as they did teaching practices at the same schools. It was a relationship that developed rather than blossomed. When they both qualified, it was a sense of inevitablity rather than that of ardour that led them to marriage.

They taught first in the urban slums of Birmingham for five years, followed by six years in the rural haven of Montgomeryshire, Myfanwy's native county, where there were statistically more sheep than people. Three years in Cardiganshire followed, before they finally moved to Llanwrtan to run the village school. It was the sort of post that Edwin had long dreamed of. He was headmaster of his own school and with his own house in a beautiful area where cultural life and good fishing (of which he was inordinately fond) were both apparent. If his wife felt demeaned by her subordinate position as general teacher combined with secretarial and domestic duties, she never showed it. They took their places in the hierarchy of village life, and were accepted.

'I'll see you later, Myfanwy', he said after they had finished their tea. 'I'll be back before dark.'

All afternoon he had been looking forward to a few hours of tranquil fishing with Edward Beynon. The coastal waters were well populated by bass, pollack and whiting all year round, but the summer brought large shoals of mackerel to grace the tables of Llŷn and beyond. He loved mackerel fishing. The fast-swimming fish cleaved through the water in elegant blue green curves, their striped backs undulating as they flashed by the hopeful fishermen in their waiting boats.

Irridescent *Scomber scombrus*, from the deeps, mused Edwin to himself as he walked along to meet Edward. You come to our shores as the water warms and there we await you with our baited hooks and bated breath. Up you come then home we go, to the lip-smacking pleasure of a fried mackerel supper.

There was no mackerel sky with its alternating bands of cirro-cumulus or alto-cumulus clouds against the blue, that evening. It was just as well, because that often presaged stormy weather. No, he reflected with pleasure, the conditions were just right for an evening's fishing.

Fishermen could never quite agree on the best method of catching mackerel, although if truth be told, it is one of the easiest of fish to land. John Prys had often expressed the view that even a bare hook or a piece of old sock was enough to tempt them. What mattered was being there when the shoal passed. It was no good sitting waiting for them. Find out where the shoal was first, then sit back and reel them in! That was his view.

Edwin Humphries favoured using a plain hook near the surface, while Edward Beynon extolled the virtues of a heavier lure and spinner at a greater depth. Small white feathers with the quills carefully stripped away could be attached to a series of hooks along the line. No additional bait was necessary and the problem was often catching too many fish, rather than too few.

'Let's get going, then,' said Edward when he saw Edwin, then spat into the sand to dislodge some of the grains that had somehow adhered to his smiling lips.

In no time at all the boat was launched and a course set for what Edward perceived to be a good area in which to fish. In this, Edwin was happy to concede to his friend's superior knowledge and experience of the coastal waters.

The destination reached, the boat sat riding the gentle swell, while the men sorted out and prepared their tackle, ready for the shoal when it passed.

It was quite some time before the shoal arrived, but once there, the boat was surrounded by sinuous flashes of blue green. *"And I blessed them unaware"*, thought Edwin triumphantly, like the Ancient Mariner in the Sargasso sea. The first catch, was soon joined by many of its flapping compatriots in the well of the boat. Then the shoal passed, and all was quiet again as the mackerel moved on in search of the small sprats which were further inland at this time of year.

'Not too bad at all', pronounced Edward in satisfaction, as he proceeded to reel in for the last time. 'There'll be quite a few households ready to buy from this lot.'

It was understood between them that, while Edwin took a share for his own use, most of the catch would go to Edward, who would then go on his regular round to sell mackerel to the villagers. It was his boat, after all.

'Duw, what's this then?', he said as the rod suddenly curved in protest.

'It's something big', said Edwin, peering down into the waters, then realised that the catch was being pulled towards them along the surface.

'Someone's lost an oar', he said, as the object bumped against the hull. He bent down to retrieve it and then placed it carefully in the bottom of the boat.

'It's brand new', said Edward, examining it closely. 'I haven't heard of anyone losing an oar, have you? It can't have been in the water all that long either by the look of it. Who can afford to lose an oar these days, I wonder?'

• • •

Werner, perched on the headland and enjoying a quiet smoke after the day's work was done, watched as the small fishing boat came back towards the land. It must be congenial to go fishing like that. What wouldn't he give to join them, to see the coastal landscape from the seaward side? He imagined the bays and the cliffs rising to the green pastures of the headland, while the restless sea between the boat and the land rocked them and reached out to stroke the shoreline in a never-ending caress.

He sighed. They would never allow him to go in a boat. He couldn't blame them. It was understandable enough. Why should they believe that the last thing he wanted to do was to escape and go back to Germany? It was inevitable that once the war ended, the prisoners would be sent back, but could he persuade the authorities to let him stay? Would Mari want him to remain?

He closed his eyes and wondered what she was doing. She would be at home now, laughing with her family and catching up with the day's events, doing all the normal things that a family does. Mari! Mari! She was so often in his thoughts. Was she thinking of him?

There had been a moment this evening, just as she left Hendy to go home, when she had turned to look back from the footpath, to where he was standing watching her by Hendy's pig-gate. Catching sight of him in the distance, she had stopped, just as time had suddenly been suspended for him, too. They had looked and then begun to move towards each other as if some irresistible, force were at work, but the sudden appearance of Beti, reminding Mari that she was expected in Pwllheli for a Land Army briefing in the morning, had broken the spell.

He sighed again, but was almost immediately cheered by the thought that he would see her the day after tomorrow. He would try to find an opportunity of being alone with her then. He would try to tell her of his true feelings and establish how she felt about him. Yes, that was it! Things needed to be spoken, to be discussed and to be agreed between them. He and Mari!

He stubbed out his cigarette on a stone and rose to return to the farmhouse. After a refreshing wash, it would be time for their evening meal at Hendy, followed by a game of chess with Peter. It was an activity that they both enjoyed, although Peter was undoubtedly the superior player. Still, he had several times been able to delay the inevitable checkmate until the game had lasted over two evenings.

The sun was just dropping into the glowing embers of the horizon now. Soon, it would be completely below the skyline and submerged in the waiting cradle of the sea. The beautiful evening star would grace the heavens. Venus, the goddess of love! The moon would also cast its glittering bridge across the waves, and the owls, foxes and bats would claim the night as their own.

He retraced his footsteps to the annexe, but stopped several times to look at the darkening night sky. As a boy, he had spent many happy hours with his father, identifying the constellations and planets. Orion the Hunter, forever in pursuit of the Great Bear, while Cassiopeia the Swan watched them across the eternal expanse of the heavens.

There was a meteor! It flashed for an instant, like a tiny pinprick in the now sable sky. If he had not happened to be looking in that patch of sky, he would never have seen it. In ancient times such things were regarded as portents, although their interpretation seemed to have been a rather hit-and-miss affair, depending upon who was the oracle of the time.

He thought once more of Mari. He and Mari. It felt good. He strode back in a light-hearted mood now, but he had yet to learn how events were to unfold,

20.

John and Megan Prys sat watching the raucous herring gulls wheeling around the ferry as it ploughed its way across the Mersey from Birkenhead to the Pier Head in Liverpool. They preferred to sit on the deck, taking in the sights, sounds and smells of the great river, watching the approaching shoreline and the Liver Building, tokens of defiance that had withstood the worst of the enemy Blitz.

They had stayed overnight with John's cousin Morfudd in Chester, after a particularly slow and tedious train journey from Pwllheli, with stops at every station. There was no need to worry about the animals. Samuel Jones would see to them.

Married to Humphrey Smith, an English ship repairing engineer, Morfudd had welcomed them warmly, glad of the opportunity to speak her native tongue as well as to hear news of her family and friends in Llŷn.

How was so and so? Who had died? Who had given birth? What marriages were in the offing? Was there to be a local eisteddfod this year? But predominant in their conversations as they sat in the cosy parlour drinking tea, was Rose the little evacuee.

'Fancy her mother leaving her like that. What's the world coming to? It's the war, of course.'

Despite her years spent in England, Morfudd's attitude to family loyalties were still essentially those of the Welsh village. Both young and old were to be looked after, as well as to meet their responsibilities to each other. The village was an extended family that cared for its own.

'You can get a bus just outside here that will take you straight to the ferry in the morning', she continued. 'It will be the Royal Iris. The Royal Daffodil was sunk at Dunkirk and they haven't replaced it. The fare is only a few pennies and it will take you straight to the Pier Head. The offices of the Adoption Society are very close, within walking distance.'

The following morning, after a hearty breakfast of tea and porridge 'to keep out the cold', the couple hugged Morfudd as their bus approached. They were carrying a picnic of egg sandwiches and a bottle of pop that she had insisted on preparing for them.

'It's no good spending good money on food over the water', she maintained, casting a disdainful shrug in the general direction of Liverpool. 'And it's the least I can do. You brought me farm butter and eggs, a real taste of Wales. I'll see you this evening. It'll be lob scouse when you get back. I managed to get some scrag of lamb from the butcher and Humphrey is bringing potatoes and carrots from the allotment.'

With her cries of 'good luck' and 'see you later' still ringing in their ears, John and Megan climbed aboard the stuffy, crowded bus that was to take them to the river.

They enjoyed the crossing with its fresh breezes and the sights and sounds of the river traffic.

'Look! There's a sand dredger', said John, pointing to a ship that represented the river's lifeline. 'If they didn't dredge the sand out regularly the river would silt up just as the Dee did in the past.'

The ferry eased its way to the landing stage, with only

a slight bump indicating that they had arrived. John and Megan, holding hands like nervous children in a strange environment, made their way up the ramp and then looked about them to get their bearings. The smells were quite different from the ones they were used to in the countryside. Here, the air was heavy and smoke-laden with a pervading odour that was all too familiar to those who lived in war-torn cities: a mixture of brick dust, cordite and unwashed bodies.

Wherever they looked, there were bombsites, craters and the gaunt shapes of dereliction. Some craters even had weeds growing in the rubble and as a result were rather euphemistically, referred to as brick fields. There seemed to be ragged children running about everywhere. Megan was horrified to see that many had no shoes, despite the fact that broken glass littered the streets.

'They do have shoes', said John, remembering something that Humphrey had said the previous evening. 'It's just that their mothers only let them wear them when they go to school. They last longer that way, Come on, cariad! It's this way.'

Megan had been about to succumb to the grubby, outstretched hands and strident appeals of the children:

'Eh missus, 'ave yer gorra penny for us?', but John, shaking his head sadly but firmly, led her away from the small predators. Not at all bothered, they immediately transferred their attentions to a couple of amused American servicemen in smart blue uniforms:

'Gor any gum chum?'

Their destination was an old, four-storey building that

had several of its windows boarded up, like a half-blind veteran that had seen better days. There was a lift to the third floor but they preferred to walk up the grubby uncarpeted stairs, not certain of how safe they would be in the lift. At the third floor they went along a dimly-lit corridor until they came to the door that they were looking for. After knocking and waiting for a while, John opened it and they found themselves in a small lobby with a counter at one side on which there was a bell.

This time, there was a response when a rather tired looking woman with henna-treated hair appeared at the sound of the bell.

'You'll be Mr and Mrs Price, I expect.'

'It's Prys. The name is Prys', said John, a distinction that appeared to make no impression on the woman.

'Come through! Mr Edmunds will see you now. There's a Mr Hughes here to see you as well'.

She led the way into a large room that appeared not to have changed since Victorian times. A kindly looking grey-haired man with a dog collar was sitting in a battered armchair, talking to a slightly younger man in a crumbled suit who was sitting behind a massive oak desk. They both stood up when the secretary announced: 'Mr and Mrs Price to see you, Mr Edmunds.'

'I'm glad you could come. Please sit down', said Mr Edmunds, gesturing to a couple of chairs facing the desk before sitting down and shuffling through some papers.

'I'm William Hughes, the Minister at Union Street Welsh Presbyterian Chapel', said the older man, coming forward to shake hands. 'I'm pleased to meet you, Mr and Mrs Prys. My friend, Elis Jones, your Minister in Llanwrtan wrote to me about you, and I'm here to help in any way I can.'

It was a great relief to the couple to find that they had an unexpected ally. They smiled at him gratefully and sat down, then looked expectantly at Mr Edmunds who continued to look through the papers. He cleared his throat several times.

'Mr and Mrs Price, thank you for coming here this morning. It might have been better if we had communicated with you by letter again, but it was felt that a face-to-face meeting was best.' He paused and shuffled the papers again, before continuing. 'Mr and Mrs Price, we have given your application a most careful consideration but I have to tell you that there are certain considerations that mitigate against you. In short, I'm afraid that your application has been unsuccessful.'

It was as if a thunderbolt had struck the room. Everything seemed to slow down in its wake. Small details such as the bluebottle buzzing against the window pane, and the frayed cuffs of Mr Edmunds's shirtsleeves impressed themselves on Megan's consciousness as she tried to take in what had been said. After what seemed to be an age, she and John burst out together: 'But why?', while William Hughes started up in shocked surprise.

'I'm afraid that you were not regarded as being suitable candidates. I'm sorry. There's nothing else to be said, and now if you'll excuse me ...'

'There's a great deal to be said', said William Hughes. getting to his feet angrily. 'You've brought them all this way, just to tell them that and what do you mean, not suitable? You've seen the recommendations and character references. They are glowing testimonials of the worthiness and suitability of our friends here.'

Mr Edmunds shifted uncomfortably in his chair.

'It's not just up to me. There are others involved in the decision and there are many factors to take into account.'

'What factors?', asked John.

Mr Edmunds, looking even more hunted, consulted the papers on his desk again.

'It's the home conditions. Our report states that there is no running water in the house. The water has to be drawn from a well. There is no electricity or gas lighting either. In fact there are no mains services at all. The lack of these basic amenities is considered to be unacceptable.'

'But the village doesn't have mains services', said Megan. 'We've never had such things, but you won't find cleaner houses anywhere, and you won't find any water that's sweeter than that from our wells and springs.'

'How many children in this city have your suitable conditions?', added William Hughes bitterly. 'Many of them only have access to water from standpipes in the street. Most of the houses are without electricity. Some have gas if they're lucky and the pipes are unbroken. You've seen the state of many of them running around the streets. When did half of them see a bar of soap, let alone have a bath? If Llanwrtan was good enough to take evacuee children from Liverpool during the Blitz, why is it not good enough now?'

'We would never let little Rose be without anything',

said Megan brokenly. 'She would always be clean, tidy and well-fed. She would always have shoes on her feet and never have to beg on the streets or run bare-footed amongst broken glass.'

Mr Edmunds fidgeted in his chair again, avoiding looking into their eyes, but rather confining his remarks to the dusty curtains at the windows.

'I do sympathise, believe me, but you see those children have parents. I'm afraid there's nothing I can do.'

'Rose does have parents, and loving ones, too', said John Prys. 'We are her parents now. It is what she wants. It is what everyone wants. We can provide everything that she needs in a loving home. How can you not see that?'

Mr Edmunds looked even more embarrassed. His gaze flitted around the room, as if trying to find an escape route from the three pairs of eyes that were looking at him accusingly.

'There's something else', he said at last, addressing the drooping pot plant on his desk. 'It was felt that an all-Welsh speaking village would not provide the appropriate educational opportunities. It is much better that Rose is in an environment with a cultural background that is familiar to her.'

'Like Australia, you mean!', said William Hughes in stentorian tones. 'For God's sake man, the little girl speaks English and Welsh. That can only be a good thing for her intellectual development. Do you not know, for example, that having a knowledge of Welsh makes the learning of foreign languages such as French that much easier because of the shared grammatical constructions? How many languages do you speak, incidentally? Only one? What a pity! I speak three. My friends here speak two. The primary school at Llanwrtan provides excellent facilities and the grammar school for the area has even had pupils who have gone to Oxford. Every village in the area has its own little eisteddfod where music, poetry, dance and recitation are celebrated. Every county has one, too, while the National Eisteddfod brings together all that is best in the country as a whole. Is that what you call a lack of cultural facilities?'

'I'm sorry, there's nothing I can do', repeated Mr Edmunds stiffly, getting to his feet to show that the interview was at an end.' I must ask you to leave now.'

'I made a promise to little Rose', said Megan with dignity as she rose to her feet. 'I never break a promise. She will be our daughter, whatever you say or do.'

'That's right, Mr Edmunds', added John. 'Rose is our daughter and we will never forsake her.'

But it was a saddened and weary couple who were seen onto the ferry by the kindly Reverend Hughes. He promised that he would continue to do everything he could and would keep in touch, but as they shook hands, it was with a sense of hopelessness and inevitablity.

Morfudd and Humphrey were horrified to hear John and Megan's news when they reached Chester. They had been convinced that the couple would be successful in their application and Morfudd had gone to great pains to provide what she saw as a celebratory supper.

The lob scouse was delicious, and everyone tried to

put on a brave face, but as they went to bed that night, Megan's tears could no longer be held back. With John's arms around her, she finally sobbed her way to sleep.

The train back to Pwllheli was just as slow as it had been on the outward journey. A concerned Morfudd had waved them on their way from the station, emphasising as if it needed telling, that they would always find a warm welcome under her roof, and not to worry, because things have a way of turning out right in the end.

'I'll find a way, cariad', said John when at last they were home in the kitchen at Ty Fron, their arms around each other. 'Don't worry now. I'll find a way.'

The following day, after seeing to the animals, John went down to the beach. He sat on one of the great blue-grey crags and stared out at the restless sea. The smell of seaweed was clean and comforting in his nostrils after the malodorous fug of the city, while the cries of seagulls were a comforting backdrop to his thoughts. There had to be a way if only he could find it. What should he do?

For a long time he sat and considered, while the surf breathed endlessly about him, as if whispering secrets he had missed while he was away from its presence. From every angle he considered the position. Along every pathway that thoughts revealed, he traversed the tangled undergrowth of obstacles.

At last a slow and steady smile of inspiration broke out across John's rugged face.

'Megan, cariad', he said when he returned to the house. 'Tomorrow, I am going to Llanystumdwy.'

21.

As she trod the footpaths to Hendy, Mari was in a thoughtful mood. She was also fairly tired. It had been quite late when she got back from Pwllheli. The Land Army briefing had not just been for a morning. It had proved to be a full, two-day training exercise. Someone had obviously cocked up with the paper work. She and the other recruits had been required to stay at a highly uncomfortable barracks just outside the town. Fortunately, a telephone message to the post office at Llanwrtan had been passed on to her home and to Hendy, so they would not be wondering what had happened to her. Her protest that it was a bit much to be treated in this way had merely brought the comment:

'Don't you know there's a bloody war on?'

She had to acknowledge that, despite the discomfort of the two days, they had provided a useful time for personal reflection. The innocent questions about Werner, that had been broached recently by Winnie and Catrin had resounded deep within her. Somehow they had shifted the emphasis on a subject that she had, until now, refused to take too seriously. Like the workings of a kaleidoscope, it was as if a focus had suddenly appeared, becoming sharp and clear, where before the vision had been blurred and confused.

The air about her had an unusual clarity, too, with the morning lark already twittering high in the heavens. It would be a fine day. The smell of mint and other crushed vegetation came to her nostrils as she walked, while a rustle in the hedge betrayed the presence of a tiny creature, perhaps a vole. There seemed to be a never-ending number of those, despite the activities of the many farm cats in the area. They would catch them and play with them, tossing the small, crumpled bodies into the air, but would never eat them. Rats and mice would be eaten with gusto by semi-feral cats, but never voles. They must taste nasty, she supposed.

She closed the pig-gate behind her as she entered Hendy's yard and patted the two sheepdogs that ran to greet her.

'Have you missed me?', she asked them, while they licked her hand, before running back to the barn from where Jacob was just emerging.

'Hello, Jacob. How are things doing? Have I missed anything exciting while I've been away?'

'You'd better ask at the house', retorted the old man gloomily. 'It's nothing to do with me.'

'What's nothing to do with you?'

Further discussion was terminated as Samuel Jones came to the door of the farmhouse and beckoned Mari to enter.

'What is it, Mr Jones? Where is everyone?', she asked, aware of a sudden cold sensation in her stomach. 'What's happened? Is everything alright?'

'They've taken them to Bangor for interrogation', he replied heavily. 'I don't know how they think we're going to manage here without farmhands. They don't think about things like that.'

'You mean they've taken Werner and Peter? Why? They

haven't done anything. Why should they be interrogated? Are they under arrest? They're prisoners of war already.'

Mari could feel the coldness growing inside her now, moving up into her chest and threatening to choke her.

'The police came for them first thing this morning. They seem to think that there's a spy in the area and he's had help from the POWs.'

'That's ridiculous!', shouted Mari. 'Even if there was a spy, which I very much doubt, they would never be involved with anything like that. Why should they?'

'They're Germans, Mari', said Samuel gently. 'They're at war with us. Their first loyalty is to their country.'

'Yes, but they're prisoners. They don't want to do anything that would get them in trouble with the authorities here. Werner doesn't even want to go back there. He wants to stay and ...' She broke off with a sob and fought to keep back the tears that were threatening to overwhelm her. 'You've got to help them, Mr Jones. Please, help them!'

Beti, entering the kitchen, quickly summed up the situation, then came over and put her arms around her.

'Don't upset yourself, cariad. It's probably a mistake. They'll sort it out, I'm sure.'

But Mari was not to be consoled.

'Of course it's a mistake but they won't sort it out. They'll just believe what they want to believe. If you won't help them, then I'll find someone who will', she shouted and ran out of the house.

• • •

In Bangor, Werner sat at a table facing a rather grubby window with tape criss-crossed across the panes. It had been a shock for him and Peter to be bundled unceremoniously into the back of a police car that morning. The two grim-faced men in an accompanying vehicle had merely told them, in no uncertain terms, to shut up when they asked where they were being taken, and why?

Samuel Jones had protested to Inspector Pugh that the Germans were not involved in anything illegal, but on hearing that a possible spy was on the loose and that national security was an issue, he had paled and gone quiet.

'How am I to cope without my workers?', he had then asked quietly, changing tack to what he perceived to be a more acceptable approach.

'I'm sure you'll be allocated some new prisoners, sir', said the Inspector. 'But it might take a few days.' He had felt rather embarrassed by the brusqueness of the military intelligence men and had protested when one of them had pushed Peter so roughly that he had fallen and banged his head against the door lintel.

'But what will happen to them?', Samuel had asked the Inspector discreetly and out of earshot of the intelligence men, as the Germans were being put in the car.

'They'll be alright, sir. Once the investigation is over, I expect they'll be transferred to a POW camp in a different area, perhaps in the North of England. All the POWs have rights under the Geneva Convention, as I'm sure you know.'

Things had moved very quickly in the last two days, thought the Inspector. Odd clues on their own meant nothing, but when seemingly disparate items were put together, a pattern began to emerge. The cave, a cigarette end, an unexplained stranger and then a discarded oar followed by the discovery of a small deflated dinghy concealed beneath some rocks. These were all facts that could not be ignored. There had to be some connection between them and possibly the German's death, but he was at a loss to know what it could be. They had to start by close-questioning the POWs.

He sat down opposite Werner and held out his cigarette case. Werner took a cigarette gratefully and leaned forward while the Inspector lit it for him. The two Intelligence men had spent over an hour firing questions at him, to no avail. He knew nothing about what they were talking about. Couldn't the idiots see that? The smoke curled upwards and he half closed his eyes as he looked at his new interrogator.

'I want to ask you a few questions and I want you to think very carefully before you answer them', began the Inspector.

'I don't know anything. I have already told your bullying friends', said Werner irritably. 'And I am only required to give you my name, rank and number.'

'I know that, but it would help us all if we could clear up this matter. My colleagues from the Intelligence Service are understandably keen to establish whether there is a spy in the area, but I am also interested in finding the cause of death of your friend, Hans.'

Werner looked at him in surprise. This was an unexpected turn of events.

'Do you think that someone caused his death?'

'I don't know yet, but there is a possibility that it was not an accident. I want to find out and I need your help. Are you prepared to help me?'

Werner frowned, gnawed at his lip then took another deep drag on the cigarette. He watched the exhaled smoke curling up towards the single, dirty light bulb.

'What do you want to know?'

'I now know from Samuel Jones that your annexe was not locked up at night so any of you could have gone out at any time. Did you ever go out after dark?'

'No!'

'Are you sure?'

'Yes, I am sure. After hard work all I wish to do is sleep', said Werner indignantly.

'What about your friends?'

'No, of course not.'

'How would you know that if you were asleep?'

Werner paused and scowled at the table, ignoring the Inspector's question.

'Can you tell me anything about Hans's state of mind?', asked the Inspector, deciding on another approach. 'Was he his normal self or did he seem preoccupied by anything?'

'What means preoccupied?', asked Werner, then looked out of the window while the word was explained to him. Two blackbirds and a thrush were busy investigating an area of grass, while the branches of a nearby lime tree swayed as if orchestrating their movements. One of the clouds looked just like a great whale that sloughed through an endless ocean of sky. Even as he watched, its shape changed and elongated as the edges became more wispy and indistinct. It was more like a giant sheep now. The blackbird gave a sudden, rounded clarion call of warning as a uniformed figure came round the corner of the opposite building, and the birds took refuge in the lime tree.

The Inspector waited patiently, never taking his eyes off the German's face. Reluctantly, Werner dragged his attention away from his window onto the outside world and thought furiously. Would he be disloyal to his friends and to his country if he answered the Inspector's questions? Was the policeman trying to trick him into revealing information that was best not revealed? Was this the soft approach after the hard methods of the Intelligence men?

'He missed his family in Germany', said Werner at last. He was sad and *einsam*'. He paused, trying to think of the English word. 'He was lonely. Anyone would be.'

'Of course', said the Inspector gently. 'I certainly would be if I were separated from my wife and children. There is no shame in that.' He lit a cigarette of his own and then continued:

'Did you talk to Hans about his family?'

'He showed us a photograph of his wife and son. That is all.'

'Did he ever talk about them?'

'No.'

'What did you talk about?'

'Just things like what he was reading, what needed to be done on the farm, that sort of thing.'

'Did Hans ever go out at night?'

'I don't know!'

'I think you do know. Did he go out?'

Werner sat, stony-faced and refused to answer.

'I can understand your reluctance to speak', said the Inspector, but please think about this. Whatever you say is not going to harm your friend now, but it could help me to find his killer.'

'How can you be sure that he was murdered?', asked Werner before he could stop himself.

'I can't be certain, of course, but I have a gut feeling that ...'

Realising that the German might not understand the expression, Inspector Pugh pointed at his midriff then patted the side of his nose.

'It is a feeling that I have, based on experience. It is what we call a hunch. I follow my nose.'

Werner nodded then considered again what he should say. Despite everything, he felt instinctively that he could trust this man but it went against the grain to cooperate with his captors. All his military training pointed to a different course of action. He thought suddenly of Mari and of his growing need of her. What was she doing now? Damn this bloody war! Would it ever be possible to have a normal life?

'Why do you need to know if he went out?'

'Because he may have met someone and that person could have been his killer.'

215

Werner frowned and considered the situation again, trying to assess all the ramifications associated with specific answers. It was like trying to memorise and predict the possible moves in a game of chess. The number of options grew with each assessment until the intricate mathematical possibilities were beyond the scope of the human mind.

'Yes, he did go out', he said at last, reasoning to himself that as the Inspector already knew from Samuel Jones that the door was left unlocked, it was hardly a revelation to hear that someone had gone out.

'Where did he go?'

'I don't know.'

'How many times did he go out?'

'I don't know.'

'For how long was he out?'

'I don't know. *Mein Gott*, I was asleep!'

'Did he tell you anything about what he'd seen?'

'No! He did not tell me or Peter anything.'

'Did you try to get him to talk about going out?'

'Yes, but ...'

'But what?'

'But nothing! We were worried about him, that's all, but he would not talk to us. One moment he was down and very sad, then next he was up and *glücklich*, I mean happy. That is all there is to it, Inspector. You have to believe me!'

Werner stubbed out his cigarette with more force than was necessary and then passed his hand wearily over his face. Would these bloody questions never end?

'Thank you', said the Inspector unexpectedly, nodding to himself as if Werner's statement had confirmed something that he knew already. He stood up and held out his hand.

'You've been very helpful, sir, and I want you to understand that I will do everything in my power to establish the truth of how your friend died.'

● ● ●

'Hello! Where are you off to in such a hurry?' said Martin, as Mari almost cannoned into him in the narrow lane. 'Hey, are you alright?', he added, seeing the look of distress on her face.

'Yes, I'm ... I'm ... I just wanted to ... Oh please, I'm ...'

'Can I help?', he asked in concern.

'No, it's ... it's ... Oh, I don't know. I ... .'

She looked up at him and he saw the unshed tears glistening in her eyes.

'I've had a bit of a shock and I don't know what to do', she repeated more calmly this time, but still with a broken note in her voice.

'Hey, come on now! Let's go and sit down so we can talk about it', he said, taking hold of her hand gently. 'If I remember correctly there's a nice flat rock over there.'

He gestured towards a copse of trees in the nearby meadow. 'Come and tell me all about it. These things are always better shared.'

'I'm supposed to be at work', she said desperately. 'Mr Jones needs all the help he can get at Hendy. I shouldn't have run off like that.'

'Well you can go back after you've told me all about it', he said firmly, leading her towards the shaded sitting place. 'Now then, start at the beginning!'

He was a sympathetic listener and in the cool, dappled shade of the whispering poplars, Mari soon found herself recounting the whole story.

'I don't know anything about this spy nonsense', she said, 'But I know that Werner is innocent, and so is Peter, I'm sure.'

'Are you fond of Werner?'

'I like them both. I work with them and I know that they haven't done anything wrong. I just know it!'

'If that's true, then there's nothing to worry about', said Martin encouragingly. 'But you're wrong about the spy. There does seem to have been someone nosing about.'

He told her about the recent discoveries and the Englishman's revelation that he had seen a stranger in the vicinity.

Ron had been mildly surprised when Martin asked him about the code manual, but said that the authorities had arranged for Edward Beynon to teach him morse code. 'That's Edward's manual', he had said. 'The high-ups thought I wouldn't be much use as a coastguard if I couldn't read any signals from an enemy submarine to a spy on land. I don't seem to have been much use anyway. I should have realised that the bugger wasn't a local man.'

Martin gave Mari's hand a stroke.

'Why don't you go back to Hendy now, and I'll make some enquiries. I've got the Inspector's card. You usually go home for lunch, don't you? Why don't you come to the Red Lion and have lunch with me later on, instead of going home? Then we can talk again and see whether we can't sort this out. Come on!'

He pulled her gently to her feet and saw that she was smiling suddenly.

'You English, you have lunch in the middle of the day, don't you? We have dinner not lunch and then a tea and supper later on. Yes, I'd like to have dinner with you, Martin. That would be nice. It mustn't be for too long, though. I have to get back to work afterwards. There's a lot to do, although Mr Jones's brother is helping there as well. I'll see you at the Red Lion, then.'

She made as if to walk away then turned back again. He was almost bowled over when she threw her arms about him and hugged him tightly.

'Thank you, Martin. I should have known that I could rely on you.'

22.

Griffith sat on a bench in the lee of the house wall at Nant, carving a wooden peg for a rabbit snare. The large bone-handled knife had been his father's and still bore his initials. All through the bad time it had been in his pocket. When the terrible noise that hurt his ears and the bright flashes that went right inside his head had been all around him, the knife had been there, its weight a comforting reminder of home. They had tried to take it away from him, but he wouldn't let them, not his father's knife. He had shouted and struggled until the doctor man had said: 'Leave him be. Let him keep it!'

The wood shavings floated to the ground in shining whorls of fragrance caught by the sun. One of the chickens came to investigate the falling particles, but soon wandered away again when they proved to be not to her taste. He glanced at her as she clucked away stiffly and grinned to himself. That old fox wouldn't get her now.

'Sut mae, Griffith?'

Catrin, Winnie, Rose and Ifan, after a strenuous morning's activity of playing pirates had suddenly realised that they were thirsty. Nant was the nearest place of sustenance so they had decided to ask Lowry Morgan for a drink. She emerged from the house, carrying a tray with a jug of water, cups and a plate of thinly sliced bread and butter.

'There's buttermilk if you prefer', she said, placing the tray on one side of the bench.

'No, this is lovely, thank you', said Rose hastily.

'Griffith, can you make me a new catapult', said Ifan, settling himself down comfortably on the ground and tucking into a slice of bread and butter. 'My old one broke.'

'Aye, I will', grunted Griffith, 'But rabbits first', he added as he resumed his whittling of the snare peg.

'Is it hard to catch rabbits?', asked Rose with interest, reaching out for a second slice of bread and thinking that the only creatures she had encountered in Liverpool were mice, rats, cats, dogs and cockroaches.

'No, no! It's easy to catch an old rabbit. He doesn't know my snare is waiting for him when he comes out to eat when the sun is going to bed.'

'Why doesn't he come out of his burrow during the day?', asked Catrin.

'He doesn't want anyone to see him, so he only comes out at night. He thinks no-one can see him then, that old rabbit, but Griffith sees him alright. Griffith sees rabbits and lots of thing in the night. He sees things that no-one else can see. They don't know that Griffith is there watching them. He sees ...'

'Can you bring some logs in for me now, Griffith?', broke in Lowry. 'Leave that snare now! It's finished anyway, isn't it? Have you finished, children?', she continued rather impatiently, looking over to where they still sat in a contented circle by the bench.

'Yes, thank you', said Ifan, leaping to his feet. 'We're going to have a snail race in my barn now. Come on, everybody!'

In a trice they had gone, leaving only dwindling laughter to echo through the canopy of leaves in the orchard.

Lowry gathered up the cups and looked at Griffith rather wearily as he went into the house. Her brother, her big child of a man, he would always be in her care. Was there never to be a respite from the perpetual watching, listening and guarding? Would there ever be a time when she could stop, just be and live her own life?

But even as the unbidden question taunted, she felt remorse sweeping through her, as if the shade of her long-lost Idris were suddenly there, watching in sorrow. She would have cared for Idris if he had come back to her, no matter how wounded and shattered he might have been. They had loved with an intensity that bridged time and distance. She would always love him. She would always love Griffith, too. He had come back from the same unremitting hell on earth. He was her brother, her only remaining close relative. She would always look after him. She would always care for him, her big child brother.

• • •

Griffith, carrying out the woven log basket from the fireside, made his way to the log pile. Big ones and small ones, not too many of one or the other. That's what Lowry had said. Lowry always knew what he should do. She was like his Mam now. He tried to remember what their Mam had been like but she was a distant figure. There was a photo of her and Dad on the parlour wall, but she looked just like Lowry. Lowry was his Mam now.

Big logs, now small logs, that's what Lowry had said. He placed them carefully in the basket and lifted it up effortlessly. Catapult! He had to make a catapult for Ifan. He would ask Lowry if he could make the catapult after they had had their dinner. He caught the enticing smell of rabbit pie as he entered the kitchen. He liked rabbit pie. He liked catching rabbits for Lowry and for the houses nearby where he was welcome. Those old rabbits didn't know he was there. They couldn't see him. There were others who couldn't see him in the dark. There were others ... He paused and thought. Bare legs and giggles in the dark. Scuffles, raised voices and a sudden scream. He had seen and heard many things before passing by without a sound. What were they doing there in the dark? It was his dark wood and his dark headland.

Some things had made him laugh, like the bare bums and stifled laughter, but the harsh voice from the bad time had frightened him. Why had it followed him here? The voice had hurt someone. It had made someone scream, just as he had screamed when the terrible thunder and the flashes were all around him. What if the harsh voice had hurt Lowry? He was glad that he had frightened the voice. Lowry was safe now.

• • •

After the strenuous game of pirates that had taken them over the headland, snail racing was a relatively quiet and relaxing occupation for the children. Arguably it did not have the same recklessness and tingling frisson of being caught and forced to walk the plank by a fearsome pirate chief, but the challenge of a race, no matter what its relative speed, was adequate compensation. If truth be told, the game had played itself out, anyway. There is a finite number of times that being made to walk a slippery plank over a water tank in the field adjoining the headland can hold its attractions. Ifan, in his role of pirate chief, had also declared that it wasn't fair that he wasn't allowed to be the victim sometimes. Why couldn't pirate chiefs walk the plank occasionally? There was nothing to say that they couldn't.

It was just at this point, when the argument was becoming heated, that Rose, glancing from the headland to the strand below, suddenly turned and gestured for them to get down.

'Shh! There's someone down there', she whispered.

They dropped down immediately and then crawled over to where she was crouching.

'It's that Englishman from the caravan', said Ifan, all thoughts of badly-treated pirate chiefs now extinguished. 'What's he doing down there?'

'He's looking for something', said Catrin, whose knowledge of beach-combing and its associated need for careful scanning on an inch by inch basis, was extensive.

'What's he looking for, d'you think?' said Rose.

'We could go and ask him', she added and then decided that this was an ill-advised procedure, judging by the shocked expressions on their faces. 'Perhaps not, then', she finished rather lamely.

'He's picked something up', said Ifan urgently.

'What is it?'

'I don't know. You were talking so much that I looked away for a few seconds. It could have been something really important. Whatever it was, he put it in his pocket.'

'But maybe he's just looking amongst the rocks for nice pebbles', said Catrin. 'I mean, everyone does that at the seaside. We could go and look for pebbles now, if you like, but it would have to be at another beach,' she added.

However, the lure of terrestrial molluscs proved to be the winner. Snails were easy to collect. The children knew where all their favourite places were. One of them was in the stone wall by Ifan's pigsty. Just under the capstone, where the mosses collected and even a small polybody fern had taken root, the snails gathered there for their daytime slumbers, oblivious of the fact that small fingers would soon detect them and bring them forth into the light of day.

Placed in a bucket lined with moss, the competitors in the forthcoming race were free to explore the sides of their prison until the race began. Any that showed signs of going over the rim were soon despatched to the bottom of the bucket again. Considerable care was taken in the selection of those that were hoped to be prospective winners.

'This one is going to be mine. It's a Nain one', said Catrin, holding up a venerable specimen of *Helix aspersa* that she insisted was a grandmother. How she had arrived at this conclusion was not disputed. Some things were beyond discussion. What was not at issue, however, was the formal ritual that had to be observed before the race began.

After the choice of competitors, the next step was to wake them up and remind them of their molluscan obligations, as well as of the fate that would overtake them if they did not heed instructions.

A solemn verse recitation is needed to arouse a snail from its slumbers, to make the grey, moist body emerge slowly from the brown, striped and spiralled shell, with four tentacles waving in disorientated splendour.

Malwen, malwen	*Snail, snail*
Ty'n dy pedwar corn allan	*Put out your four horns*
Neu mi tafle'i di	*Or I'll throw you*
I mor mawr Pwllheli!	*Into Pwllheli's great sea!*

It was a formula that never failed. Although the larger pair of tentacles were eye stalks that regarded the children more in sorrow than in anger, the snails would nevertheless cling onto the starting line on the side of the barn in reluctant cooperation.

Ready, steady, go, and they were off! Only they weren't! Despite encouragement, protestations and threats, the snails were oblivious of any concept of lane discipline. Even those that began to go up the wall of the barn would soon veer off to the right or to the left. Had there ever been a clear champion that adhered to the straight and narrow path of salvation? No, not in living memory had there ever been one that did not favour the wide and rampant primrose lane to destruction, such as that depicted in the framed print from *Pilgrim's Progress* that hung in Ifan's parlour. So, the winner was always the one that went farther up than the others before it too succumbed to temptation. Once patience was exhausted, the game was deemed to be over and the snails were tipped into the undergrowth to seek out their damp and supposedly secret refuges once more.

'It's time for your dinner, Ifan', called his mother suddenly, appearing around the corner of the barn.

'TTFN', called Catrin, Winnie and Rose, as they too hurried off to their respective dinner tables.

• • •

Mari nodded to the surprised Ceri as she made her way to the corner table where Martin awaited her. There were no other customers in the dining room, unlike the bar where several of the locals had gathered, as was their wont at this time of day.

Martin rose to his feet and held out his hand in greeting. He smiled and squeezed her hand before pulling out a chair for her. His hand was firm and warm. Despite herself, she squeezed his hand in return.

'I'm glad you could come. I thought that we could talk more privately here than in the bar. How are you now?'

'I'm alright now, thanks', she began, feeling slightly embarrassed at the thought of how she must have seemed in the lane, then she paused as Ceri came to the table, notebook at the ready.

'It's vegetable broth to start with and then there's Mam's special omelette to follow. It's made with real, fresh eggs, not that tasteless dried egg that the government wants us to use. It's got potatoes, tomatoes and onions in, and there's salad to go with it. Is that alright for you both?'

'That sounds wonderful', said Martin enthusiastically.

'Right you are', said Ceri. 'I'll bring you some bread and butter as well. What would you like to drink?'

'Tea for me, please', said Mari, trying to avoid Ceri's increasingly questioning look. 'No really, I have to get back to work', she added to Martin, as he held out the drinks list for her perusal.

'Half of bitter for me, then, please', said Martin. 'Now then', he continued as Ceri went back to the kitchen. 'Let me bring you up to date with things. I telephoned the Inspector but he's apparently in Bangor today. I left a message for him to ring me when he gets back to Pwllheli. I'm sure he will do. He seems a decent enough chap.'

'Bangor! That's where Samuel Jones said they were being interrogated', said Mari. 'Oh Martin, what will they do to them, do you think? Will they let them come home again?'

'I don't know', he said, taking hold of her hand again. 'But I'm sure that they won't come to any harm. I'll speak to the Inspector this evening and then we'll know exactly what the situation is. If you like, I'll try and persuade him to come here tomorrow lunchtime - Welsh dinnertime that is - so we can go through things with him. I'll try and think of a way to excite his interest, to make sure he comes, although, come to think of it, there are a couple of things ...' He broke off and frowned slightly. 'Yes, why didn't I think of that before?'

'Think about what?'

'It's just something fairly trivial, but I need to check it out. No, we'll talk about it later', he continued, sensing that she was about to protest. 'Look, there may be nothing to it, but it's something I'd like to think about.'

'Why can't I think about it as well? Isn't that why I'm here, so we can put our heads together? Why are you leaving me out?'

'I'm sorry, I didn't mean it like that. Of course,we're in it together! I just didn't want to raise any false hopes.'

'Tell me, then!'

'Well', he began rather hesitantly. 'It's the dogs, you see. It's ...'

But the arrival of Ceri bearing two bowls of thick broth, followed by a large plateful of bread and butter, effectively halted the conversation.

'How long do you think they'll take to catch him, that spy I mean?', said Ceri, reluctant to go back to the kitchen just yet. 'What on earth was he doing in Llanwrtan anyway? There's nothing here that would interest a spy.'

'Well, it's a quiet spot with plenty of little coves where someone from a submarine could easily paddle ashore in a dinghy', said Martin.

'But why would he want to come?'

'It's probably just a dropping off point, en route to somewhere else nearby, or even somewhere in England. He could be going anywhere.'

'This broth is delicious. Please tell your Mam it's lovely', said Mari, anxious to get rid of Ceri.

'Now, where were we?', said Martin, as a reluctant Ceri went back to the kitchen. 'I know, we were talking about you, weren't we?'

'No we weren't! It was about dogs', said Mari firmly.

23.

There was no let-up from the hot, searing pain that scythed through his brain. There was light, then darkness, then light again. Crimson waves pounded though his head and body. He tried to move his legs, but to no avail. He thrashed his arms about in desperation and tried to open his eyes. Anything to get away from that tide of madness, those jagged rocks that cut into his body and the pounding that reverberated with every move. But the effort was too much and he screamed in agony until a prick in his arm brought welcome respite. He sank back into the encompassing darkness.

Later, much later, he rose again to the surface. There was light ahead. He must use his arms to propel his body towards it, but a searing bolt of pain made him scream again. Why couldn't he use his arms properly? What was the matter with him? The light dimmed and he was looking at the sea. There were tall cliffs and jagged rocks. There was a pleading voice that followed him wherever he went, like a wraith that pursues, sidles and worms into every crevice, burning its way into his flesh. The tears that rose from the heaving surf were salt in his wounds.

'Go away!', he screamed. 'Leave me alone!'

The rocks, the cruel crags that bit into flesh were like a hungry carnivore that has waited long to sate its appetite on the unwary. The splintered bones, shattered on the rocks, were like an offering on the altar of the sea.

'Go away!', he screamed again, 'I can't take you with me, you fool. You'll spoil everything.'

'What's he on about now?', said Nurse Wilson, tucking the patient's flailing arms back under the covers. 'All that mumbo jumbo. Sounds a bit like Welsh, doesn't it?'

'Could be. There are a lot of them in the city', said her colleague vaguely, entering the appropriate data on the chart at the bottom of the bed. 'Although he seems to have an Irish name', she added with more interest. 'That's probably why he's ended up here.'

Nurse Wilson nodded in agreement, as if this blanket assertion were a logical explanation to account for the misfortune of having being run over in the street.

'Yes, it's definitely Welsh', she said. 'Me and my brother used to go on holidays there before the war. We stayed in a caravan. Nice it was too, although my mum seemed to spend all her time cooking, while my dad went fishing. Me and my brother, we must have explored every rock pool in the area, for crabs and starfish and those sea anemones that you could squeeze to make them spurt out water. We had a great time and Dad would sometimes take us out in a rowing boat. We never got on with the local children, though. They used to throw pebbles at us and tell us us to go home. Then they'd shout all sorts of things in Welsh. We gave as good as we got, though.'

She passed her hand over the patient's forehead as he began to mutter again in an increasingly desperate way.

'What do you think he's saying, poor chap?'

'Load of nonsense, I expect. It's probably just as well that we can't understand him. The things they come out with while they're under anaesthetic usually don't bear repeating.'

But Nurse Wilson looked rather doubtful as the patient continued to thrash about and call out.

'Perhaps we should mention it to Dr Evans. He's Welsh, isn't he? It might have a calming influence on him if someone talks to him in Welsh. I'll have a word with him, if you like', she added, thinking of the crinkly-haired intern with the gorgeous, velvet brown eyes.

• • •

'Look, I've already told you that there's nothing to worry about', said Martin. 'Your friends are not going to come to any harm. I was enjoying hearing about you, for a change.'

They had finished their meal at the Red Lion and he was doing his best to prolong Mari's stay before he lost her to the afternoon's work session at Hendy. 'Tell me some more about you', he pleaded.

'There's nothing to say about me that you don't know already', she protested.

'Tell me about your daughter then. She seems as bright as a button and is obviously going to be nearly as beautiful as her mother when she grows up.'

He smiled and took hold of her hand again. 'Look! I don't care whether Winnie was born in or out of wedlock. It's none of my business, or of anyone else, come to that. What matters is the here and now, and there's nowhere I'd rather be than here and now with Mari Evans, WLA of Llanwrtan in Llŷn.'

She laughed and took her hand away, then picked up her teacup to finsh her tea. 'You're impossible, but thanks

232

for that, and thank you for dinner and for your company. I really enjoyed myself and you've made me feel a lot better about things. But, I really have to be getting back now. I feel I have to make it up to Samuel Jones after running out on him. It's the least I can do.'

'Alright, but I warn you that if I don't see you again soon, I intend to scour the village until I find you. You will come here tomorrow, won't you? The Inspector should be here as well. '

He paused, took hold of both her hands this time, and said softly: 'You mean a lot to me Mari, you know that don't you? I was meant to come here and I was meant to meet you. It's written in the stars.'

'Oh get away with you!', she said rather uncertainly, standing up to retrieve her coat and to cover her confusion. 'I'd better be going now.'

'I'll see you tomorrow, then', he replied, escorting her to the door. 'Don't forget now, it's written in the stars!'

• • •

'Has he been telling you his wicked fantasies, then?' grinned Dr Evans, giving Nurse Wilson a knowing look through his dark eyelashes.

'If he has, he's been wasting his time on me, because I can't understand a word he says', she retorted, giving him an equally suggestive look. 'I think he's one of your compatriots, isn't he?'

The patient stirred and began to call out urgently again. His head moved from side to side, quickening in pace as his words emerged ever more precipitously.

Nurse Wilson passed a soothing hand over his forehead and then turned to look at Dr Evans who was frowning as he took the patient's pulse.

'That, Nurse Wilson', he said grimly. 'Is neither Welsh nor English. If I'm not mistaken, that's German!'

• • •

Inspector Pugh replaced the telephone, pursed his lips and gazed thoughtfully at the photograph of his wife and children on the desk. It was going to be another late homecoming, that's for sure. Sorry Anwen, cariad, he thought. I know I promised, but these things happen. I'll make it up to you. I seem to live according to the dictates of the telephone these days. Who'd be married to a policeman?

'Come on, Bob!', he called to his junior colleague who was about to take a large bite out of a tomato sandwich. 'We're going to Liverpool.'

As the saloon car bowled along the quiet, green lanes that would soon merge with the trunk road to England, he settled himself more comfortably in his leather seat and looked out of the window. Bob was a good driver, if a somewhat stolid companion, content to drive in silence unless his superior officer chose to converse.

A flock of sheep grazed in a field on the left, their corporate whiteness leavened by the occasional black sheep in their midst. Inspector Pugh grinned to himself. The black sheep of the family. He'd been called that too. His siblings included two schoolteachers and a chapel minister, but he had chosen a career in the police force, much to his family's chagrin. Yes, of course, it was necessary to have police officers, they had conceded. Society needs law enforcers, but why did they have to come from the Pugh family? There was no precedent for such a thing. But he had persevered and they had gradually accepted his strange choice of career. At least Anwen had accepted him for what he was. Not for her, the ill-concealed 'if only' attitude that still occasionally manifested itself at family gatherings. She didn't like the irregular hours - of course she didn't - but she understood their necessity and she always made it clear that she was proud of him. Their two children were proud of him too. Anwen! He was a lucky man, there was no doubt about that. He'd make it up to her when he got home.

They were now passing a field of cows, Welsh Blacks and crosses, standing or sitting as was their inclination. He'd always thought that cows sitting down in a field was a sign of rain to come, or was it the other way round? This lot didn't seem to know, anyway.

In the distance, a farmer was ploughing, with an inevitable train of seagulls following and swooping in the wake of the tractor, like a hungry white cloud. They passed another field thick with Rhode Island Red hens, ranging almost in unison as they investigated the riches of the pasture. Heads down! Peck, peck! A fox would have a field day with that lot.

He shifted his weight slightly, closed his eyes and thought back to the events of the last two days. That young pilot, Martin Taylor, had been insistent on seeing him, so insistent that he had finally agreed to drive out to the Red Lion at Llanwrtan. He'd been surprised to find the young Land Army girl from Hendy there with him.

'Oh Inspector, you must help him! He hasn't done any-thing wrong', she'd burst out before he had time even to sit down. He had felt rather irritated at the thought that he'd been called out on an emotional whim. Didn't they realise how busy he was, for heaven's sake? But Martin Taylor, perhaps sensing his irritation, had intervened quickly.

'I think I might have some information for you Inspec-tor. It's about the fire. It may not be important but I thought I ought to let you know. You did say to call you if I thought of anything that might be useful, and you did leave me your card.'

'Yes, I did, but could you not have told me on the tel-ephone, sir?' said the Inspector rather wearily.

'Well, I suppose so, but speaking face to face is always better, it seems to me. There's always the possibility of forgetting something and then remembering it only after putting the receiver down. I hope you don't think I've inconvenienced you, Inspector.'

'No, not at all, sir', said Pugh with more gallantry than he felt. 'Now, perhaps you'll let me know what this is all about?'

'Well, it was something that someone said in the bar the other evening. He was telling this shaggy dog story that seemed to go on for ever.'

He paused as the Inspector, who knew all about the local proclivity for long shaggy dog stories, nodded, with a faint smile.

'It wasn't so much the content of the story', he contin-

236

ued. 'It was the fact that it really was about a dog. I suddenly remembered it when I was having lunch with Mari the following day. By association, I suppose, I thought about the other dogs.'

'What dogs?', said the Inspector as Martin paused.

'The sheepdogs at Hendy. Their kennel is outside the house and they would have heard a prowler. But they didn't bark, Inspector. I checked up on that. They didn't bark. Don't you see? They didn't bark because they must have known the arsonist. He must have been a local man.'

The Inspector nodded slowly as he considered the implication of what he had heard.

'I do believe you're right sir. Well done! Yes, it would have to be a local man or someone living or working at Hendy. That would include - let's see now - the family, the German POWs, Jacob Lewis, and you Miss', he added, looking at Mari.

'You can't think Mari had anything to do with this?', said Martin indignantly. 'That's absurd.'

'It's alright', said the Inspector soothingly. 'I don't suspect you, Miss. I don't think it likely that the family or Jacob or the POWs had anything to do with it either. That leaves ...' He paused and frowned. 'There's the Englishman in the caravan, of course. Do you know of any other local people who might have been out at night and who would fit the bill?'

A slight gasp made them stop and look round. It was Ceri bringing in a tray of drinks from the bar. She stood with a slightly frozen expression on her face, then hurried forward to place the tray on the table.

'Is anything wrong?', said the Inspector.

'No sir. It was something you said just now. It reminded me of something, that's all ... someone ... it's ...'

'Yes? Go on!'

'It's probably nothing at all.'

'Let me be the judge of that!'

It had taken a great deal of persuasion to get Ceri to explain what she meant. Several times she had been on the point of explanation, only to back down again.

'It can't really be important. It's probably just my imagination. I don't want to get anyone into trouble. It's not right to tell tales about people, is it?'

It had taken the combined efforts of all of them to persuade Ceri to reveal what she knew, but it was Mari's final observation that had clinched the matter.

'What was it you were telling me recently about a good detective never hesitating about putting his cards on the table?', she had asked, knowing that this was the latest observation to have impressed the film-loving Ceri.

Yes, things had fallen into place after that, thought the Inspector, as he opened his eyes for another look out of the car window. They were on the trunk road now and travelling at a respectable speed. Fields and livestock had been left behind, to be replaced by houses, terraces and garages, with occasional copses of trees, straggling fences and trimmed hedges to relieve the monotony. Apart from the odd cyclist, the only traffic seemed to be made up of army vehicles, their camouflaged presence like a perennial reminder of autumn, defying any seasonal brightness. The whole world seemed to lack colour these days.

Drabness was everywhere. When would it all end?

But, first things first, thought the Inspector, turning his mind once more to matters in hand. The latest revelation would have to wait until he got back to Wales. There were more urgent matters to attend to now. There was a man with an Irish passport who had been involved in a traffic accident in Liverpool. Amongst the contents of his pockets was a torn bus ticket for a Pwllheli bus and he was apparently in hospital speaking garbled German.

The peremptory telephone call telling him to come at once had been from military intelligence. They were used to issuing orders and going over the heads of the police authorities, it seemed. No doubt, t'was ever thus.

There had to be a connection, though, didn't there? Spies, dinghies, caves, cigarette ends, bus tickets, speaking German, fires, dogs and sudden death. They were all interwoven threads that produced a tangled web of deceit and deception, but perhaps the time had come at last for the process of unravelling to begin.

He yawned. Leave no stone unturned, he thought. That had always been his motto if you wanted to tie up loose ends. And with that somewhat jumbled metaphor in his mind, the Inspector slipped into a comfortable doze.

Bob turned to look at him with a grin, as the first gentle snore emerged from his recumbent companion. Not long to go now. They were nearly at the Mersey Tunnel.

24.

Mari tried to concentrate on what she was doing; making muslin caps for the cheese truckle before it was finally bound, ready for storage. This was a good one, with no discernible cracks to conceal air spaces that could make the cheese swell up during its ripening phase. In three months time it would be ready to eat, although the flavour would be mild. Six months in store would produce a mature, more full-bodied flavour that was more to her taste. Hendy had a good reputation for producing fine cheeses. They had even won prizes at the dairy shows held before the war.

What was Werner doing now? Were he and Peter still being held in Bangor, or were they already far away in some English camp? She had been so looking forward to introducing him to the Madryn trail tomorrow. It was to have been a surprise for him. It would have been ...

She sighed. Martin seemed to think that the Germans would be alright. Surprisingly, so did the Inspector. He had even gone so far as to suggest that the focus of attention would soon move away from them. Well, no, he hadn't actually said that, she admitted to herself, but he had come very close to it. A nod was as good as a wink, they said.

She took a bowl of thin flour and water that had been mixed to a fine paste, and began to paint the cheese with it before applying the muslin caps. Once in place, top and bottom, they were then held in place by a tight muslin bandage pasted around the sides. There, it was done!

She carried the cheese over to the storage shelf and placed it next to the one wrapped last week. Each cheese in the long line was dated and a careful log kept of relative storage times. Each one was also turned regularly.

Martin had been so helpful. She didn't know what she would have done without him. He'd even made her laugh, despite the overwhelming sadness that she felt inside. He was such good company too. When he smiled, the corners of his eyes crinkled up. She suddenly recalled his hands holding hers and his voice breathing huskily: 'It's in the stars.'

• • •

Martin smiled at Ceri and picked up his beer. He looked around the bar and then headed towards his favourite corner seat by the fire.

'Mind if I join you?', he asked Sergeant Thomas, who was deep in conversation with Edward Beynon.

'Not at all', said the Sergeant. 'We were just talking about this spy business. Have you met Edward Beynon?'

'No, I haven't but I'm very pleased to do so now', said Martin, shaking hands with the fisherman. 'You'll be the source of that excellent mackerel I had for supper the other evening, I think. Very tasty it was, too. There's nothing quite like mackerel straight from the sea, is there?'

'You're right there', said Edward. 'The shoals have been good this season, too. Some years are better than others, of course, but we can't complain this year.'

'Where's Ron?', said Martin to Sergeant Thomas, before turning to look about him as if the Englishman were about to materialise.' He doesn't seem to be around.'

'I heard he went back to Bootle', said the Sergeant, although he didn't mention that he was going back the last time I spoke to him. Must have been a sudden decision.'

'Do you know when he's coming back to the caravan?' asked Martin in surprise.

'I don't think anyone does, but then Ron is a bit like that. He's a very friendly chap, but he comes and goes when the mood takes him. One minute he's here, the next, he's gone and nobody knows quite when he'll be back, but he always does - in his own time, that is. It's been quite some time since he went to Bootle, mind you. Maybe he had some business to attend to.'

'Did he not mention it to you either, Edward?' said Martin, turning to the fisherman. 'I mean, you and he shared the coastguard watch, didn't you? I seem to remember him saying that you'd taught him Morse Code. He said that the manual he had belonged to you.'

'So that's where it is', said Edward. 'I was looking for it the other evening. Yes, I helped him with the code, although there hasn't been much call for it. It's mainly used for communication with the islanders on Bardsey, in case of emergency. There's no telephone line there, of course. There's a little hut on the hill at the tip of the mainland at Aberdaron. Every evening a morse message is sent from there to whoever is watching on the island, to make sure that all's well. Years ago, the islanders used to light signal fires if they needed help of any kind. Flashing messages with the code system is a big advance, although it's a cold, draughty job for the one who has to go up to the hut. We take it in turns.'

Edward stopped and took a large draught of beer before continuing: 'When war broke out there were ructions about it in Whitehall, I can tell you. A very smart chap appeared one day and said we had stop sending morse messages immediately. *"Otherwise, how do you chaps know that a German submarine isn't intercepting your messages?"* he said.' Edward did a fair imitation of the said officer's accent, that drew smiles from his listeners.

'I said to him, sir, I said. I don't think they understand Welsh on German U-boats. It's an unbreakable code as far as they're concerned. That stopped him in his tracks, straight away, but he said, *"You'll hear more of this, I can promise you"*, and then he went back to England. A few weeks later we had an official communication telling us that, in future, any messages to and from the island had to be in Welsh, not in English, otherwise it would be viewed as a grave breach of security. We were, of course, happy to comply with official orders.'

Edward finished his recital with a roar of laughter, and then glanced rather apologetically at Martin, in case he had inadvertently caused offence, but was relieved to see that the young Englishman was joining in whole-heartedly in the general merriment.

'Jesus! I can just imagine it', he said when he had stopped laughing. 'We get blokes like that trying to tell us what to do all the time. Most of them have never even been up in a 'plane.'

He broke off as Edwin Humphries and William Jones,

the Choirmaster, approached the table.

'Please don't get up', said Edwin to Martin who, alone of the assembled company, was making an effort to get to his feet. 'Don't let me disturb you, gents. It was just to check whether you're up for the Madryn trail tomorrow.'

'Yes, indeed, we need everyone in good voice when we get to the top', added William Jones. 'Although you might find it a bit much with your leg the way it is, Mr Martin. The Vicar says that he'll drive you up part of the way and then you can just do the last bit. He's taking old Guto Rowlands from the post office as well. He's been going on the trail for more years than anyone else in the village. He's over a hundred, they say.'

'Well, I'll certainly give it a go, whatever it is', said Martin nobly, not sure that he wanted to be classified in the same group as a centenarian, 'But you'll have to tell me what the Madryn trail is. I'm afraid I've never heard of it.'

'You've never heard of it?' exclaimed William Jones in shocked surprise. 'I thought everyone knew. It's one of our most ancient traditions hereabouts.'

'Yes, but we don't exactly advertise the fact, do we?' said Edwin Humphries. 'I didn't know anything about it either, when I first came to the village.'

He turned to Martin and continued: 'Garn Fadryn is that hill you can see from here. It's a prehistoric site that some say is the cairn or burial site of the giant Madryn, one of the local deities in ancient times. There are still remains of round houses near the summit and in the 12th century, a castle was built there by the sons of Owain

Gwynedd. The trail is a kind of pilgrim's route to the top, no doubt going back to heathen times originally, but these days, a Christian service is conducted jointly by the Minister and the Vicar. Most people take a picnic with them and it's a nice day out in the fresh air, as long as the weather is fine. There's a great view from the summit and the forecast for tomorrow is good, it seems.'

'That's settled then', laughed Martin. 'Please tell the Vicar that I'll be pleased to take up his kind offer of transport, Mr Jones.'

• • •

'It's disgraceful', said Bethan to Enid next door. 'How can they be so stupid at that adoption society? Anyone could have told them that John and Megan Prys would be ideal parents for little Rose. Why don't they listen to common sense?'

'Common sense and regulations are not necessarily good bedfellows', said Enid wearily, thinking back to the trauma of losing her husband at Dunkirk, and how long it had taken bureaucratic red tape to heed the financial needs of a widow with a young son. 'If in doubt, they'll always opt for regulations', she continued. It's the safe approach for them.'

The whole village had been shocked to hear the news, that John and Megan's application had been turned down. It had seemed such a certainty, too. Edwin Humphries was particularly cross with the authorities. Everything had been done by the book. Nothing had been left to chance. He had written to complain in no uncertain terms, but he doubted whether it would do any good. Once rampant officialdom got the bit between its teeth, there was usually no turning it. No, the only way to stop a runaway horse was to seize its bridle from the side, he continued to himself, reluctant to drop the metaphor just yet. Some miraculous intervention, a sideways feint was the only possibility now, but here, metaphorical inspiration as well as pragmatic solutions deserted him.

The Minister and the Vicar had also sent letters of complaint, and a petition to sign had been organised in the post office. Virtually everyone in the village had signed it already, and many had had to be dissuaded from signing more than once.

• • •

It was Herbert Johnson, the same supercilious officer from military intelligence whom he had met before. Inspector Pugh felt almost like a suspect by the time their meeting came to an end, but he had finally managed to get him to see things from a slightly different perspective. Dealing with the Liverpool police had been far more straightforward. Once they had established that the hospital patient was not only German-speaking, but had in all probability made his way from the Llŷn area, there seemed little doubt that he was a spy. They had been happy to turn the case over to the intelligence men. Let them get on with it!

Interviewing the man was problematic. He had still not regained consciousness and the medical staff were reluctant to let anyone try, at least not until there was some sign of improvement. This they doubted, in view of the internal bleeding that they had been unable to stop. The intelligence men had to be content with providing an armed guard at his door and a German-speaking agent, with notebook at the ready, at his bedside. So far there was little to report.

'It's just a jumble of words and phrases, sir', reported the agent. 'Although he keeps coming back to the same things. He wants to get away. Someone's following him. Rocks and the sea, and so on.'

'May I see your notebook?', asked Inspector Pugh, hoping that no-one would realise his role in the proceedings was now officially at an end. Bob, his deputy, had already taken himself off to the police canteen for a quick meal before their departure.

The agent looked at his superior, who nodded his agreement, and then handed it over.

Yes, it all fits, thought the Inspector, skimming through the precisely written comments. That poor bastard Hans must have thought he'd be going with him.

'What do you make of it?', asked Johnson.

'Quite a lot', said Pugh thoughtfully. 'Yes, quite a lot.'

'Are you going to share your revelations with us?' said Johnson rather peevishly.

'Yes, of course, but perhaps we should go next door, sir.' He looked at the patient who appeared to be fast asleep, but what if he were really awake and listening?

When they were seated rather uncomfortably next door, in what appeared to be a small storeroom, the Inspector continued:

'Imagine this scenario! Our friend here comes ashore,

probably from a submarine, and paddles to the beach in a dinghy. He may, or may not, have had signal help from the shore. That's an aspect that hasn't been established, but my own feeling is that he was coming in blind.'

'Why do you think that?', broke in Johnson.

'Because he appears to have had an accident. He lost an oar, probably because he collided with the rocks. There are some that are just below the surface of the waves there. The dinghy that we found hidden also has damage that points to a rock collision. If he'd had help from the shore, that would not have happened. They would never have signalled that as a suitable landing area. He was lucky to have made it.'

Johnson nodded and then said: 'Go on!'

'So, there he is ashore. He manages to drag and hide the dinghy, but the paddle has gone. We later find both. Now what? He needs to establish his precise location, but what if he has managed to lose some of his kit - maps, food and so on? What then? He's probably soaking wet and needs to find a hiding place. His luck is still holding because, by some miracle, he finds a small cave. How long he remains there, we don't know but he seems to have had help and some provisions from someone.'

'Who?', said Johnson sharply.

'I can't prove it, but I suspect it was the German POW Hans. The prisoners weren't locked up at night and he had taken to wandering about outside. There's no evidence at all that the other two prisoners were involved in any way. They knew nothing about it.'

'God's teeth, those bloody incompetent Taffs!', shouted

Johnson, oblivious of the fact that he was speaking to a member of the same race. 'How do you know that he wasn't the shore contact in the first place?'

'I don't sir, but I doubt it very much. You see, he was apparently suffering from quite severe depression and could think only of his wife and child. I think they met accidentally. The spy here must have been over the moon at finding such an unexpected ally. He must have persuaded him to get some supplies and information. Unfortunately for him, Hans must have assumed that he would be going with him. He was obsessed with the idea of getting back to his wife and child. It wouldn't have been too long before the spy realised that he was dealing with a very disturbed man. In the notebook, if you recall, he wants to get away, but someone keeps following him. Hans posed a threat that had to be removed, so the poor chap was pushed over the cliff. The cruel jagged rocks and the sea that the spy's been mumbling about refer to that.'

Inspector Pugh paused and lit a cigarette. 'He cold-bloodedly pushed him over then went back to the cave. We know he was there because of the cigarette end we found. He must be a cool customer not to have left the area immediately.'

'Why do you think he waited?'

'He reasoned, correctly as it happened, that there would be search parties looking for a German POW, and that when they found him, they would assume that he'd fallen accidentally. There would be no reason for them to look any further. So, he waited until the body was found.

Then, when everything had calmed down and the coast was clear, he upped and left.'

'Bastard', breathed Johnson, 'But what about this fiery missile business? He wouldn't have thrown it. It must have been Hans who started the fire. Maybe in his confused state he thought it would divert attention from an escape, although the opposite proved to be the case. What do you think, Pugh?'

'I'm sure you're right, sir', said the Inspector in a rather non-commital way, while looking casually at the shelves on which various sheets, pillow cases and towels were neatly stored. 'We'll never know for sure, but it's a reasonable assumption.'

'Now, all we need to find out is why he was here and who his contact was in Liverpool.'

'That's your department, sir', said Pugh, getting to his feet. 'I don't think I can be of any further use to you here. Intelligence work is outside my remit, after all.'

'Yes, of course. I take your point', said the somewhat mollified Johnson, standing up and reasoning that for a country plod, his companion had done quite well. 'Thank you for your help and cooperation, Pugh. It's much appreciated.'

'Thank you, sir', said the Inspector, then paused at the door. 'I expect that it will be alright to take the other POWs back from Bangor now. They're doing good work on the farm, for our war effort after all, and they're quite innocent of all this. If you could give me the appropriate paperwork, sir, I'll take them off your hands. You've more important things to deal with, I'm sure?'

Johnson hesitated for a moment, frowned and said:

'I'm not sure about that, Pugh, although you're probably right; they haven't actually done anything wrong. It would be one lot of paperwork I could usefully do without, I suppose.'

The Inspector waited patiently while his companion considered the options.

'Look here, Pugh!', he said finally. 'It would have to be on the basis that the prisoners are locked in at night, every night, from now on. You'll have to make sure that those villagers understand that. There's to be no more of this treating them like equals nonsense, d'you hear me?'

'Of course, sir. I'll see to it myself, sir. You can be assured of that. Thank you very much, sir.'

As they emerged into the corridor, they became aware of running footstops heading for the patient's room.

'You'll have to wait outside', said a nurse, attempting to block their way in.

Ignoring her, Johnson pushed his way past to where a doctor and several of his staff were working furiously over the recumbent figure of the spy. For several minutes they continued until, at last, the doctor turned and said: 'He's gone, I'm afraid.'

'Damn it! Did he say anything before he died?', said Johnson, turning to the agent sitting with the patient.

'No, sir, nothing at all.'

'Damn it!', said Johnson again. 'Now we'll never know what he was up to.'

'No, sir', said Pugh.' But he won't cause you any more trouble either.'

25.

The Sunday of the Madryn trail dawned with a luminosity that heralded well for the walk to come. As the light gradually increased, there was much studying of the cloud cover, for if there was enough blue sky to make knee breeches for a gander, then all would be well.

Catrin and Winnie had been awake since dawn, and had several times been sent back to their bedroom on the grounds that it was still too early for them to be up and about. It was only Nain's final warning that she would make them do the morning's milking if they got under her feet one more time, that was effective in curtailing their enthusiasm. So, they sat, wrapped up in blankets on the wide window-seat of the bedroom, accompanied by Llwydyn the cat's kneading, furry approval.

It was a good spot from which to keep an eye on any comings and goings outside. So far, there was little to see, apart from Mari going out to the cows and Bethan coming in with supplies from the barn. Nain was preparing the picnic in the kitchen. Only when these tasks were completed and it was time for breakfast, would the girls be allowed back into the kitchen. After breakfast, they would be responsible for the washing up.

'They would give us the worst job, wouldn't they?' said Winnie. 'It's not fair for Nain to make the picnic on her own. I'd have liked to do it, too. I mean, she may pack something we don't like.'

'But we like everything', said Catrin, for whom the

idea of disliking food was an alien concept. 'Nain makes nice picnics', she acknowledged generously, 'But it is mean to expect us to wash up after breakfast. After all, she's not going to Garn Fadryn, is she? It stands to reason that the washing up should be done by those not going, not by those who have all that walking to do.'

No matter how worthy the claim, however, it would be a brave soul who dared broach such a subject to the venerable matriarch.

Nain had made it clear that, this year, she would not be going on the trail. Rather she would be joining Ifan's grandmother, Ellen Rowlands, next door. It being a Sunday, naturally precluded taking her knitting or crochet work with her, but the prospect of a cosy chat with her old friend was an attractive one. Nain's deafness was no barrier to those who were well versed in the art of such communication. Discussions would invariably include a general appraisal of everything that was currently happening in the village, followed by an in-depth examination of specific characters, their strengths and their weaknesses. The two Nains were united in the view that gossiping, as a negative activity indulged in by those who had nothing better to do, was to be avoided. Impartial discussions, on the other hand, were useful and pragmatic. It was arguably a finely-drawn distinction, but to both women, a day where every prospect pleases beckoned with pleasurable anticipation.

All over the village, picnics were being packed, haversacks adjusted and shoe laces doubly checked. The starting point was outside the chapel. The Choirmaster was there already, handing out hymn books as people arrived.

'And no leaving them behind in the bilberry bushes!', was his injunction to the younger members of the congregation, who were known to be remiss in such matters.

'I want the same number coming down the hill as went up there in the first place.'

Catrin and Winnie soon met up with Ifan and Rose while Bethan and Mari chatted with some of the other early arrivals. If only Werner could be here, thought Mari wistfully. He would have loved it, especially the view from the top. From there it was possible to see the whole peninsula laid out in a sweeping panorama before them, with sea on either side and the Rival mountains behind. Beyond and farther into mainland Wales were the high and mysterious mountains and the dark lakes of Eryri. One day, she would show him. One day, they would explore the places of legend together. One day ...

'There's the Vicar', said Bethan, as an old Morris 8 came wheezing up to the chapel. The Reverend Walters got out, leaned forward to speak to the other occupants of the car and then went to find the Minister. Some of the bulkier items, such as the portable lectern that they would need for the outdoor service had already been taken up in Hendy's van, but the heavy bible and smaller items were to be carried in his boot. With three passengers, he hoped there wouldn't be too much strain on the old girl.

His smiling wife, sitting in the front passenger seat, turned round to address the two men in the back: 'Are you comfortable there?'

'We're fine, thank you, Mrs Walters', said Martin, trying to ignore the fact that old Guto's walking stick had somehow become entangled with his own, and was pressing painfully against his knee. He shifted his weight a little to relieve the pressure on his leg and then took advantage of the movement to push Guto's stick to a more acceptable position. He hoped the journey up the track wouldn't take too long. He wasn't sure which was preferable, a struggle up the hill on his own or sharing a conveyance with Guto.

'Here we are, then', said the Vicar, returning and opening the boot so that one of the chapel deacons could unload his burdens into the space. 'We're still a bit early', he continued, going round to the front. It will take the walkers at least an hour to get to the top, so we don't need to start just yet. Do you want to stretch your legs in the meantime?'

Guto, to whom the concept of stretching his legs was as unacceptable as swimming around the headland, shook his head and announced that he would stay where he was, thank you very much. Too much exercise was bad for his legs. As it was a Sunday, he would pass the time here, in quiet contemplation instead. With that satisfied pronouncement that carried the distinct odour of smug sanctity, he promptly fell asleep.

Martin, who had just spotted Mari in the throng, nodded eagerly and got out of the car.

'Good morning, ladies', he said, addressing Mari, Bethan and Ifan's mother, Enid. 'It's going to be a fine day, I think.'

'I didn't know you were coming', said Mari, unable to

conceal her pleasure at seeing him. 'Will you be able to manage the walk uphill? I mean, it's quite steep for your leg to cope with.'

'Don't worry!', he laughed. 'I'm not going under my own steam. The Vicar is kindly giving me a lift in his car. I'm a bit of a fraud really.'

'You're not a fraud', said Mari. 'At least you won't be as long as you remember to take a pebble with you.'

'A pebble! What for? Why a pebble?'

'To place on the cairn at the top, of course.'

'Of course! I should have known. It's part of the proceedings, I suppose.'

'It is.'

'Shall we meet up at the top, then you can show me what the procedure is? You could be my translator, too. That would be useful.'

'Alright', laughed Mari, turning to look about her for a moment. 'I think we're being lined up to start now, so we'll see you at the top! Don't forget, it's a small pebble, not a great lump of rock you need to bring.'

Martin waved to the column as it began its slow, burgeoning way to the summit, then turned towards the car.

A pebble! Find a pebble first! Rough, smooth, jagged, rounded, bluish-grey, greenish-brown, with or without flecks, white with sandy bits. What a choice! Here's a nice one! This will do! He slipped the smooth, brown-flecked stone into his pocket, then made his way back to the car.

'That's a shell, you've got, not a stone', said Winnie, examining Rose's offering with a critical eye. 'You're supposed to have a pebble, not a shell. Look, we've all got pebbles', she added somewhat ungraciously, gesturing towards Catrin and Ifan who rather reluctantly showed their stones. Neither wished to become involved in a controversy at this stage of the proceedings.

'I don't think it matters. It can be a shell if you like', said Ifan hesitantly.

'It's a very pretty shell.' added Catrin diplomatically, wondering whether to give her cousin a shove.

'Yes, it is, and why can't it be a shell?', said Rose stubbornly. 'Who says so? I'm taking it to the top anyway.'

But a small doubt niggled, like an irritating grain of sand that has worked its way between wriggling toes, and a few minutes later, she ran a little way back to where John and Megan Prys were walking along, hand-in-hand.

'Does it have to be a pebble or can it be a shell', she addressed the pair, holding up the small pink and grey cowrie that she had selected during a recent visit to the beach. 'Winnie says that it has to be a pebble, but this is such a pretty shell.'

'Give it here', said John, holding out his hand and taking it from her carefully. He held it up for Megan to see as well, and then gave it a thorough examination.

'Hmm! If I'm not mistaken, this is a very special shell. In these parts we call it a gwichyn pen voel - a bald-headed winkle shell - because it does look a bit like a head with no hair, doesn't it? You only find these on a few special beaches in Llŷn, and they bring good luck. If you have one of these in your purse, it will never be empty, they say. No, it doesn't have to be a pebble, and I think this is a very suitable choice, but you may want to keep it for your own purse, unless you find another one for that later. It's up to you, of course.'

He handed the shell back to Rose, who wrapped it carefully in her handkerchief before putting it in her pocket.

'Thank you! I'll take this and leave it at the top today and I'll find another one for my purse next week', she said and ran back to where she had left her friends.

'A wise choice', smiled John to Megan. 'Yes, indeed, a wise choice.'

The Morris 8 was not best equipped for traversing the rough pathway. Martin reasoned to himself that it was only the combined presence of a lady and a gentleman in holy orders that stopped him from using a few choice expressions whenever they hit a rut. Each time, the walking sticks became entangled again, Guto would sway across until he was leaning heavily on his fellow passenger, his nose dripping unconcernedly onto Martin's jacket. Martin had also cracked his head at least twice against the side of the car.

Strangely enough, the journey appeared to hold no trepidations for the old man. Each time they hit a rut, Guto would shout out gleefully: 'We shall have no fears because Jesus Christ is on our side!', a comment that was swiftly followed by a cackle of ribald laughter.

The Vicar, unable to decide whether this was a genuine expression of Christian sentiment or a comment of more dubious origin, kept a discreet silence. His wife, one hand clutching her hat, the other gripping the side of the seat, looked out of the window and kept up a series of gentle but rather breathless platitudes on such things as the prettiness of the lambs this year, good fortune with the weather and what an excellent turnout it was today. None of the comments required an answer.

At last, they arrived at the parking spot from which no further progress was possible by car. It was now only a matter of fifty yards or so to the spot where the congregation had gathered. It was a great relief to Martin to see Guto's grandson Dai Rowlands with his wife Blodwen from the post office, coming to claim Guto. The Minister and chapel deacons were also arriving to help the Vicar and Mrs Walters to their allotted places, and to carry the bible and various items for the service.

Martin straightened his jacket and checked to make sure that his lapels were relatively free of the journey's detritus, then looked about him. Several people nodded and smiled at him, obviously gratified to see the English RAF hero in their midst.

'Hello! You made it then?,' said a welcome voice. 'We've kept a place for you here, although it's standing only. There are a few flat rocks further back to sit on, but they're really for the older people. Will you be able to manage?'

'Of course I can, especially with you by my side. What more could any man ask than to ... '

'You behave yourself now', grinned Mari.

The service was essentially a simple one, but in this high place of rocks and sky, it seemed to have an eerie quality of timelessness that spanned countless ages, thought Martin. He could understand nothing of what

259

was being said or sung, but was touched by some elemental quality in the ceremony. He found himself wondering what were the roots of such a gathering? Could it be pre-Christian in its origin? Probably! Many Christian rituals had indeed been grafted on to existing and ancient beliefs. According to the Vicar, *Englynion Y Beddau* (Stanzas of the Graves) referred to in the 13th century Black Book of Carmarthen, lists the names and burials of people living long before recorded history. Their burial grounds were in remote places such as this, on hills, moorlands and headlands, remote from the dwellings of men.

His thoughts were interrupted by the next hymn which was sung with the usual heart-felt gusto under the keen direction of the Choirmaster. Unconfined by roof and walls, the blended voices soared effortlessly into the realms of cloud and sky. Martin could almost imagine the sound travelling further, ever further, outwards and upwards, past flocks of wheeling birds, beyond the boundaries of earth, finally joining the eternal music of the spheres.

After the last hymn and the final blessing, the congregation wended the short way to the topmost point of the hill, where their stones were added to the cairn. Rose placed her shell in the middle of the pebbles. It tinkled its way through the gaps between them until it found its own secret niche. As she turned away, she received a broad wink from John Prys.

Martin realised with annoyance that he had left his picnic in the car, but Mari was insistent that he should share the food they had brought, rather than walk down to the car park and back again.

'Don't argue! We've got plenty here. Let's sit over there!', she added, indicating a spot on the leeward side of the hill. 'There should be room for all of us on this blanket.'

She proceeded to unroll a woollen tartan blanket taken from her haversack, while Bethan and Enid busied themselves with cups, and various packs of carefully wrapped sandwiches.

He sat down gratefully, content to watch the others, especially Mari, as they organised the children and the distribution of the food. Her head moved this way and that, the dark curls bobbing against her forehead and cheeks as she turned and spoke and laughed. She was so beautiful, he thought. It seemed incredible that they had not even known each other a short while ago. Now, he could not imagine being without her. The last thought brought with it a sense of shock, like a small jolt felt somewhere in his chest. Was that true? Had she really become so important to him?

He thought suddenly of the letter that had come for him yesterday morning. It was to inform him officially that he would no longer be flying on active service. The doctors had ruled against it, while emphasising that a more static role was perfectly feasible for him. He'd be flying a bloody desk, that's what they mean, he thought bitterly.

He loved flying! Despite the dangers and the ever-present stress, he loved it. Now, that would all be behind him. He would have to sit out the war, counting paperclips in some bloody office. He was to report for his new duties in a week's time. He had told no-one yet, not even Mari. What was there to say, anyway? But he must say something. He could not just up and away as if they had never met. He must speak to her.

And with that thought, another more radical one appeared, as if a door had suddenly opened somewhere within his deeper consciousness. Through that portal, he caught a sudden glimpse of the two of them together, really together. She was his girl after all, wasn't she? Was that a real possibility? He was certainly keen on her, but something in him had not yet committed itself fully to the idea of a permanent relationship. But, as he continued to look at her, the vision grew clearer and his own words echoed in his mind: *"It was meant to be. It's in the stars."*

Mari was his girl! He was sure of it now. He would speak to her. After declaring himself, he would ask her to marry him. They might not be able to marry immediately, but an engagement could take place straight away. When they were married, she and Winnie would come to live with him. His new posting suddenly seemed less burdensome. They would be together. They would be happy. A new chapter of his life was about to open. He would ...

He suddenly became aware that the others were looking at him.

'Come on, sleepy head! Did you want another sandwich, or not? It's only the third time I've asked you', said Enid cheerfully. 'What on earth are you dreaming about?'

'I'm sorry! I was miles away', he said in confusion,

taking the proffered sandwich. 'I'm not usually slow in coming forward where food is concerned', he continued with a laugh and then bit into the bread to avoid further comment on the subject.

The others carried on where they had left off, but Bethan continued to look at him in a rather questioning way. Then, she glanced at Mari and back again. Oh no! If what she was thinking was true, there could be untold problems and heartaches ahead.

'Can we play Spitfires now?', said Ifan. 'It's alright, Mam', he added, sensing the protest that was about to come from his mother. 'I know it's a Sunday but we can make it a quiet game.'

Quietness was not an attribute that Enid would normally have ascribed to Spitfires, and was about to say so when Martin came to the rescue.

'I've got a much better game', he said, hauling himself up. 'It's called Madryn ducks and drakes. Now, I balance this small rock on top of this other one, then we draw a line a few yards away - here - beyond which we cannot go. The idea is to collect some more stones - say three each - and then we take it in turns to throw them and try to knock the rock off its base. We get one point for each time it's knocked down, and the winner is the one with most points. How about that?'

It was a good game, with several more of the village children coming to join in. As soon as it was well under way, Martin turned to Mari and whispered: 'I have something to say to you, something private. Shall we walk a little way along here, as if we were going to get a better view of the headland?'

'You're very mysterious all of a sudden', said Mari. 'Come on then! It's a pretty spectacular view, isn't it? Oh!' she added as a new thought struck her. 'Have you heard anything from Bangor? Has the Inspector said anything?'

'No, it's not that, although I'm sure we will hear from him during the week. No, it's something else, something about me - about us.'

"Curiouser and curiouser, said Alice", she laughed. 'Now, you really are being mysterious. What is it?'

'I have orders to go back in a week's time.'

Her face clouded over. 'Oh Martin, I'm sorry to hear that. Won't they let you stay a bit longer? How can they ask you to go back to flying again when your leg is still not properly healed?'

'That's just the point. They want me to go back, but to a desk job. They won't let me fly again.'

'But that's wonderful, Martin. Now I won't need to worry about you being shot down. You'll have a nice, safe job. You've done enough for your country already.'

'Mari, listen to me! I really wanted to fly again. Don't ask me to explain why, but I really did. Anyway, as things stand, I can't, so I have to make the best of it.'

He paused and gazed about him. Here, over a thousand feet above sea level, even the skylarks appeared to be flying low over the peninsula. Far out at sea, a ship crawled along the horizon, while gulls wheeled above the beaches, like tiny petals of white blossoms tossed by the undiscriminating winds. He found himself envying their freedom to explore the skies.

'Oh Mari, what I want to say is that I don't want to leave you, but I have no choice. I must go back, but I need to know something first. Is there any chance for me? I mean, will you be my girl? Will you write to me?'

'Of course, I'll write to you', said Mari. 'We're friends aren't we? What are friends for?'

'Yes, but what about the other bit - about being my girl? Will you be my girl? Mari, I need to know.'

He spoke fiercely this time, aware that his anger was increasing. He thought of the efforts that he had made on her behalf to bring the two Germans back from Bangor and suddenly hated Werner with an intensity that almost frightened him. Damn the German! Let him stay where he was, instead of coming back here and wheedling his way into Mari's affections again. He was ...

'Martin, you're hurting me', gasped Mari in shocked surprise, pulling her arm away from the tightening grasp of his fingers. 'We're friends, of course we are, but we've only just met. I don't know what to say. I can't think straight at the moment. Can't we just leave it that we're friends for the time being, and see how things go. Meanwhile, we can write to each other and ... ?'

'It's him, isn't it?', said Martin bitterly. 'It's that Werner, you're always going on about, isn't it? It's that damned German.'

'I'm not always going on about him, as you say', said Mari indignantly. It was you who offered to help me, if you remember. As for being your girl, you haven't exactly given me time to think about the possibility, have you? You just drop something like that on me and then want an immediate answer. What do you expect me to say? We were having such a nice day, and now you've gone and spoilt it.'

She turned away with a slight sob and without once looking back, walked away to rejoin the Madryn ducks and drakes competition that was approaching its finale. Groups of people were now clearing up and preparing to head down the hill to their homes. He watched Mari's retreating back miserably, but was so caught up by the power of his own conflict, that he was quite unable to follow. For a long time he stood alone amidst the chaos of his thoughts and emotions, then headed slowly back towards the Vicar's car.

'Mari, I'm so sorry', he whispered wretchedly, to himself, as he stumbled along, a sentiment that was almost immediately replaced by another wave of anger: 'Damn that bloody German.'

• • •

Thankfully, it had been Bethan's turn to see the girls to bed when they returned to Pant Uchaf that evening. Mari was grateful for that. All she wanted to do was to be by herself and try to make sense of the emotional whirlwind that seemed to have blown up in her face.

Nain had wanted to know all about the trail walk, but a warning shake of the head from Bethan, who was standing behind Mari, had alerted her against pursuing that line of questioning. So, she had changed the subject, rather telling them of her day with Ellen Rowlands, next door, and of the snippets of interest gleaned from their conver-

266

sations. She knew that Bethan would explain things to her later, after the girls were in bed.

The children had needed no encouragement to go upstairs that night. Within fifteen minutes, both were fast asleep, hurling the magic pebbles of their dreams into distant cairns within the ancient and enchanted mountains.

Mari sat in her nightdress on the stool in front of the dressing table and studied herself as she brushed her hair. She saw that there was a slight bruise on the arm that Martin had grasped so tightly. She had never seen him angry before. But it wasn't just anger, she realised. He had been truly and deeply upset. He must care for her, she mused, but he had not actually said so, had he? She thought back again to their exchange. No! Not once had he said that he cared for her in a special way - that he loved her. What was painfully obvious, however, was that he was very jealous of Werner.

But, there was no cause to be jealous. As far as she could recall, she had not said or done anything that would give rise to that ugly emotion, that green worm that could so easily inveigle its way into the unwary heart.

Why was green so often associated with envy?, she wondered suddenly, going off on one of those unpredictable tangents that present themselves when thought processes come into play. Green was also the colour of nature and of truth. Green was a positive colour. It was one of her favourite colours. It went well with her colouring, everyone said so.

She put the hairbrush down and looked at herself in

the mirror again. 'For heaven's sake, what are you rambling on about?', she said impatiently. 'This nonsense isn't getting you anywhere.'

She got up and went to sit on the bed, just as there was a slight tap on the door and Bethan's voice said: 'Mari, can I come in?'

• • •

After two double whiskies Martin knew that he had had enough. It was more than enough he realised, as he swayed to his feet from the bedroom chair on which he was sitting. The bar was closed on Sundays but John Rowlands, the proprietor, realising that his guest was in a very despondent state, had produced the spirits from some secret source, reasoning that as it was for medicinal purposes, the law was not being broken. It was also being served in the guest's room, not in a public area.

Martin's distress was so obvious that John had felt it incumbent upon himself to talk to him for a while, once his wife and Ceri had gone into the kitchen. In his experience, a sympathetic ear was all that was necessary in such cases. There was no need for extraneous talk or - heaven forbid - the giving of advice! No, just being prepared to listen quietly, without too much comment, that was what was needed.

Even so, he had not expected to be taken into the Englishman's confidence so soon. It had been with some sense of relief that Martin had told him that orders to rejoin his unit had arrived, but that they would not let him fly.

'What's the use of a pilot who can't bloody fly a plane?',

he said bitterly. John had tried to reassure him that a ground role was also important, but soon realised that he was wasting his time. After taking the whisky up to Martin's room, he had discreetly wished him good night and then gone downstairs to rejoin his family.

Martin eased himself onto the bed and thought back to the exchange between him and Mari. What had he said that had offended her? There must have been something. Yes, he had been a bit abrupt with her, he supposed, but the thought of that bloody German with her had made him so angry.

He had desperately wanted to tell Mari of his feelings for her, but everything had come out the wrong way round somehow. Why was it so difficult to speak openly about how he felt? He had never had this difficulty before. He was popular with women, wasn't he? Flattery, laughter, jokes and general banter had always gone down well. He liked women and they liked him. He enjoyed their company and their conversations. Unlike many men, they said, he actually listened to their views, and didn't tell them what to do all the time. He'd never thought about that before, but he supposed that it must be true.

So, why was it different with Mari? Their initial meetings had gone well. They had laughed, joked and talked, and she had been genuinely grateful for his help. Yes, she would be, said a small bitter voice inside him. She's been using you to get her lover boy back. She doesn't care a hoot about you.

'Stop it!', he told himself, punching his pillow in exasperation. 'For God's sake, stop it!'

They had shared something, he was sure of it, but somewhere along the line, things had gone wrong? Where had they gone wrong? It had to be when he had tried to make his feelings clear to her on Garn Fadryn.

But had he communicated any of his feelings at all? He thought back to what he had actually said and with a growing sense of dismay, realised that he had not put into words anything substantial. Had he at any point said that he loved her? No! Had he said that she meant the world to him and that he wanted to spend the rest of his life with her? No!

What had he said? He groaned out loud as he recalled the self-pitying way in which he had described not being allowed to fly in future, and the adolescent manner in which he had asked her to be his pen-pal girl. He was a grown man, for God's sake, but he must have sounded like a forlorn schoolboy. On top of everything else, he had even hurt her arm. It didn't bear thinking about.

He must see her again before he left. This time he would describe his feelings properly, not hide behind an emotional facade. The first thing was to write her a note and apologise for his behaviour. That was the least he could do.

26.

The subject of why Monday was named after the moon - *"and who has the right to decide that anyway?"* - had been instrumental in making Catrin and Winnie late for school that morning. The porridge had also taken longer than usual to make and serve up. That combined with the last-minute search for Winnie's spelling book, left in the barn, made them unusually late.

Mari had already left on her early start to Hendy, so it was down to Bethan and Nain to get the girls on their way to meet scholastic retribution. For retribution would surely follow if they arrived at school after nine-o-clock in the morning.

The usual punishment was having to stay in at morning playtime and clean whatever happened to be in particular need of ablution. The most unpopular task was cleaning the pots used for mixing paints, especially if the paint had hardened around the rims. On this occasion, however, fortune smiled on the tardy two for the only thing that needed cleaning was the nature table that stood at the side of the schoolroom. A quick tidying and dusting was all that was necessary to bring the display back to a pristine condition.

Mrs Humphries, coming to inspect the table, would almost certainly have found them something else to do, for it was well-known that fairness was not a characteristic to be found in her nature, but on this occasion, her husband was with her. As quick as as a blink, Catrin seized the opportunity that presented itself for a diversionary tactic, and asked him: ' Why is Monday named after the moon, sir?'

'That is an interesting question, Catrin', he said, his eyes beaming with pleasure behind his glasses, while his wife sniffed her disapproval. She had experienced these tactics before, but her husband seemed to delight in applauding the inventiveness associated with such ploys. She sniffed again, but realising that she had been outmanoeuvred, walked away to the staff room.

'It is the ancient civilisations that we have to thank for naming our weekdays, of course', continued the Headmaster enthusiastically. 'So many of our descriptions come from them, although there does seem to have been something of a disparity between the Roman and the Northern gods. Our Welsh word for Wednesday is *Dydd Mercher* - the day of Mercury from the Romans - while the English name *Wednesday* comes from the Northern god Woden from the Vikings. However, everyone seems to be agreed that Sunday is named after the sun.'

He smiled with pleasure again and continued: 'Come to think of it, you should both be out enjoying the sunshine now, so off you go!'

When the cousins emerged triumphantly into the sunshine, they found Rose skipping at the side of the playground while Ifan and George were busy kicking a ball to each other. They appeared not to have a care in the world, but Catrin knew, as they all did, that Rose's bid to stay in Llanwrtan as the adopted daughter of Megan and John Prys had failed. They had tried to talk to Rose about it, but she seemed not to believe the news.

'Don't worry! Everything is going to be alright, just you wait and see!', was her reply to every cautious query and comment.

'How can you be so sure?', asked Winnie, despite a warning look from Catrin.

'Because it was my special wish that I took to Enlli. The shell I carried to Garn Fadryn was special, too. John Prys said so. He said we must never give up hope, even when there seems to be no hope left.'

And with that, they had to be content.

• • •

Mari found it difficult to concentrate on her work at Hendy that morning. She seemed to be filled with a sense of sadness that permeated everything. Wherever she looked, there seemed to be no escape from a cloying cloud of greyness. Beti was the only one who understood something of her situation, because she had arranged things in such a way that the two of them would be working together in the dairy, then later with the chickens and finally with preparations for dinner in the kitchen. Mari was staying at Hendy until the evening rather than following her usual practice of going home for dinner. With so much work to do, it was a reasonable compromise.

The outdoor work, with the sheep, pigs and cattle, was left to Samuel, his brother and old Jacob. Although nothing was said, everyone knew what a gap had been left by the departure of the Germans. It was true that they knew nothing about farming and animal husbandry when they arrived, but they had been quick to learn and to pull their weight in the daily routines. Now, without their help, the timetable had to be reallocated again.

Selecting chickens for next season's breeding flock from the current laying flock was an activity normally undertaken by Jacob, so the news that he was being usurped in this by Beti and Mari was not well received.

'It's not just about choosing those that look healthy and well feathered', he said grumpily. 'There are different things that apply to cocks and hens. Proper records need to be kept and consulted and, most important of all, respect should be paid to what traditional experience has taught us.'

'You're absolutely right, as usual, Jacob', said Beti hurriedly, aware from Mari's loud intake of breath, that she was about to react impatiently. 'Thanks to you, we have excellent records to consult, and your list of homilies should prevent any crow-headed hens or narrow-backed and thin-chested cocks being selected.'

'You mind that you drop each cock on the ground'. said the old man, somewhat encouraged by her comments. 'A good one will stand his ground and talk or crow at you, while a poor one will squeal, ruffle up his feathers and run away.'

'We'll certainly remember that', said Beti, giving Mari another warning glance. 'If there's anything we have doubts about, we'll definitely come and ask you straight away.'

And with that reassurance, Jacob was relatively content.

Throughout the rest of that morning Mari's thoughts and actions were confused, but Beti made many allowances for what she recognised as some sort of emotional crisis taking place in the other woman. She was not the sort to pry and ask questions, and knew that sympathetic silence could often be the most effective approach.

As far as Mari was concerned, she was glad of the opportunity to sort out her thoughts, and to ask herself questions that might otherwise have been obscured by prosaic needs or surface emotions.

She thought back to what her sister Bethan had said the previous night.

'You've got yourself into a right muddle haven't you?'

'What do you mean?'

'I mean that not content with giving Werner the run-around, you're now doing the same thing with Martin!'

'I am not!' said Mari indignantly. 'What sort of person do you take me for? I've just been friendly that's all.'

'Friendly! Is that what you call it? Mari, it's a word that can cover a whole range of scenarios, and, you see, you can't . . . '

She paused. 'What I mean to say is that you have to be particularly careful, especially where men are concerned. 'You're a very pretty girl Mari, and it's easy for you to give the wrong impression. Don't forget that both Werner and Martin have been involved in war, and a pretty brutal war too. They probably see things in a different way from us. Everything is more immediate. Life and death - they are separated only by a hairline. One minute life and all that involves and then death - everything gone.

Everything just blotted out for ever.'

Her voice broke suddenly and Mari saw that there were tears in her sister's eyes, and knew their source.

'Oh Bethan, cariad, don't cry. Richard will always come back to you. The tide of this awful war is turning and the U-boat packs are fewer and less effective than they were!'

She reached out and hugged Bethan, stroking her hair away from her forehead.

'I know we were talking about me and that you mean well, but there's really no need for you to worry about me or Richard. You're right, I have been in a bit of a muddle but things are clearer now - and that's probably thanks to you as well.'

Yes, she was clear in her own mind now, thought Mari as she walked home from Hendy that evening. Things had fallen into place for her. She knew what she must do.

However, the last thing she expected when she got home, was a letter from Martin. There it lay on the kitchen table; a cream envelope written in a rounded, flowing hand that she recognised as his. He had beautiful writing. She had once complimented him on it.

'Megan Prys brought it from the post office for you, as she was going to the village anyway', said Nain. 'Aren't you going to open it?'

Mari took up the letter, but made no move to open it.

'Where are the girls?', she asked.

'They're in the tree house with Ifan and Rose. I've told them to be back by supper time.'

Mari nodded. 'I'm going upstairs for a while. I've got a bit of a headache, but I'll be down soon.'

Martin's letter was brief and to the point. An apology for what he acknowledged as his boorish behaviour, followed by an explanation as to what had caused it. He loved her, of that he had no doubt, but he was also duty bound to follow instructions and take up his new posting. Would she consider him, despite everything? He would always love and protect her, and would accept Winnie as his own child. He loved her. He loved her.

She read the letter through again and then decided to respond in kind. She found writing paper and an envelope and began:

'My dear Martin, . . .

● ● ●

Werner and Peter looked round the annexe in pleased surprise. There was no trace of the fire-damage to be seen. Although the broken window had been repaired and most of the mess cleared up before they left, the scorch marks and general damage had been difficult to disguise. Now, a transformation had happened. The walls were newly whitewashed and there were new covers on the divan beds. Someone had been busy in their absence.

It had come as a shock that Monday evening, when Inspector Pugh and his deputy had arrived at the barracks where the Germans were being held in Bangor. They had assumed that the document the Inspector had with him was authorisation to return them to the prisoner of war camp in England, from which they had originally been sent to Wales. But no, it turned out that they were being taken back to Llanwrtan, to resume their work at Hendy farm. They still could not believe in their good fortune.

Although full of questions, they had heeded Inspector Pugh's urgent instructions to keep quiet and to do exactly as they were told. This had included being handcuffed and escorted out to the car by two armed guards. Here, they were officially handed over, once the chief security officer had assured himself that the Inspector and his deputy were both suitably armed. Once in the car and on their way, however, the handcuffs were removed.

'I take it that we have your word, both of you, that you will not try to escape?', said Pugh, a question that brought immediate and enthusiastic agreements from the prisoners.

'I'm afraid it's no good asking me any questions', he continued. 'Because I'm not prepared to tell you anything. I'm not in a position to do so, anyway. You are enemy prisoners after all. All I will say is that the culprit has been dealt with and the incident is now closed to my satisfaction. If you have any sense, you'll accept that justice has been done, and make the best of things from now on. This war can't last much longer.'

With that, they had to be content, and they were! Werner leant his head against the car window and looked out at the increasingly familiar landscape. He was going home. He was going home to Mari. With that thought filling his mind and his heart, he dozed contentedly.

Beti had quickly organised supper for them when they arrived unexpectedly at Hendy. It was a cold collation but, compared with the food they had endured at the barracks over the last few days, it was a veritable feast.

The others had obviously eaten already. After a nod and an indecipherable grunt, which they took to be a form of welcome, Jacob took himself off to his bedroom where he could address the muse in relation to the poem that he was currently working on. The Germans looked at each other and smiled. Yes, it was good to be back.

'I expect you'll want to turn in early, too', said Samuel Jones pointedly. 'It'll be an early start in the morning. My brother has been helping out while you've been gone, but he can't be here all the time.'

'How is Mari?', asked Werner, no longer able to contain himself. 'Does she know that we are back?'

'I shouldn't think so. After all, we didn't know until you turned up just now. She's been working hard, too - we all have - to keep up with the work load. She's a good girl, is Mari. Now, I've got these damned forms to fill in for the Ministry of Agriculture.'

He took off the glasses that he wore only for such tasks and wiped his forehead wearily before putting them on again, rather crookedly. He shuffled the pile of forms that had been placed at one end of the dining table and then frowned. A note of embarrassment was evident in his voice as he spoke:

'Oh yes, there's one more thing. I've been told that, in future, you must be locked up in the annexe at night. The authorities weren't too happy about that door being left unlocked. It's one of the conditions they specified before they would agree to let you come back here. Inspector

Pugh went out on a limb for you, you know. He's a good man, so don't let him down. If you get caught short during the night, you'll have to use a bucket.'

It was a compromise that they accepted with good grace. As they went out, Samuel called after them:

'That's alright then. I won't lock up until I go to bed, and that's likely to be some time yet, unless I can get these forms sorted out.'

Outside, the night air was soft and balmy, with the fragrance of hay, old roses and a residual trace of cows carried on the breeze. They breathed deeply and appreciatively and stopped to look at the night sky.

'I think it will be fine tomorrow', said Peter. 'Now, what about a game of chess?'

Beti, coming back after locking up the chickens, stopped for a few words : 'I'm glad you're back', she said gently. 'My husband has been run off his feet, trying to keep up with everything. Mari will be glad too. She was very worried about you, telling everyone that something had to be done to get you home.'

She paused when she saw the delighted expression on Werner's face and frowned slightly. 'I mean she was worried about both of you', she continued. 'She thought it wasn't fair that you should have been taken away when you hadn't done anything. She and Pilot Officer Taylor have been working on your behalf.'

'Why should he help her?', broke in Werner before he could stop himself. 'It's nothing to do with him.'

'Well, they've been seeing quite a lot of each other. I suppose he just wanted to help', said Beti rather lamely.

'He's quite keen on her, I think.'

'How do you know that?', said Werner rather aggressively, shaking off Peter's warning hand on his sleeve. 'How do you know it?', he repeated. 'Has she said so?'

'Well, no', said Beti, wishing that she had never brought up the subject. 'It's just that they've been going out together, that's all.'

'Where have they been going? Has she told you that they are going out together?'

'No, of course not. It's not my business.'

'Then it may not be true', he persisted. 'If he has been chasing after her, it is not a surprise. She is a very pretty girl, but that does not mean that she is keen on him, as you put it. Why do you say these things?'

'Stop it, Werner!', said Peter urgently, pulling at his arm again. 'You have no right to speak in this way to Mrs Jones. Please excuse him, Mrs Jones.'

'It's alright', said Beti. 'I'm sure Werner meant no harm. Let's leave it at that, shall we?' She patted Werner's arm sadly and then went into the farmhouse.

'I'm sorry', called Werner at her retreating back, but if she heard him, she made no gesture of acknowledgement. 'I'm sorry', he repeated brokenly, then turned and strode off towards the stable block.

'Where are you going?', called Peter.

'I'm going for a piss. Where do you think I'm bloody going?'

27.

As soon as she saw Inspector Pugh approaching, Lowry knew. She had tried to push the knowledge away into some dark corner of her mind where it could stay, secure from pursuing thoughts and prying logic. Let it be forgotten, she had thought. Let it lie as in a shaded area of the secret woods, where countless drifting leaves obscure, conceal and finally inter until all traces have been forgotten. But, he knew. She could see it in his face. He knew!

'Good day, Miss Morgan', he said courteously, doffing his trilby hat. 'Is Griffith here?'

'Do you want to see him?'

'No, it's you I came to see.'

'Why me?'

'Is there something you want to tell me?'

'You'd better come in', she said, holding the door open for him. 'Would you like a cup of tea?'

'That would be very nice, thank you.'

He gazed around the cosy kitchen as she made the tea. The sunlight streaming through the window gleamed on the willow pattern plates and copper lustre jugs on the oak dresser. On one side of the dresser was a framed photograph of a young man in first world war army uniform. Holding his arm was a pretty girl with laughing eyes. In a photograph on the other side was a ram-rod straight soldier, gazing at the camera with all the pride of a young man ready to do battle for his country. On the wall was a framed sepia photograph of a middle-aged couple, posed in that formal and unsmiling manner typical of the Victorian era, effectively concealing the human warmth that lay beneath.

The kitchen was spotless. There was a faint smell of lavender polish that he rightly assumed came from the recently polished dresser. A grandfather clock ticked steadily in the corner, while a comfortable black and white cat lay curled up on a cushion on the wooden armchair by the range fire. On a small side table was a large, bound family bible where he knew the details of family births, marriages and deaths would be recorded. He had a similar one in his own home.

The deep windowsill, set within the thickness of the cottage wall, had a small vase of marigolds, like captured sunlight in a moment of stillness.

He reached over and stroked the cat, which twitched its ears and answered with a lazy purr before resuming its slumbers.

'Here you are, Inspector.'

He drank his tea gratefully, while Lowry sat opposite, hands folded rather decorously on her knees, waiting for him to speak.

He put his cup and saucer down on the table and addressed her gently.

'There's no-one else but you to look after Griffith, I take it?'

'No, I'm all he has. He's all I have, too.'

'Have you ever considered that he might be better in a home?'

'That would kill him', she answered angrily. 'This is his home and it always will be while I'm here to look after him. He's happy here and he's accepted by the villagers. They all know that he would never hurt anyone.'

'But he did hurt someone, didn't he, Miss Morgan?'

'Not in the way you mean. He never intended to hurt anyone. He was frightened, badly frightened. He ...'

She stopped as her voice broke and emotion threatened to engulf her. She gripped her handkerchief tightly and looked around the room before gazing down at the tiled floor.

'Tell me what you know, Inspector', she continued, seemingly heedless of the fact that he was supposed to be questioning her.

'I think that he was responsible for throwing a fiery missile through the window of Hendy's annexe where the German prisoners of war were sleeping. Why did he do that?', said Pugh, content to go along with the way the interview was progressing.

'I told you, he was frightened. He'd heard a German voice one night when he was out, and he thought he was back in the trenches again. '

'But he must have heard the POWs speaking German to each other on previous occasions. Had he shown any signs of being afraid of them then?'

'No.'

'So why should this be any different?'

'He said it was another voice. It was harsh and threatening and had made someone cry. There was a scream. He was afraid. He was afraid that the voice would hurt me, too. He had to stop it, he said, before it came here. I suppose that in his confused way, he thought that it had come from Hendy's annexe. Anyway, you seem to know the rest, Inspector.'

'Yes, I think I do', said Pugh. 'What he heard was the voice of someone else speaking harshly to Hans, telling him that he could not go with him. Who that person was, you have no need to know. When Hans became persistent, he pushed him over the edge of the cliff. That was the scream Griffith heard.'

'What will happen to Griffith, Inspector?', said Lowry in a voice that threatened to break again. 'Will they send him to prison?'

'What Griffith did had nothing to do with the death of Hans. His only crime is that he started a fire that was put out quickly and that harmed no-one, although there was some damage to the room. Mr Jones is not disposed to bring charges about that. No, I don't think he will go to prison, Miss Morgan. You, however, have withheld information that could arguably have been useful to us much earlier than was the case. That is a serious offence.'

For several minutes she gazed at the floor, then took a deep breath and addressed him again: 'How long will I be in prison, Inspector?', she asked calmly. 'It's just that I need to know so that I can try and arrange for someone to look after Griffith while I am away', she added.

Inspector Pugh smiled gravely at her and then paused for a moment before speaking: 'Miss Morgan, what I am about to say is extremely serious and is in absolute confidence. Is that clear?'

'Yes.'

'I need to be assured that Griffith will never do such a thing again. That means you will have to be extremely careful in watching him, all the time. I know that you do so already, but now I'm asking you to be even more diligent than before. It's a great deal to ask of anyone, I know that, but it's absolutely vital. Do you understand?'

She nodded and then, without taking her eyes off his face, whispered: 'Can you assure me that the owner of the harsh voice has gone for good?' When he nodded, she continued: 'Then, you have my word, Inspector.'

She looked at the photographs on the dresser and the wall, as if evoking their presence from the past to witness the events of the present. She reached out and placed her hand on the family bible.

'On the memory of my parents and everyone and everything that I hold most dear, I swear it.'

'Thank you', said the Inspector gently.

For a long moment they sat and looked at the fire in the quiet, ticking kitchen, then he continued: 'There's one final thing, Miss Morgan, and it is this. It is vital that we agree between ourselves, that this conversation never took place. No-one must ever know of it. Is that understood and agreed?'

The shock was evident, but soon the startled surprise in her eyes gave way to tears that ran unchecked down her cheeks as she nodded dumbly.

'So', continued the Inspector briskly, 'If anyone should ask, why I came to see you today it was quite simply to buy some of that excellent peppermint tea which my wife tells me you have. *"If you're going to Llanwrtan today, don't forget to get me some of that peppermint tea"* - those were her last words when I left this morning, so I'd better make sure I remember otherwise there'll be trouble when I get home.'

As Inspector Pugh got into his car, clutching his bag of peppermint tea, Griffith suddenly appeared.

'Rabbit for you, for your supper', he said, thrusting the furry body into the car, before turning hastily and running back to join Lowry at the gate. They both waved as the car turned into the lane.

28.

The laughter of the children playing in the farmyard at Ty Fron carried into the house where Megan Prys and Eluned Thomas were sitting by the fire in the kitchen.

'That letter I had', said Eluned. 'It was to say that they're coming to collect Rose next week. George is going back with them, too, according to Blodwen at the post office. It seems that they've traced George's father in a German Prisoner of War camp. I'm glad for young George's sake, but oh, Megan, it'll break my heart to see Rose leave the village. I can't bring myself to tell her. Only yesterday she was telling me how excited she is about coming to live with you. She said to me: *"Mrs Prys will be my Mam and you'll be my Nain, Mrs Thomas"*, and then she gave me a great hug, the little lamb. Isn't there anything we can do?'

'We've tried everything, Eluned', replied Megan sadly. I don't know what else to do, although John keeps saying that we mustn't give up hope. He seems to think that there's still a chance, that some miracle may happen, but I don't know ...'

She dabbed at her eyes with a handkerchief and turned to look out of the window. The children had now formed a line and were taking it in turns to throw a ball against the wall of the barn, with the next in line having to catch it before it bounced on the ground. She remembered how she and her friends had played the same game when they were children, and on the same wall, too. She sighed and got up to refill Eluned's cup, just as John came in. He had been splitting logs all morning, then stacking them in a pile under the eaves at the side of the house where they would dry out, ready for use the following year. It was a task that was tiring, yet satisfying. The smell of the wood was redolent of warm summers, while the resin was a harbinger of the comforting flames that would keep the worst of winter at bay.

He gave them a weary smile then joined them by the fire, stretching out his legs in a relaxed manner and accepting gratefully the cup of tea that Megan had poured out for him. He enquired after Eluned's health and then listened carefully as she recounted again what she had told Megan.

'I'm glad about the boy', he said. 'He deserves some good fortune. Hopefully he will settle in well when his father returns.'

'If only we could say the same about little Rose ... ', began Megan and then paused for the other two had turned their heads towards the window. The silence was unexpected. Had the children gone? She got up and looked out of the window and saw that they were standing silently watching as two large cars drove into the farmyard.

'John, who is it?', she asked as the other two joined her at the window.

'Let's find out', he said.

The door of the first car was open already. A short, stocky and rather self-important man got out and stood by the car as two other men emerged. Eluned recognised one immediately as the evacuee allocation officer from Bangor, but who were the other two?

The second man was tall and silver-haired, while the third was a fair-haired young man who seemed to dance attendance upon him.

'That's our local MP', said John of the silver-haired man. 'I recognise him from his posters.'

The fair-haired young man came towards them eagerly.

'Mr and Mrs Prys? My name is John Edwards and I'm the local agent for this constituency. May we come in?

'Of course', said Megan, but who ...?

But instead of coming towards the house, the MP had gone to the second car where a chauffeur was just opening the passenger door for a middle-aged man in a beautiful suit. Once he was out, he and the chauffeur turned to assist a third man, while the MP stood ready to give further help if that were necessary.

The man who was helped from the car was old and frail and moved with the aid of a walking stick. He came towards the house slowly yet determinedly, then stopped when he reached the children.

'Good day to you all', he said courteously and smiled at the chorus of 'Good day, sir', that he received in reply. 'Is there a little girl called Rose here?'

There was an uncertain pause and then Rose put up her hand hesitantly, following a hurried and whispered conversation with her friends, that had included an encouraging shove from Winnie that propelled her forward.

'That's me, sir. I'm Rose.'

'So you're Rose. I've heard a lot about you. Good things too. I understand that you like living here. Is that so? Are you sure you wouldn't rather go back to Liverpool?'

'No, sir. I don't want to go back. I want to live here?'

'And where exactly would you like to live?'

'Here, at Ty Fron, sir.'

'And who would you like to look after you?'

'Mr and Mrs Prys, sir. I want them to be my Mam and Dad. I don't want to go to Liverpool or Australia, sir.'

The old gentlemen smiled benignly, patted her cheek, then he turned towards the door of Ty Fron.

'May I come in?', he asked gently.

Megan and Eluned stood as if frozen. Was it really who they thought it was? Was he actually here in Llanwrtan asking to come in to Ty Fron?

But if there were any doubts, they were soon cast aside when they saw the fine leonine head with its magnificent sweep of white hair, walrus moustache and the noble bearing that was apparent despite age and ill health. Here was someone who was immediately recognisable, not only in Wales, but throughout Europe and the world.

'Oh please come in Mr Lloyd George, sir. It's such an honour to have you', said Megan. 'Come in and sit down! Would you like a cup of tea, sir?'

She led the way in and was about to show everyone into the parlour, but the great man made his way to the wooden armchair by the fireside and sat down gratefully.

'This will do fine', he said. 'The kitchen is the heart of

a Welsh household, and as for that cup of tea, it would be most welcome, Mrs Prys.'

Megan and Eluned busied themselves getting out the best crockery and then making a fresh pot of tea, while John got extra chairs from the parlour in order to seat everyone. It was quite a squeeze but they managed.

It had been a surprise to David Lloyd George to learn that there was a smallholder from Llanwrtan who had come to see him in Llanystumdwy some weeks previously. His housekeeper had been adamant that Mr Lloyd George did not receive visitors without an appointment.

'I'm sorry, I don't have an appointment, but I would be most grateful if you could ask the gentleman if he would see me', said John. 'It's a matter of great importance and he is the only man who can help me.'

'I'm sorry but it's out of the question', said the housekeeper and proceeded to close the door.

'Please', said John holding onto the door. 'Please tell him that my name is John Prys and he once presented me with an eisteddfod prize for recitation when I was a boy. He told me then that I should always be true to what I believe and never to give up when difficulties arise. I've never forgotten that. Please tell him. Please!'

The housekeeper paused and looked him up and down again, chewing her lip and frowning as she tried to decide what to do.

'Wait here!', she said abruptly.

In a short while she returned and said rather loftily:

'Mr Lloyd George will see you in the study. Mind you

wipe your boots and don't tire him out! He's not a well man', she added, as if an element of face-saving were required in relation to their earlier exchange.

John took off his cap, wiped his boots carefully and followed her into the comfortable, book-lined study. A log fire crackled cheerfully in the hearth, its flames picking out the brass plates on the walls and the silver photograph frames on an antique desk under the window. A large tortoiseshell and white cat was curled up comfortably in front of the fire.

'Sit down!', said the old gentleman after the housekeeper had introduced John. 'Sit there where I can see you!'. He indicated a wing chair by the fire, opposite to his own. 'I hear that you are a reciter of note.'

'A reciter but not an orator, sir.'

Lloyd George smiled and said: 'Tell me why you wish to see me!'

John recounted the whole story from start to finish, trying to be succinct but without omitting any important details. His listener paid keen attention, his eyes fixed on John's face, nodding every now and again, occasionally pursing his lips, but never interrupting the recital.

John felt that he was in the presence of an acute and formidable mind, able to absorb information and weigh facts in a precise and analytical way. When he came to the end he added simply: 'I came to see you sir, because they will listen to you.'

He leaned forward and handed Lloyd George a large envelope . 'This contains all the correspondence and other documentation. There are character references as well, from the Minister, the Vicar and the Headmaster of the village school.'

Lloyd George leafed through the documents, nodding as he did so.

'Well, you seem to come highly recommended, Mr Prys. I will obviously have to study these thoroughly and consult other people, but you must realise that I have no official capacity. There is no reason why anyone should listen to anything I have to say. I have no standing anywhere at all these days. I am just an old man living out his days in retirement.'

'You will always have a place in the hearts of the Welsh people, sir. You did more for ordinary folk than anyone. No one else would have given pensions to the poor.'

Lloyd George smiled again.

'That was a battle I enjoyed, I can tell you. They thought I was an upstart who didn't know his place, who had no right to invade the corridors of largely inherited power.'

'I once read a speech that you gave in Cardiff on St David's Day years ago', said John. 'You spoke about this area. You said that, in Roman times, Caernarfon would have been the Bulawayo at the fringe of the Roman empire. You said the Roman conquerors spoke a language that has since died, and which children now only learn in schools. You also said that the so-called barbaric language spoken by the conquered people then, did not die. It is the ancient language that we still use today. But, sir, the adoption society seems to think that a Welsh-speaking family and village cannot offer the right environment for little Rose.'

'Do they indeed? Well, I didn't do too badly, coming from a similar environment', chuckled Lloyd George, putting the papers back in the envelope. 'Leave these with me, Mr Prys', he continued. 'I will see what I can do, but I can make no promises. You are a good man, I can see that, and I would like to help you, but it would be irresponsible of me to raise false hopes.'

Now standing in the kitchen at Ty Fron, John thought back to the conversation he had had with Lloyd George at Llanystumdwy. Unbelievably, here was the great man himself sitting at his fireside, enjoying a cup of tea, chatting amiably in Welsh and laughing with Megan and Eluned as if they were old friends.

'Mr and Mr Prys', we have had a further committee meeting to consider your application.'

It was Mr Willows, the head of the adoption society, the man in the beautiful suit who had accompanied David Lloyd George in his car.

'It was felt that certain factors had not been fully taken into consideration when the first decision was made. Now, I am glad to tell you that your application has been accepted and that we are happy for you to become Rose's adoptive parents.'

John and Megan looked at each other and then at the circle of faces in stunned disbelief. Then Megan felt John's arm going around her shoulders while tears of joy began to well up inside her. She managed to choke out the words:

'Thank you, sir. Thank you Mr Lloyd George, sir. Thank you everyone.'

There were handshakes and congratulations all round and then it was time for the distinguished party to leave. The farmyard was now crowded with villagers who had been alerted by their children. A collective sigh arose when they saw the old man. He beamed and waved to them as he made his way to the car, stopping to shake hands every now and again. When he came to where Rose stood with Catrin, Winnie and Ifan, he stopped and said to her: 'Go inside, mach i! Your Mam and Dad are waiting for you.'

'Three cheers for Mr Lloyd George', shouted Samuel Jones and a great chorus of acclaim broke out. It continued as the cars wended their way out of the farmyard and down the narrow lane where some people were still running to see the great man himself.

It was an event that the villagers were to recall for many years to come. It was an event that John and Megan Prys were to recall with poignant memory two years later, when they and their daughter Rose, along with hundreds of other Welsh people, stood in a lane at Llanystumdwy as the funeral cortege of David Lloyd George, recently ennobled to Lord Dwyfor, went past with his coffin resting on a humble farm cart as he was taken to his last resting place. All her long life Rose was to remember him with great affection and was often heard to remark: 'Lloyd George knew my father. My father knew Lloyd George. And I did too.'

29.

Mari set off early as usual. There were still some of the poultry to be selected, once the dairying tasks had been completed. She felt in a strange, almost detached mood, where one half of her was delighting in the twittering rapture of morning, while the other side was moved by an ever-present sadness.

She suddenly caught sight of the robust figure of Ron walking back to his caravan from Hendy. A few minutes later they came together on the path.

'Ron, I thought you were in Bootle. No one seemed to know what had happened to you. You didn't tell anyone you were going did you?'

'No, I didn't. It was a spur of the moment thing I suppose. You see I had lost something. It was of no great value to anyone else, but it was of sentimental value to me. Years ago, my late wife Dorothy had given me a pocket watch and I had dropped it on one of the beaches. I spent ages looking for it, even though it would most probably have been smashed beyond repair by the tide. Anyway, once it was clear that it had gone for good, I decided to buy a replacement. The same shop in Liverpool is still there after all these years. It was a gesture by a romantic old fool, I expect.' He removed the watch from his waistcoat pocket and showed it to her.

'It's lovely', said Mari gently, running her fingers over the glossy metal. 'And you're not a fool Ron! There's nothing wrong with romantic gestures either. They give meaning to our lives, it's said.'

'Yes chick, I think they do,' said Ron, retrieving the watch and putting it in his pocket.

'I expect you'll be in for a busy day today, so I won't keep you any longer.' Walking on Ron stopped and turned.

'By the way, the German boys are back.'

'What! Why didn't you tell me before?' cried Mari, thunderstruck by the news.

'Sorry, I didn't think. They got back late last night, apparently.'

'Are they all right? Are they back to stay?'

'I don't know, why don't you go and see for yourself?'

Mari carried on, quickening her pace until she was running, running, almost skimming over the vegetation of the path to the pig gate. Werner was home! Werner! There he was! She could see him on the other side of the gate, by the tractor.

He looked up and saw her, her face shining with happiness. He felt his heart thumping, but with a sudden bitterness realised that her delight was not because of him but because she had found love with that English pilot.

He couldn't bear to look at her, so he threw his cigarette away and stomped off around the corner of the barn.

'Werner,' she called after him. 'What's the matter? Aren't you glad to be home?'

'Yes, thanks for your help and that of the others', he said curtly. 'Now I have some work to do so please excuse me.'

He turned, almost knocking old Jacob over as he went.

'Duw, he's in a state,' said Jacob. 'Must be a matter of the heart I'd say.' He winked and went on his way, calling the dogs to accompany him.

She stood, stunned, in the farmyard, thinking back to her correspondence with Martin. Why was everything going wrong? She turned and walked into the kitchen of the farmhouse where Beti was finishing drying the dishes.

'Hello cariad,' said Beti. 'I'm sure you're glad to see the boys back again. We had no idea they were coming until they arrived late last night. Have you seen Werner?'

'Yes, but he didn't seem to want to talk to me,' said Mari bitterly. 'I don't understand what's going on.' She suddenly burst into tears and Beti put her arms around her.

'What is there to understand?' said Beti quietly. 'It's a matter of choice, don't you see? That's all it is. They both love you, that's obvious, but where do you stand in all this?'

'Yes, I know now,' whispered Mari, but is it too late?'

'Don't be silly' said Beti turning towards the hob. ' I'll make you a nice cup of tea and . . .'

But when she turned back, she heard the outer door slamming and the kitchen was empty.

Werner stood looking out over the fields, trying to steady the churning confusion inside him. So preoccupied was he that he didn't hear the steps behind him until the voice spoke.

'Werner, oh Werner, please talk to me. I was so looking forward to seeing you again.'

He was silent for a moment, finding it difficult to look at her. Then, slowly he turned and said, 'It's that pilot, Mari. You love him and I can't bear it. I suppose that I cannot blame you for he has everything that I have not. He *is* everything that I am not. He will make you happy. What can I possibly offer you that could compete with what he has to give?'

He turned away and gazed out across the fields in the direction of the sea. 'I have no wish to go back to Germany when this war is over, but I must if there is no future for me here, although my heart will remain.'

'Aren't you forgetting something?' asked Mari, putting her hand on his arm so that he turned to face her once more.

'What have I forgotten?'

'The most important thing of all. You say that Martin has everything, and it's true. He's handsome, clever and reliable. He's good company and he makes me laugh. He's an extremely nice man but there is one thing that you have which he does not.'

'What is that?'

'My love', she answered simply. 'It's you I love, not him. Can't you see that?'

Werner stood stock still, amazed by her revelation. Stunned disbelief played across his rugged features as he considered the implication of her statement, then a slow smile spread across his face and lit up his grey eyes.

'Is it really true that you love me, Mari? You really love me and not Martin?'

'Of course, I do. I've loved you since before Martin ever arrived here. I'll always love you, Werner.'

She leaned forward and kissed him gently. 'You're the one for me. There's no-one else.'

He grasped her hands in his and looking into her eyes declared: 'Mari, I have nothing to offer you but my love. But always I will love you, my sea girl. I will work hard to make a home for us here at Llanwrtan if they will let me stay. And they will let me stay, I know it. Winnie will be as my own child and I will look after you both to the end of my days. Will you marry me?'

There was a pause that to Werner seemed endless before Mari replied.

'Of course I will. I thought you'd never ask.'

Catrin, Winnie, Ifan and Rose, creeping up behind the haystack at Hendy, were just in time to see Werner take Mari in his arms. For a few moments they watched them, then diplomatically retreated to Ty Fron's barn to discuss the situation.

No-one saw the solitary figure of a young man with a walking stick who had been watching Mari and Werner from a distance. Slowly, he turned away and sadly made his way back to the village.

'He kissed her on the lips again, not on the cheek', said Winnie happily, when they were sitting in the barn once more.

'He'll have to marry your Mam now', said Rose with great solemnity.

'It must have been the wish of his heart that we took

to Enlli', said Catrin thoughtfully.

'Come on, that's enough about kissing. Let's go and play Spitfires', said Ifan.

The gnats weren't biting today. It was a truce declared under the eye of a soporific sun. But the chorus of the grass played on.

Llanwrtan

This novel is a work of fiction and the village of Llanwrtan exists only in my imagination. Apart from some well-known historical figures, the characters bear no relation to anyone living or dead.
If you need to refresh your memory, here is a list to refer back to, of the houses and their inhabitants.

Pant Uchaf: Catrin Hebon, her mother Bethan, her father Richard and her maternal grandmother Lisa Evans. Also living here are Mari Evans (Bethan's sister) and her illegitimate daughter Winnie.

Ty Nesaf: Ifan Davies, his widowed mother Enid and his maternal grandmother, Ellen Rowlands.

Ty Fron: John and Megan Prys, a childless couple.

Hendy: Samuel and Beti Jones and their agricultural labourer Jacob Lewis (who is also the village bard). Mari, who is in the Land Army, works here. There are also three German POWs billeted at the farm - Werner, Peter and Hans.

Ty Capel: Rev Elis Jones, Minister of the chapel and his wife Catherine.

Ty Gwyn: William Jones, Choirmaster at the chapel and his wife Sarah.

Red Lion: Proprietors John and Jane Rowlands and their daughter Ceri. Martin Taylor is an English visitor staying at the inn.

Vicarage: Rev. Roger Walters, Vicar of the church and his wife Mair.

Post Office: Blodwen Rowlands, postmistress. Her husband Dai, the postman, and his ancient grandfather Guto.

School House: Edwin Humphries, headmaster and his schoolteacher wife Myfanwy.

Bwthyn: Eluned Thomas, an elderly widow and her son, Sergeant Thomas of the Home Guard. Rose Wilson an evacuee from Liverpool is boarded here.

Nant: Lowry Morgan, the village herbalist and her brain-damaged brother Griffith.

Hafan: Edward Beynon, a local fisherman.

Holiday Caravan: Ron Harris, a retired English businessman from Bootle.
Pwllheli Police Station: Inspector Pugh

Epilogue: Three years later

The summer of 1946 was a fine one. The war was over and there was a new government with urgent priorities to find jobs for the returning armed forces and provide accommodation in the badly damaged towns and cities. The wartime regime of rationing was, if anything, stricter than before, with no prospect of any relaxation in the future.

However, life in Llanwrtan remained much the same, with small changes returning the little community to peacetime activities. Most of those who had left the village to serve their country were home again and everyone was looking forward to better times ahead.

Life for German POWs who chose to remain in Britain was not easy. There was still resentment against Germany and the loss of life that Hitler's regime had brought about. For Werner, however, Llanwrtan was a haven where he was accepted and respected for his hard work and pleasant manner. Despite all odds, he and Mari were married and there was a new baby on the way. Though continuing with farm work, Werner had begun a fledgling repair business for clocks and household items and also worked part-time at a local garage.

Peter, the other POW, had left Llanwrtan the previous year, and had been in a holding camp in England, waiting to return to his shattered country. He and Werner kept in touch and the summer of 1946 finally led to his return to Germany.

At the Red Lion, Ceri now happily married to Rhys, had taken on the day-to-day running of the guest facilities. Two unexpected visitors that summer had been Martin accompanied by his English wife Stephanie. He and Werner finally made it up over a modest meal with their wives, where many toasts for the future were made in English, German and Welsh. At a nearby table, Bleddyn, the surviving son of Beti and Samuel Jones of Hendy, was celebrating his recent engagement to Ifan's widowed mother.

John and Megan Prys began a small B & B enterprise at Ty Fron. To their daughter Rose's delight, their first visitors from Liverpool that summer had been George and his father.

Rose, Winnie, Catrin and Ifan had left the village school and now attended the grammar school for the area, catching the school bus outside the post office each morning.

Richard, Catrin's father returned safely from the Atlantic war. He and Bethan were now expecting their second child, yet another sign of the burgeoning new life and a bright future for the village.

Catrin's Nain was still hale and hearty but old Guto at the post office had finally died and no-one knew whether he had reached a hundred years or not.

Lowry and Griffith continued much as before, and Inspector Pugh in Pwllheli, received a well-deserved promotion to Superintendent.

Appendix I

Although this is a work of fiction, some of the incidents are based on real events as well as on local legends. As I have quite shamelessly adapted them for my own purposes, it is only right that I should list them here and confess where I have made alterations.

Adoption
There was a scheme to send orphans to Australia but most were sent in the period immediately after the war. The Adoption Society, which in the book is situated near the Pier Head in Liverpool, is a figment of my imagination and bears no resemblance to any real organisation of the time.

Bardsey
There is, of course, a holy island of Enlli where legend has it that Merlin is buried. Some also claim that it is the last resting place of King Arthur. Twenty thousand 'saints' are also reputed to have made their last pilgrimage there. There are still old people who remember that local fishermen would doff their caps in respect when passing the island. Today the Pilgrim's Route from Clynnog Fawr to Bardsey is a popular tourist trail.

Cloak of Invisibility
One of Merlin's gifts is reputed to be the cloak of invisibility. If so, it has certainly protected the traditional culture of Wales from the outside world. (It has often been said that when you live next door to a powerful neighbour, the best way to survive is to make yourself invisible). There are probably more bards per head of population in Llŷn than there are anywhere in Wales, and probably in the world, but can you spot them? They could be filling your petrol tank, serving you in the shop or looking after the sheep.

David Lloyd George
The great man did not go to live in Llanystumdwy until 1944. His help with Rose's case is, of course, fiction but he is still regarded as a heroic figure in Wales, for having championed the rights of ordinary people.

Eating the Yeast
Yes, it actually happened to a now elderly Llŷn lady who has asked to be kept anonymous. As she herself has commented: *"You know, we were really innocent in those days and didn't know anything."*

Evacuees
There were English evacuees in Llŷn. Although Rose is a fictional character, there were some evacuees who became fluent in Welsh and were adopted by their boarding families.

Fox Hunting
It is within living memory that the risk of being evicted for killing the landowner's fox was lifted from some Llŷn small-holdings. My mother remembered a local poacher being given 'unofficial' payment for trapping a fox.

Garn Fadryn
Garn Fadryn is a prehistoric site and hill that rises to just over 1000ft.

German Prisoners of War
Werner, Peter and Hans are fictional characters, but there were German POWs in Llŷn, although most came after the Normandy landings. In my village they were sometimes entertained to tea on Sundays and were not locked up. One of them repaired my aunt's watch. They also sang in Welsh in the chapel.

Gwichyn Pen Voel
The small bald-headed cowrie or periwinkle shell is found on some of Llŷn's beaches, but you have to look carefully to find it. It is a symbol of good luck and a purse containing one is never empty. I have one in my purse, but I am not going to tell you on which beach I found it.

King of Enlli
Enlli did have a King with a gilt crown and coronation provided by Lord Newborough. (The crown is now in the Liverpool Maritime Museum). The story of the King who abdicated and took the crown with him to the mainland, only to have it reclaimed by the angry islanders, is also true.

My uncle, Owen Jones of Craig-y-Don in Abersoch, who had a boat, used to take visitors to the island. He remembers the system of asking the King's permission to land and of pay-ing a shilling to the official 'Carrier' unless you were a local.

Legend of the Monk and Skylark
This is an old Welsh legend. I have borrowed it and transferred it to the fictional village of Llanwrtan.

Loss of Land under the Enclosures
It was a traditional custom in Llŷn that if you built a dwelling on Common Land and had smoke coming out of the chimney within 24 hours, the land was yours. My great, great, great grandfather Robert Roberts built his cottage, and acquired his 4-acre smallholding in this way but it, along with neighbouring properties, was taken by a large estate in 1817, under the Enclosures Act.

The story my mother told was that the heads of all the independent holdings were invited to a supper at the 'big house' and then asked to sign a paper as proof of attendance. This they did, in all innocence, but as they could not read English, they did not know that they had signed away their properties. They were subsequently issued with eviction notices unless they agreed to pay rent.

Morse Code Messages to Enlli
This story is quite true. A relative by marriage, Henry David Williams of Rhydlios, describes the incident in his self-published book *Ynys Enlli* which was also published in an English language version called *Across the Bardsey Sound*.

Postman's Round
The reference to the postman who took his inspector the long way round, rather than along the footpaths, is quite true. My mother remembers the event taking place in the 1930s.

Ram in the Boat
This actually happened when Richard Williams of Glan Aber, transported the ram from Abersoch. However, it was being taken to St Tudwal's island where he kept a flock of sheep, not to Bardsey. In the novel, Edward Beynon is fictional.

Snail Racing
I'm glad to say that children in Llŷn still play snail races and have not forgotten the old rhyme to make the snails wake up.

Spy in Llŷn

Unlikely as it might seem, there was a German spy in Llŷn, although he was an incompetent one. He knocked at the door of our house, one morning, asking my mother the way to Pwllheli. There were no road signs at the time.

In all innocence she gave him instructions as to where to catch the bus and he went on his way. Some time later she mentioned him to her uncle, Sir Evan Jones, who called while on a visit from Llan Ffestiniog. When he heard the story he immediately went to the post office, which had the only telephone in the village, and rang the police. They caught the spy a short while later.

I don't remember the incident, but my mother often told us the story. He was such a nice man, she said, even though he was a spy and anyway, she had been brought up always to help a stranger at the door.

Storms on Enlli

Storms frequently cut off the island from the mainland. My mother's uncle, Rev. William Jones, was the Minister at the chapel there for 29 years, until he and his family retired to the mainland at Garn Fadryn.

The island relied on the mainland for many of its supplies, including the basic commodity of flour. Although they did grow some cereal crops, these had to be taken to the mainland to be milled. Lord Newborough had given the islanders the option of either building them a mill or a chapel. They had chosen to have a chapel!

The incident of praying all night actually took place and there was indeed a wooden cask of flour washed up on the beach the following morning. It was a story that my mother often recounted.

Appendix II

Modern Welsh is derived from what was the original language of Britain and is one of the oldest living languages in Europe. Its survival has been nothing short of miraculous. Over the centuries it has survived being banned both in schools and as an official language, being ridiculed as a peasant tongue and being ignored as a serious historical and cultural source.

It survived because it remained the common language of the hearth in many areas such as Llŷn. In 1588, Bishop Morgan's translation of the Bible from Hebrew and Greek sources into Welsh during the reign of Elizabeth I (who herself spoke Welsh) ensured the standardisation of the language throughout Wales.

In recent years, its increasing recognition as an official language and the fact that it is taught in the schools, has not only stopped the decline that was threatening its existence, but has actually increased the numbers of those speaking Welsh.

To echo the words of the National Anthem: 'O bydded i'r hen iaith barhau'. (Long may the old language survive).

The alphabet
There are 28 letters in the Welsh alphabet (see below). Apart from the letter y, their pronunciation never varies.

There are seven vowels: a, e, i, o, u, w, y.

Some letters are double: ch, dd, ff, ng, ll, ph, rh, th.

The following letters are not found in Welsh: j, k, q, v, x, z, but they may be borrowed for certain names, eg, Jones, Vaenol.

Where a vowel sound is long, a circumflex is placed above it, eg, Llŷn (See below).

Pronunciation
a (*ah*) **b** (*bee*) **c** (*eck*) **ch** (*ech* as in Scottish lo*ch*) **d** (*dee*)
dd (*eth* as in o*th*er) **e** (*e* as in h*e*avy) **f** (*ev*) **ff** (*eff*) **g** (*egg*)
ng (*eng*) **h** (*ah-itch* - with *ch* as in *ch*utney) **i** (*ee*) **l** (*ell*)
ll (see below for *Ll*anwrtan) **m** (*em*) **n** (*en*) **o** (*o* as in t*ow*)
p (*pee*) **ph** (*eff*) **r** (*er*) **rh** (*rhuh*) **s** (*ess*) **t** (*ti*) **th** (*eth*) **u** (*ee*)
w (*ooh*) **y** (*eeh* or *err* depending on context).

In descriptions, the adjective always follows the noun, eg, Ty Gwyn (House White) unlike the English, White House.

Llanwrtan - *Llanoortan* ('ll' is an aspirated sound produced by putting the tongue against the back of the upper teeth and expelling air through the side of the mouth).

Pant Uchaf - *Pant Ichav* (the 'ch' sound as in the Scottish loch)

Ty Fron - *Tee Vron*

Ty Nesaf - *Tee Nesav*

Glossary of Welsh words and local expressions

Ach y fi - An expression of distaste.

Cariad - Love

Duw - God

Diawl - Devil (a common swear word)

Diolch yn fawr - Thank you very much

Enlli - Bardsey island.

Gwichyn Pen Voel - Bald-Headed Winkle or Cowrie shell.

Jarff - A local expression for one with a big opinion of himself.

Lloegr - The Lost Land (England).

Llŷn - Peninsula in North Wales.

Mach i - My little one (a common expression of endearment).

Mam - Mother

Myrddin - Merlin

Nain - Grandmother

Oes yna bobl? - Are there people? (said when knocking at the door before entering a house).

Saeson - English (from Saxon).

Sut mae? - How are you/how are things?

Tir Mawr - Big land (Enlli islanders' name for the mainland).

Twp - One who is stupid

Ty - House

Ty bach - Little house (outside lavatory)

Tyd yma! - Come here!

Tylwyth Teg - Dynasty of the Fair One (Fairies).

In rural Wales, people are often identified by their first name followed by the name of their house, eg, Catrin, Pant Uchaf.

Appendix III

If you would like to learn more about Wales, Llŷn and Welsh culture, the following are recommended sources:

A History of Wales. John Davies. Penguin. 1990. The best and most authoritative coverage available on the subject.

Wales. Jan Morris. Penguin. 1998. A beautifully written book that is accurately described as *Epic Views of a Small Country.*

Llŷn. Elfed Gruffydd. (Adapted from the Welsh by Gwyneth Owen). Carreg Gwalch. 2003. Essential coverage of the history, culture and natural history of Llŷn.

The Literature of Wales. Dafydd Johnston. University of Wales Press. 1994. A fascinating and concise overview of Welsh literature - *'the oldest attested vernacular literature in Europe'* - from the 6th century to the present day.

Singing in Chains. Mererid Hopwood. Gomer Press. 2004. Cynghanedd poetry has been described as, *'one of the unsung glories of European civilisation'.* This delightful book (with CD) provides an accessible key to one of the world's oldest verse forms that is still widely written and read in Wales.

The Language of the Blue Books: The Perfect Instrument of Empire. Gwyneth Tysin Roberts. University of Wales Press. 1998. A comprehensive study of the 1847 Report into the State of Education in Wales that stigmatized the Welsh language as, *'a great evil'.*

Neighbours from Hell: English Attitudes to the Welsh. Mike Parker. Y Lolfa. 2007. An excellent portrayal by an Englishman living in Wales. He is also the author of *A Rough Guide to Wales.*

The National Eisteddfod. Held each year and alternating between north and south Wales, this is the major cultural festival, and covers all aspects of life in Wales. www.eisteddfod.org.uk

BBC Wales. Comprehensive coverage of Wales and Welsh life, including national and regional events and also learning the language. www.bbc.co.uk/wales

S4C. Welsh language television channel. www.s4c.co.uk

Bardsey Island Trust. www.bardsey.org

Rhiw.com An excellent website for the Llŷn Peninsula. www.rhiw.com

Katie Thear was a founder and first editor of the magazine *Practical Self Sufficiency* in 1975, known today as *Country Smallholding*. She has also written extensively for other magazines and newspapers.

Her books include:

The Home Dairying Book. *Broad Leys, 1978.*

Practical Rabbit Keeping. *Ward Lock, 1982.*

Part-Time Farming. *Ward Lock, 1982.*

Practical Chicken Keeping. *Ward Lock, 1983.*

A Kind of Living. *Hamish Hamilton/Channel 4, 1983.*

Home Dairying. *Batsford, 1983.*

The Family Smallholding. *Batsford, 1983.*

The Complete Book of Raising Livestock and Poultry (with Alistair Fraser). *Pan Macmillan, 1988.*

Goats and Goatkeeping. *Merehurst, 1988.*

Home and Farm Dairying. *Broad Leys, 1988.*

Incubation. *Broad Leys, 1997.*

Starting with Chickens. *Broad Leys, 1999.*

Free-Range Poultry. *Whittet Books, 2002.*

The Smallholder's Manual. *Crowood, 2002.*

Starting with Ducks. *Broad Leys, 2002.*

Starting with Geese. *Broad Leys, 2003.*

Cheesemaking and Dairying. *Broad Leys, 2003.*

Starting with Bees (as Peter Gordon). *Broad Leys, 2004.*

Organic Poultry. *Broad Leys, 2005.*

Starting with Goats. *Broad Leys, 2006.*

Keeping Quail. *Broad Leys, 2007.*

Starting with Turkeys. *Broad Leys, 2007.*

(Dates refer to the publication of the most recent edition).

Broad Leys Publishing Ltd

(Established 1975)

We are small, specialist publishers of fiction and non-fiction books with a rural interest.

For a complete list of our titles please contact us at:

Broad Leys Publishing Ltd
1 Tenterfields
Newport
Saffron Walden
Essex CB11 3UW.

Tel/Fax: 01799 541065

www.blpbooks.co.uk